AINSLEY KEATON

The Beachfront Retreat

VINCI

BOOKS

By Ainsley Keaton

Sconset Beach

The Beachfront Inn

The Beachfront Surprises

The Beachfront Reunion

The Beachfront Secrets

The Beachfront Girls

The Beachfront Sunsets

The Malibu Girls

The Beachfront Christmas

The Beachfront Retreat

Vinci Books

vinci-books.com

Published by Vinci Books Ltd in 2025

1

Copyright © Ainsley Keaton 2023

A CIP catalogue record for this book is available from the British Library.
Paperback ISBN: 9781036703783

Chapter One

Samantha

Samantha was very excited. She was working her very first A-List wedding! Fiona Kennedy was *the* hot actress of the day. Fiona had been working for the past 10 years and everything she touched was box office gold. She had just won the Academy award for best actress for her turn as Mary Queen of Scots. And she was marrying somebody who was just as hot and of the moment. Luke O'Neill had projects lined up with Martin Scorsese and Christopher Nolan, and was in talks to star in the next Tarantino. No doubt about it, this was royalty marrying royalty, and Samantha was making the wedding cake for the big shindig.

She got the job because of Camille Hudson, who was one of Samantha's oldest friends in Los Angeles. Camille knew Samantha's brother Jackson from his days of waiting tables, and Camille worked alongside him as a server. Samantha met her about 6 years ago when she came out to visit Jackson, and they kept in touch over the years, and when Samantha moved to the Los Angeles area Camille was the first person she called. Turned out Camille Hudson was best friends with Fiona, and Camille gave Fiona Samantha's name and the rest was history. Everybody would be there, and Samantha would be meeting the crème de la crème of the Hollywood scene.

The wedding cake she made for Fiona was beautiful but traditional. Three tiers, raspberry flavored icing dyed white, French vanilla cake with a raspberry center. The cake was covered in flowers and butterflies. It was one of Samantha's masterpieces, and she knew this cake would be one of many that she would make for the A-list crowd. Of that, she had no doubt.

She met Fiona, and she was very impressed with her. Fiona was very down to earth, giving her a hug when she first met her. Fiona was very excited about the cake, although something seemed a little bit off. Fiona wasn't as excited as Samantha would've been if she was in Fiona's shoes. Then again, Samantha didn't know Fiona well, so maybe that was just how she was. Maybe she just wasn't a spaz-out- bounce-off-the-walls type like Samantha herself.

No matter. Samantha would make the most of her opportunity. Fiona was kind enough to invite her to the wedding, because she was Camille's friend, so she would go with bells on and Grayson in tow.

Grayson would be just as excited as Samantha to meet everybody. David Weiss, the original showrunner for *Game of Thrones,* would be in attendance and Grayson *loved* that show. Grayson was a cosplay geek for the show, dressing up as different characters. He had met quite a few of the actors and actresses during various Comic-Cons in San Diego. So, when Samantha told Grayson that she scored an invite to the wedding of the year, he squealed with delight just like a woman would. Samantha love that about Grayson – he never was embarrassed to show his geeky side.

So, both Samantha and Grayson were bouncing off the wall about the big event. It would be the highlight of Samantha's year.

Maybe her entire life.

Chapter Two

Fiona

"I can't breathe," Fiona Kennedy complained to her best friend and platonic soulmate, her ride-or-die, Camille Hudson. She was staring at herself in the mirror - flowers woven throughout her curly red hair, a beautiful fitted white dress, bodice cut and flowing over her trim 5'2", 110-pound figure. Her freckles were covered by her expert makeup artist, Bella Lancashire, who also fitted her with some eyelash extensions, as usual. She always had to wear eyelash extensions. Otherwise, on the big screen, nobody could see her eyes. And her eyes, the color of the Caribbean in the areas where the water is clear green, not blue, with flecks of hazel around the pupil, were what millions of moviegoers paid to see. That and her 1000-watt smile that positively lit up the screen, or so the movie critics always said.

She was shaking and ready to puke. Camille was sitting on the floor in front of her, holding her hands to steady her.

"Come on, girl, you're just panicking," Camille said, smoothing a lock of hair off Fiona's forehead, a motion that always used to calm her but didn't anymore. At this moment, nothing could calm her.

"Right. I'm panicking. I'm like Carrie Bradshaw when she tried on the wedding dress before she was supposed to marry Aidan. Remember when she got that rash? I probably also have a rash."

"You don't have a rash," Camille soothed.

"How do you know?"

"Because you'd be itching," she said. "Are you itching?"

"No."

"Then you don't have a rash." Camille shook her head. "Fiona, what is this really about?"

Fiona took a deep breath. "My publicist set this up, you know," Fiona said. "This whole thing was stupid Amelia's idea."

Amelia Katz had been Fiona's publicist since she was an 18-year-old actress new to town and had just gotten her first big part in a movie that became a surprise box-office smash. Amelia thought it was time for Fiona to marry Luke because they were starring in a movie that would be released in the fall and had "Oscar" written all over it. Fiona and Luke had been together for the past eight years, and Amelia said they should be married, so Fiona went along with it. Against her better judgment and way against her gut.

"I know," Camille said. "You've told me that 100 times. But you've also told me you're marrying Luke because you want to. Now, what is this about? Are you only marrying Luke because your publicist said it was a good idea to get hitched at this point in your career, or are you marrying him because you love him?"

5

Fiona shook her head. "What is love? Nobody's been able to define that. I guess I could answer that question if I knew what love was. But I love you, I know." Fiona knew she loved Camille because she would step out in front of a bus for her. That was her standard for love – be willing to sacrifice anything for that person. But it was different with Luke. If she loved him, it would be romantic love, and Fiona didn't know exactly what that was about. So she didn't know how to answer that question.

She knew she wouldn't step out in front of a bus for Luke. If he was dumb enough to wander out into traffic, that would be on him. So, what did that say? And what did it say that she was panicking about taking vows with this man?

She felt like crying. Everybody was there. They were getting married at the Malibu Garden Estate, a luxury palace surrounded by cliffs - Fiona, the most popular actress in the world and current Oscar winner, the modern-day Julia Roberts, or so the press dubbed her, and Lucas O'Neill, another A-list actor who just grabbed the lead in a new Scorsese film. The paparazzi were everywhere – in hovering helicopters, outside the gates, and even a few inside the gates. Her publicist set that up, too, inviting a few choice reporters and photographers in so they could give breathless detail to the millions of adoring fans.

She couldn't just run, although she wanted to. If she ran, her face would be splashed over every magazine imaginable. *People* would be okay because they would be professional and would be sure to run a tasteful photo on the cover. They would report the "runaway bride" angle responsibly. But every other rag would run the worst possible picture of her. They would run a still from one of her movies where her makeup was smeared, giving her a raccoon look, her hair like a drowned rat. There were a few of those photos to go around, and those would be the photos that would stare out at her from *In Touch*, *The National Enquirer*, *Star* and *Life & Style*. They would briefly turn away from the latest "Brad and Jennifer getting back together" story, which was always BS, but nobody cared, to splash her face on the cover and dig up as much dirt as possible from as many "sources" as they could, so they could drag her through the mud. And they would just make stuff up like they always did.

Yet running was exactly what she wanted to do. This wedding was wrong. It couldn't be wronger, and that wasn't a word, but Fiona didn't care. Wronger. Nothing could be wronger than this. She knew just how wrong it was in every fiber of her being, in every cell of her body.

Camille was still looking at her with worry in her big brown eyes. Fiona and Camille went way back to when Fiona worked as a waitress at the Water Grill Restaurant, Fiona's first job when she got into the city. Camille was still working there as a server because she loved it, and she never had the ambition to get into the movie business, unlike most young servers and bartenders.

Camille became Fiona's only family, Fiona's parents having been killed in a car accident when she was only eight years old. She was in the car's backseat when her parents were killed and was in critical condition and on life support for a month. After that, it was a series of foster families, none of whom were bad but weren't her family. Mothers and fathers were not fungible, so Fiona never took to her various foster families over the years. But they meant well, all of them. They provided her shelter, food, clothing, and tried to provide her with the love and affection Fiona could never feel for them.

"You're avoiding the question," Camille said. "I asked you if you're marrying him because you love him, and you came back with a question to my question. You asked what love is." Then Camille hummed the old Howard Jones song *What Is Love.* Camille and Fiona often had Sunday brunch at a restaurant that played old 80s tunes, and they loved every one of them, even though the songs were popular before both of their births.

"Well, I guess that's your answer," Fiona said. "If I can't answer definitively that I love the guy, then I must not."

"So, you're just marrying him because your publicist told you to?"

"No, not entirely. I really want a family. Someone to be my person. That's really it. I want so badly to belong to somebody."

Camille had tears in her eyes. "Oh, Pippi," Camille said, using her nickname for Fiona, after Fiona showed her a picture of herself at 10. Young Fiona looked exactly like the actress who played Pippi Longstocking, minus the silly braids that stuck up in the air. The name stuck between the two friends and usually came out when Fiona was having a hard time, which she certainly was at that moment. "Love, you belong to me," Camille said. "I'm your person. It's not the same as what you're talking about, but I'm your person. And I always will be. And you don't have to go through with this. You don't."

Fiona swallowed hard. "But I do. I have to. If I don't, the tabloids will roast me alive." She looked at herself again in the mirror. She wouldn't cry and smear her makeup. And then she put her head down on the vanity. "My wedding day wasn't supposed to be like this. I'm supposed to be happy, over the moon. I'm not supposed to feel like I'm going into an execution."

Camille put her hands on Fiona's shoulders. "Look at me," she said, and Fiona obeyed. "You don't have to do this. Because if you do, and you guys get divorced, you'll still get roasted over the coals. You know how the stories go. It's always the woman's fault when the power couples break up. Heads you lose, tails they win. Always. So you might as well rip the Band-Aid off now instead of later. God forbid after the two of you have kids."

Fiona thought about having kids with Luke and visibly shuddered. That thought really made her want to puke. "No. There can't be kids, never between us."

"You see. There's also your answer. If you say there won't be children emphatically, he's wrong for you. Completely wrong for you."

"But he can be my family. He can give me the stability I've never had before. I need that, Camille. I know, I know, you're my family. But I want somebody who'll legally be my family. I know that sounds ridiculous and even sounded ridiculous in my head, but that's how I feel."

Camille just sighed. "Okay. I want to talk you out of it but can't tie you up and gag you if you're determined to do this." And then she looked around. "I have to get out there to wait for you."

Fiona desperately wanted her to not leave. She didn't want to be alone and certainly didn't want to walk out there alone. She didn't have anybody to walk down the aisle with her because Camille was her maid of honor, so she couldn't walk her down. She didn't feel close enough to anybody else to ask them, even though the director of her current movie, John Wilkinson, offered to do just that. "You're like my daughter," he said gruffly, touching Fiona's heart.

But she didn't feel like he was her father, so she politely declined the offer. So, she would go out there alone.

She heard the music begin and walked out into the crowd of people waiting for her. The scene couldn't be more stunning - Luke was waiting for her at the altar, which had a backdrop of rolling hills behind which the sun was setting. There were 500 guests and at least 100 reporters. The guests included a Who's Who of current A-List actors, actresses, and directors. Anybody who was anybody in Hollywood was there, looking at her walking down the aisle with a bouquet of wildflowers. Her hands shook wildly, and she felt like a death-row prisoner going to her execution.

I wish I were a death row prisoner going to my execution. That would be so much better because, after the execution, it's all over. But I might be stuck with this guy for the next 60 years. She felt startled to think that, in her head, death was preferable to this.

But she was an Academy Award-winning actress. She just won the top statuette for Best Actress for her turn in the Mary Queen of Scots biopic. Her role as Queen Mary garnered the best reviews of her career, a career that spanned some 30 movies over 10 years, most of which featured her in a starring role. She starred in everything from light rom-com to action-adventures to independent movies, which were her favorite roles.

So, as an actress, she could put on the face everybody was expecting from her. And that was the face of an excited bride, elated to marry the man of her dreams. The little orphan who somehow made it to the very top of the elite world of Hollywood and now was marrying the handsome actor who swept her off her feet.

She put one foot in front of the other, the beautiful, blushing bride. She finally got to the altar and faced Luke.

He was a very handsome man. There was no disputing that. Dark wavy hair, a straight Roman nose, and perfect teeth framed by full lips. Olive skin, as Luke was considered

"Black Irish," referring to the Irish people who are descendants of the Spanish Armada and had darker hair and eyes than most other Irish people. Eyes that brought to mind a snifter of perfect cognac. Eyes that a girl could get lost in, but, somehow, Fiona never lost herself in them. She didn't really know why.

Of course, he was handsome. He was a leading man. He was supposed to be the Yin to her Yang, the Alpha to her Omega. They were the glorious power couple, the two people everybody looked up to because they were perfect together and completed each other.

When she got to the altar, she heard some audible sighs from the audience. She looked out into the crowd and saw the look on so many women's faces. The look that said they believed in true love, now that Cinderella and her Prince Charming were making everything official. She felt guilty making these women believe this was a fairytale come true when it was anything but.

As she looked into Luke's beautiful Cognac-colored eyes with a hint of green around the pupil, the opposite of hers, which were clear green with hazel around her pupil - even their eyes complemented each other, swoon! - she didn't hear a word he said to her. She knew he was waxing poetic about the moment they met, how he was swept away, and how she changed his life and he couldn't live without her, or some such nonsense, but she wasn't listening to him.

All she could think was, why? Why didn't she love him like she should? There was nothing wrong with the guy at all. He was passionate, intelligent, funny, and even-tempered. He rubbed her feet after a hard day and could make the most amazing gnocchi with vodka creme sauce and pancetta, her favorite Italian meal, and that was just one of the many wonderful dishes he had in his repertoire.

He played the piano like a concert pianist. The only other actor Fiona knew about who could play piano that well was Dudley Moore, who was popular in the 80s and classically trained on the instrument. Luke drew baths for her and sometimes joined her in their beautiful sunken tub.

He was so perfect on paper. But he never gave her butterflies.

She realized he was looking at her expectantly, a sure sign he had stopped reciting his vows, and it was her turn.

Oh, God. Could she get through this? Could she recite her vows like she was reciting movie lines? Could she play the role demanded of her, the role of the blushing bride thrilled to death to be marrying her Prince Charming?

She opened her mouth, but nothing came out. Her voice was finally failing her.

She finally just squeaked out the bare minimum as she promised to love and honor him. She almost choked on the "till death do us part" portion of the rather prosaic vows, but she screeched out that part as well. There was no reciting of a Kahlil Gibran poem or the famous words of 1 Corinthians 13 about love being patient and kind. No, there were just the bland words about loving and honoring but not obeying. No way would her feminist heart allow her to say anything about obeying anybody.

Luke's eyebrows crinkled slightly after Fiona choked out her vows and then turned her head to the minister conducting this farce. The look on his face said *is that all you're going to say? Nothing personal? After all I said to you?* His eyes looked troubled, breaking Fiona's heart just a little.

Damn, he deserved somebody better than her.

When she heard the applause, she realized it was a done deal. She was married to Luke. She wasn't Mrs. O'Neill - they'd agreed she wouldn't take his name, both because her feminist heart wouldn't allow her to and because the name Fiona Kennedy was famous. Her fans knew her by Fiona Kennedy and was its own brand. So, no, she wouldn't change it, not for Luke or anybody.

Now it's time to get through the damn reception. She would have to be on that evening. She would have to smile and make sparkling conversation with all 500 people invited to the reception. She'd have to laugh at un-funny jokes, throw the bouquet, somehow look madly in love during the first dance, and just get through the whole thing without tossing her cookies.

As the two walked down the aisle together holding hands, Fiona holding her bouquet up in the air with a big smile, everybody applauding and looking at them with tears in her eyes while they threw rose petals at their feet, Fiona couldn't stop thinking one thing and one thing only.

What the hell did I just do?

Chapter Three

Fiona

The reception went as well as possible. The cake was beautiful and delicious, as was the spread of lobster Newburgh, new potatoes, asparagus, and lots and lots of bread. During the reception, Fiona found Samantha Flynn, the cake maker, and hugged her. She was truly thrilled with the cake, perhaps more thrilled with it than anything else in that room. She was certainly more thrilled with the cake than she was with her new husband. And it was her favorite - raspberry icing, raspberry filling. Fiona couldn't get enough of anything and everything raspberry.

"I'm so excited you loved it," Samantha said, literally jumping up and down. "Oh, I wish my mom was here. She loves your movies."

Fiona smiled and tried to sound pleased that Samantha's mother was a fan. In reality, she heard 100 times a day that somebody or another had all of her movies memorized, and Fiona was tired of hearing it. But she would never, ever let any of her fans know just how tired she was of all the adulation.

"I'm so glad your mom likes my movies," Fiona said, holding Samantha's two hands in her own.

"Oh, she does, and I do too," Samantha said. And then she proceeded to recite lines from Fiona's movies, and Fiona smiled and laughed, even though she'd heard her own movie lines recited to her almost as many times as she'd heard about such-and-such being her biggest fans.

A tall, handsome man in glasses came up to Samantha and shyly put his hand out to shake. "I'm Grayson, Samantha's boyfriend," he said. He seemed much shyer and more reserved than Samantha and seemed tongue-tied, which Fiona was also used to. She was accustomed to all different types of reactions to meeting her and always fantasized about the day when she could just be herself. Fiona Kennedy, just a face in the crowd.

Fiona chatted with Samantha and Grayson for a while. She guaranteed she'd give Samantha's name to everyone she knew, which wasn't a lie. Samantha squealed with delight upon hearing Fiona's promise. Fiona laughed a little, gave her a quick hug and then moved on.

Fiona conversed with everybody there, but she clung to Camille, who had a date of her own but made time for Fiona's various freakouts over the evening. It wasn't quite like the movie *Melancholia*, where Kirsten Dunst's character not only disappeared during her wedding reception to take a bath but also had sex with a random guy, but it was close. Fiona did all she could to avoid her new husband, making an excuse to Luke that she couldn't talk to him because she was so busy talking to everybody else. She looked googly-eyed at Luke during their first dance to the Radiohead song *Creep*. Yes, it was an odd choice, but both loved that song and felt like weirdos in their own way. And Luke thought Fiona was special, so the song fit him well. Fiona, not so much, but she felt like a creep and a weirdo, so the song had meaning for her.

And, of course, she talked to the press. She had to make sure they made glowing reports about her. Amelia would expect nothing less, so Fiona gushed about how wonderful Luke was to anybody who would listen and could write some good articles.

Finally, after an exhausting 9-hour reception that went on until 3 AM, Fiona and Luke headed home. She knew Luke would ask her why she was so distant, and she'd just have to lie to him. Pretty little white lies that would spare his feelings.

The following Monday, the two were back on the set. It was the last day of filming, after which there would be a wrap party. Fiona was secretly happy that this was her last movie for a while because she was ready for a break. She was working like a dog, 17-hour days on the set, and she needed a break. She hoped and prayed that if she could take a little breather away from her life, she could look at Luke with different eyes. Maybe she was just tired, so she was in a bad mood, which made her look at Luke without love in her heart. She didn't really know.

For Luke's part, he stayed at the wrap party while Fiona went home. They still had separate homes, Fiona living in a six-bedroom home in Malibu that was on cliff above the ocean, Luke living in Beverly Hills in a 20-room mansion, but they would soon look for a place together.

But the next morning, Fiona got the shock of her life.

Chapter Four

Hallie

Hallie was so happy with her new job at the Malibu wellness retreat. She couldn't believe her good fortune when she actually got the job, and as her car climbed the mountain to go to her retreat, she thought about everything that led her to this point. How ironic that her lived experiences would lead her to such a lucrative and responsible position as this one.

All her life, she suffered from low self-esteem. That was the source of most of her problems – a toxic marriage, a drinking problem, chronic insomnia, a rift with her daughter, weight gain. She never felt worthy. She always felt entitled to scraps, so she stayed married to Nate for too long. She was depressed for so long that, at some point, she'd forgotten what it was like to live without blackness.

All that changed with the move to Nantucket and Willow's acupuncture therapy. Willow explained that the energy centers in her body were blocked, which was why she couldn't accept positive things in her life. And, sure enough, once the acupuncture opened up her energy centers and chakras, and the energy started flowing freely within her body, she felt more positive about life in general. Somehow, acupuncture accomplished what years of therapy never did.

The upshot was that she could get this job at this wellness retreat because of her lived experiences and completing her online integrative nutrition course. She overcame years of negative self-talk that led to many destructive impulses, so Annie McCormick, the retreat director, hired her. Annie saw that Hallie was ready to use her background to help others.

Hallie arrived at the retreat, anxious to meet the six clients she would be working with. However, when she got to the retreat, Annie informed her there was a change in plans.

"Hallie, change in plans," Annie said. "I know you usually take six clients under your wing. But I want you to take on only one."

One client, not six? Hallie had no idea how that would work.

"I don't understand?" Hallie started to feel anxious. She'd been there for the past few months and thought she'd done well. But maybe not if Annie was already reducing her workload.

"Well, here's what I was thinking," Annie said. "I'd like for you to go along with the other counselors with their client meetings. Go on hikes with the clients, participate in group counseling sessions, eat meals with the clients, and so forth. The only difference is that you won't take six clients this time like the other counselors. But we have one client, Pete, and he's extra. In other words, he's the 25th client here, and usually, we only have 24 people here. So each of our four counselors has six clients. But you'll only have one."

At first, Hallie's mind went to a very dark place. She immediately started with her negative self-talk that was so ingrained in her brain for so long. Was Annie just letting her down easily? Was she about to be fired? Was Annie only assigning her one client because she wanted her to quit?

She finally nodded, trying to hide her distress. "Of course, that sounds like a good plan. I guess my hours will be the same as ever?"

Annie nodded her head. "Yes. You'll still be working 8 to 5, but you'll be only working with Pete. He's the only person who wasn't assigned a counselor when he got here. We over-booked. I'm sorry. Things aren't usually this chaotic. You probably think we're not managing the place right, over-booking like that. I assure you, this has nothing to do with you. You're great."

Hallie just nodded. This was a setback, but she was determined to overcome it. "Okay. Well, maybe I can meet Pete."

"Yes. Currently, he's not staying in one of the cabins because, as I said, he's extra. So he'll be staying at the main house. We set up a room for him there. He's in the main room right now. So, you can meet him now."

Hallie followed Annie to the main hall. There, sitting in a chair, not talking to any of the people who were congregated in the hall, was an overweight man. His head was bowed, and he concentrated on looking at his hands instead of making eye contact with anybody. His shoulders were slumped, and the expression on his face was extremely sad.

Hallie wasn't sure why he wasn't talking to the other people because this was social time – it was the time between breakfast and the first hike of the day. Everybody else was chatting and getting to know each other because they were all new to the retreat. Everybody came to the retreat at the same time and left at the same time, as there was an interest in the group being cohesive. And cohesiveness was difficult to maintain when new people constantly circled in and out of the group. As it was the first day for everybody at the retreat, the clients were excited to get to know each other. Pete was one of six men joining the retreat group. The rest were women. But everybody, the men and the women, were actively trying to get to know everybody there.

But Pete needed help fitting in with the group. Hallie's heart immediately went out to him. She knew what he felt like, being an outsider constantly looking in. When she was growing up, she moved around a lot. She went to two different kindergartens, two different first grades and two different second grades. It wasn't until she was in the third grade that she finally was settled into a school. By then, all the other kids had formed their own cliques, none of which involved Hallie.

When she saw Pete looking longingly at the other clients talking to one another, as if he wanted to join in with the conversations but felt like he couldn't because he assumed he'd be rejected, Hallie felt a lurch of recognition. That was how she always felt growing up. It wasn't like she chose to be a loner. She didn't. But whenever she tried to get in with a group of kids, they excluded her. She finally assumed that she'd always be excluded, so she never tried.

And that was the look on Pete's face. He was biting his bottom lip, his eyes trained on the other clients who apparently didn't even know he was sitting there. And then he kept looking at his hands, his shoulders still slumped. Once or twice, he shook his head, and it looked like he wanted to cry.

Annie looked over at Hallie and then pointed at Pete. "Pete will be your one client for these six weeks," she said. "So, when you hike with the other clients, you'll talk to Pete. And maybe Pete won't participate in group therapy if he doesn't want to. But if he does, you can sit in the group with him." And then she whispered. "I feel Pete will need a bit more one-on-one than many of our clients. That's why I wanted you to be paired with him specifically, one-on-one."

Hallie nodded. Suddenly, the motivation for Annie pairing Hallie up with Pete looked very different. Annie seemed to sense that Hallie might bring Pete out of his shell, and it was obvious that if Pete was just one of a group of people, he'd get lost in the shuffle. He seemed inward, and Hallie felt his insecurities and loneliness. It was palpable from where he sat.

So Pete would have his very own counselor. Hallie. He seemed to need personal attention. Once Hallie realized what was happening, she felt much better about the situation.

"I see," Hallie said. "So, Pete was basically an add-on that wasn't supposed to be here, and that's why we're paired up together. It seems like this will be a good situation for Pete and me. Maybe I won't be overwhelmed with the needs of six people, and maybe Pete will feel uncomfortable being part of a group. I feel he's the kind who won't talk very much."

Annie looked relieved that Hallie wasn't upset by the change in plans. "Yes, pairing you with only one person was a good idea. And I also thought Pete might not be comfortable being a part of a group. I just get those vibes from him."

As Hallie looked at Pete, who was still looking at his hands while occasionally looking at the group with longing eyes, Hallie knew Annie was right. At least at the moment, it was obvious that Pete wouldn't do well in a group.

Hallie took a deep breath and then went over to Pete. To Hallie's surprise, he welcomed her company when she sat beside him. He smiled at her shyly.

"Hello," Hallie said to Pete. "My name is Hallie Gleason, and I'm a counselor. I've been paired up with you. One on one."

"My name is Pete Peters." Then he laughed. "Yes, thank my parents for naming me Peter Peters."

Hallie had to have a laugh, too. "Hey, it could be worse. Your name could be Ima Hogg. You know, there was actually a woman named that. She was a socialite in Texas and actually quite attractive."

Hallie wanted to mention that the aforementioned Ima Hogg was also slim, in contrast to her name, but she didn't think it was appropriate to say that to Pete, who was so obviously struggling with his weight.

Pete smiled at her. "I remember hearing about that poor woman named Ima Hogg. I even looked her up on Wikipedia, and I found out there are other people in the world with unfortunate names. I think it mentioned people named Ima Hooker, Ima Pigg, Ima Nut and Ima Butt. Why do parents do that to their kids?"

"Why indeed?" Hallie said, relieved that the ice had broken between her and Pete. "Have you had breakfast yet?"

Pete shook his head. "No. I'm trying to lose weight, so I don't want to eat all the time."

Hallie lightly put her hand on Pete's arm. "Pete, I know what you're saying. Some experts say intermittent fasting is a good tool for weight loss. But I don't want you to be afraid of food. That's one of the destructive tendencies we all have when we gain a bit of weight. Food becomes the enemy. And when food is the enemy, our relationship with what we put into our mouths doesn't serve us well. I think that's one of the reasons why at this ranch, everybody has to eat regularly. We're trying to establish a healthier relationship with food."

Pete just nodded. "I'm sorry. Please don't report me." And then he shook his head and stared at his hands again.

What an odd reaction. Hallie wondered what Pete meant when he begged her not to report him. "Pete, I don't understand. Why would I report you? And who would I report you to?"

"I just don't want to be in trouble. That's all."

Hallie's hand inadvertently went to Pete's forearm again. Pete's expression and demeanor tugged at Hallie's heartstrings. "Pete, of course, you won't be in trouble. But everybody is encouraged to have breakfast here on the ranch. And don't worry, the breakfasts we serve are nothing but healthy."

Hallie had Pete's file in her hand. She looked in the file to see if there were any food allergies or sensitivities she needed to know about Pete. Also in the file were lists of foods that Pete simply didn't care for. The menu at the ranch was tailor-made for each client, according to their preferences, sensitivities, and allergies.

Pete shrugged. "I got here late, so they didn't try to force me to have breakfast. But I also feel like every bit of morsel of food I put into my body will do nothing but make me bigger. I don't know. It seems like I just think of food and gain 10 pounds."

Hallie looked again at Pete's file. As all the clients did before they came to the ranch, Pete had a complete physical and blood work done before arriving. Pete didn't seem to have any physical issues. His hormone levels were within range, and his thyroid seemed to function fine. Everything seemed to check out. So there wasn't an obvious reason Pete would have problems with losing weight.

At least Pete didn't seem to have any *obvious* physical issues. So, Hallie deduced that Pete was like many people - he was unaware of how much he ate. People with a dis-regulated relationship with food must be made aware of how many calories they eat daily. They usually overeat without even thinking about it. And then they just assume that food, in general, is the enemy because they think they're not eating much, yet they're still gaining weight. In reality, they eat way more than they think.

"I know where you're coming from," Hallie said. "And I also know you were asked to keep a food journal. I hope you feel comfortable sharing your journal with me."

Pete nodded and silently got a small leather book out of his satchel. "Here," he said. "Read it and weep. I didn't hold back as much as I wanted to. You don't know how tempted I was to write every day that I ate nothing but fruits, vegeta-bles, and grilled fish. But I had to be honest."

Hallie smiled. "Thank you for sharing. I hope you don't mind if I read this through before we hike. In the mean-time, I know you're supposed to eat breakfast before going on this long hike. Otherwise, you could get low blood sugar, which could cause many problems. So, why don't you and I go down to the cafeteria, and we can get some food?"

Pete and Hallie walked to the cafeteria. Hallie would

have breakfast with Pete, so she chose granola with blueberries and yogurt. Pete chose polenta topped with pears and blueberries with yogurt on the side.

"You and I both got blueberries," he observed.

"Yes, blueberries are one of the things this place really likes to push. It has a ton of antioxidants and vitamins and all kinds of good stuff." Both Pete and Hallie also chose green tea for their beverage, which also had a lot of antioxidants.

"I guess I have much to learn about nutrition," Pete said. "I admit, I don't know much about it. I haven't really learned much about food and what it does."

Hallie and Pete sat down, and Hallie dug into her breakfast, which was delicious. She had learned to appreciate a simple granola, fruit, and yogurt breakfast. On the other hand, Pete looked at his polenta topped with fruit with disdain.

"What do you usually eat in the morning?" Hallie asked him.

He shrugged. "I don't know. Sometimes I grab a donut and coffee or eat some kind of cereal. Other times I get a bagel and cream cheese."

Hallie opened Pete's journal and read what he wrote down for his breakfasts. At first, when Pete mentioned cereal, Hallie thought that didn't sound so terrible. The donut and coffee, not so much. The bagel idea was marginally better than the donut, but only marginally, as bagels are nothing but simple carbs and had no nutritive properties.

But, unfortunately, when Pete mentioned cereal, he meant Frosted Flakes and Frosted Shredded Wheat. It wasn't exactly Captain Crunch, but it certainly wasn't great.

"I hope you don't mind if I glance over your journal over breakfast," Hallie said. "I don't want you to think I'm ignoring you. Unfortunately, the hike starts in less than 20 minutes, so I must multi-task here."

"No, go ahead," Pete said. "Read away."

Hallie looked through the first week of food logs and saw the problem. Pete wasn't eating a ton, but his eating could've been better. A lot of pasta, bread, and sugar was written on these pages. Pete also ate a lot of potato chips with ham salad sandwiches on white bread and called that lunch.

A typical day for Pete started with a cheese Danish and coffee in the morning, followed by a chocolate milk mid-morning, a ham salad sandwich with potato chips for lunch, a snack cake of some sort mid-afternoon, followed by a dinner of pasta, garlic bread, and dessert - usually chocolate cake. Sometimes he ate pizza for dinner.

Hallie nodded. Pete ate a lot of simple carbs and sugar, with very little protein, aside from the ham salad. And no fruits and vegetables. He didn't even get veggies on his pizzas, such as mushrooms or black olives. His pizzas usually had pepperoni, sausage, or hamburger, if not all three.

Hallie saw the problem. Although Pete totaled up the calories for every day's meals and ate only around 2500 calories a day, which wasn't terrible for a man his size, he was eating all the wrong things. His body wasn't processing all those simple carbs, sugar and grease very well. Nobody's body processes crap food very well, and when you don't eat anything nutritious, which was the case with Pete, your body just doesn't work efficiently.

Hallie thought back to her childhood again, which was a difficult one, not because her family life was chaotic or depressing, because it wasn't. Her parents were very loving, yet clueless. And the fact that they were clueless was why

Hallie moved around so much when she was a young girl. Her parents moved around Kansas City without regard to school districts, so they never cared that when they moved down the street to a new rented house or apartment, Hallie would start over yet again in a new school.

And her mother needed to be more conscientious when packing Hallie's lunches or preparing breakfast for young Hallie. Breakfast was Captain Crunch or Fruity Pebbles. Hallie lived on fluffernutter sandwiches for lunch – peanut butter and marshmallow fluff on white bread. These fluffernutter sandwiches, bags of potato chips, and Hostess Ding Dongs were a staple in Hallie's lunches. It was the 1970s, and, to be fair, many parents served their kids sugary cereal and packed the same things in their children's lunches. Back then, nobody knew about the benefits of organic food or how bad white bread was for your body, let alone packaged cupcakes. And Hallie was very thin growing up because she was active and had a good metabolism, so it wasn't like the bad effects of such a terrible diet showed on her body.

The 1970s were also when ham and pickle roll-ups were considered the height of sophistication. In other words, people were clueless in the 70s. And, as Hallie looked at poor Pete's journal, the only thing she could think of was that Pete would've been right at home at the Gleason house. It was almost as if he was raised by Hallie's mother, Linda Gleason, a mother who always meant well but was reliant on Hamburger Helper, frozen pizzas, and eating out to feed Hallie and her brother, Ron.

"So, what do you think?" Pete asked anxiously as he watched Hallie look through his journal. "I don't eat a lot for a man my size. That's what I always told Laura, but she never believed me."

"Laura?" Hallie asked. "Is that your wife?"

27

Pete shook his head, and his hands were now shaking. "Ex-wife. She never loved me. She only loved my bank account, never me." He took a deep breath. "I should've known when I met her. She's slim and beautiful. I should've known she would've never looked at a guy like me if I was broke."

Hallie struck a nerve. That much was plain. "I'm so sorry you had a bad marriage." She felt Pete's marriage to Laura was probably part of his problem. She probably did a real number on his self-esteem, but then again, Laura might've been just the last person in a long line who did a number on poor Pete's self-esteem. Specifically, if Pete had always been heavy, he probably was bullied in school.

It was all such a vicious circle when you're young and overweight. You get bullied for being overweight, which makes you sad and angry. You eat more because you're eating your feelings. And then you gain more weight, you get bullied more and more, which causes you to eat more and more, which makes you gain even more weight.

Hallie wondered if Laura was a bully, much like Annie was bullied by her husband. One thing was for sure, if an overweight person marries the wrong person, the person who won't be supportive but has his or her own issues and takes them out on the overweight spouse, that can prove disastrous.

Pete shook his head. "That's okay. I won the lottery, you know. Three million dollars. I thought it was the greatest thing ever because nothing good had happened in my life. But it wasn't a good thing because these women who never would've looked at me before were looking at me. I was always a fat kid dreaming of dating a cheerleader. When I won all that money, I felt my dream was coming true as all these former cheerleaders were trying to get my number.

But they only wanted to spend my money on their boyfriends and themselves."

Hallie closed her eyes as she imagined the beautiful Laura. She didn't have a picture of the woman, but she could imagine her appearance. She pictured a woman with a Botoxed face, a fake rack, and tons of makeup. She probably insulted poor Pete daily and slept with every gym rat in sight.

Hallie knew it was all such a stereotype, but she thought she probably was on the money with her visualization. Those plastic-botoxed women were the kind who would marry a man just for his money. After all, how could they pay for plastic surgery if their husbands were poor?

"Do you have a picture of Laura?" Hallie asked. She was curious if her visualization was true or not.

Pete nodded and brought out his phone. "I know I have to give this phone up soon enough, but I have it right now." He looked at his phone, rifling through his pictures, and then hit on one of Laura. "Here she is."

Hallie looked at the picture and saw just how right she was. Laura had huge blue eyes framed by obviously fake eyelashes, fish lips enhanced with some filler, cheekbones that looked like implants, and big brunette hair.

Hallie nodded and handed the phone back to Pete. "She's very pretty," Hallie said.

"She should be," Pete said. "I paid enough money for her to look like that." Then he sighed and shook his head. "I'm sorry. That was uncalled for. I hope you don't tell anybody I said that about Laura."

Hallie heard the words coming out of Pete's mouth and realized he was desperately trying to appease Hallie and anybody else who might hear him. Obviously, he had a lot of buried resentment and hurt, but he was hesitant to show that side of him for some reason. She would have to drill down into his issues and excavate why he felt so little about himself that he would marry a plastic woman who only cared about his plastic credit cards.

"It's okay," Hallie said. "You have to understand that, here at the ranch, you're not supposed to censor yourself. That's the whole point of being here. You're here to get in touch with your inner self. Even if you don't like your inner self, you still need to contact him. There's a hurt child inside us all. Sometimes the hurt child is buried deep, and you must do a lot of work to bring him to the light. But the only way you'll get in touch with the hurt child is if you're willing to not judge your feelings as being wrong. So, please, don't apologize for thinking angry thoughts about people who've wronged you."

Pete nodded, but it was obvious to Hallie that he wanted to apologize to her again for saying mean things about the plastic and apparently unfaithful Laura.

"I'm just very sorry. My mother always told me that if I didn't have something kind to say about somebody, don't say anything at all," he finally said.

"Okay. I understand the impulse to not say unkind things about your ex-wife. But the anger doesn't go away if you don't get it off your chest. You just internalize it."

Pete took a deep breath and continued to eat his polenta and pears.

"By the way, how's your breakfast?" Hallie asked.

He shrugged. "Okay. It's not a Danish or pancakes or even Frosted Flakes, but I suppose it's okay."

Hallie knew Pete would prefer eating a stack of pancakes with butter and maple syrup, a big bowl of Frosted Flakes, or a Bear Claw doughnut. Who wouldn't?

Given the choice, Hallie suspected most people would prefer to eat delicious and addictive junk food.

Her work was cut out for her with Pete. She would have to find a way to change his entire mindset regarding food. That would start with him finding a way to verbalize his feelings, which also seemed difficult for him.

Pete would be a challenge, that was for sure.

But Hallie was welcoming the challenge.

Chapter Five

Hallie

After breakfast, Hallie and Pete went hiking with the rest of the group. Hallie tried to encourage Pete to open up with the other group members, who talked to one another as they hiked through a beautiful forest of trees. They were making friends, and Pete wasn't a part of that group.

It didn't help when Hallie introduced Pete to a couple of people in the hiking group. Everybody who she introduced Pete to was polite enough, but most of them were busy bonding with other people, and they didn't really seem interested in including Pete in the conversation.

So, Hallie and Pete talked to one another exclusively on the hike. Which wasn't such a bad thing, considering Hallie was trying to get past the armor that Pete obviously had around him as a protective shield. In Hallie's experience, most people had a protective shield around them of some sort. Some people's shield was made up of papier-mâché, so it was easy to pierce. Other people had a reinforced concrete and metal shield, and nobody would ever get through it.

Hallie needed to learn what kind of material made up Pete's shield. Did he construct his shield with papier-mâché, concrete and steel, or something in between? Hallie hoped there would be some way to pierce his armor and get to the root of his self-destruction. That was what Pete was doing, in the end, with his junk food habit that wasn't doing him any favors. He was self-destructing just as sure as somebody who was an alcoholic, chain smoker or drug addict was self-destructing.

The problem was that there was no way he could give up food cold turkey. With other addictions, the addicted person could get clean or stop drinking, smoking, gambling, or whatever. After going through rehab and counseling, addicted people could walk away from their addiction and never have to face it again if they didn't want to. The compulsive gambler doesn't have to return to the casino. The alcoholic doesn't have to go to a bar or a party if he or she wants to avoid alcohol. The drug addict could just drop their playmates, leave the playground, and never return.

In other words, with most addictions, it was possible to avoid the addictive substance. Not so with food addiction. Obviously, you have to eat to stay alive. So there was no way to avoid the addictive substance in this case. Add to that the constant ads touting the addictive substance, junk food. You couldn't turn on the television without seeing a beautiful piece of pizza, a giant hamburger or a bag of chips and soda. And Hallie knew most restaurants didn't exactly cater to people trying to lose weight, to say the least. How difficult would it be for somebody like Pete to go to a restaurant to see all his favorite foods on the menu, knowing he should order the salad but not finding that option appealing? Not only that, most restaurant salads weren't exactly healthy anyhow. Many were just as laden with fat and calories as any other dish on the menu.

The challenge for Hallie would be to change Pete's mindset completely when it comes to the issue of food. She had to find some way to show him how to make better choices and not feel deprived. Changing his mindset completely might be the only way Pete could lose the weight and keep it off, other than lap band surgery. And Hallie didn't believe in lap band surgery, as that surgery did nothing for the root of the problem, which started in the brain. She'd heard of too many people who had lap band surgery but still found a way to overeat the wrong things, which meant they either didn't lose the weight or gained it all back after some initial weight loss.

At any rate, the lap band was also bad because all it did was make a person feel full after eating a small amount. But, since it does nothing to address the psychological roots of overeating, it could lead to depression because the over-weight person no longer had an outlet for unaddressed mental challenges.

So, as Hallie and Pete walked along on the hike, Hallie engaged Pete in conversation. She had some idea about why Pete was currently overeating – he was in a bad marriage with a woman who did a number on his self-esteem and probably made him feel terrible about himself. But she had to know more about Pete's problems. She wasn't quite clear when his weight issues began. Did they just begin recently with the bad marriage? Hallie wasn't sure, but the clues pointed away from that hypothesis.

She asked him about his background, hoping to glean some useful information.

"So, Pete, tell me a little about your mom and dad," Hallie said.

Pete shook his head. "My dad was a triathlete, and my mother was a former beauty queen who has stayed 120 pounds her entire life. They live in San Francisco in the Pacific Heights area in a home worth millions. Not that I will ever see any of those millions because they've told my brother and me that all their money will go to charity after they die. Of course, I don't need their money now because of the lottery win."

Was there something there? Hallie tried to detect a bitter tone to his voice that would belie his feelings about his parents, but she didn't detect this note. It was somewhat odd that his parents would cut both him and his brother out of their will in favor of giving it all away to charity, but, at the same time, it wasn't exactly unusual. Many parents want their children to earn their keep because they believe that just giving kids a trust fund wasn't healthy for them. People need to have a sense of respect and pride in their accomplishments, and wealthy parents leaving millions of dollars to their offspring defeated the purpose because it would inevitably lead to those children losing motivation to earn their own way.

Interestingly, his parents apparently didn't have the same weight issues as Pete. His parents probably had a healthy diet and exercise program, especially his father, the triathlete.

"Does your brother have any issues with his weight?" Hallie asked Pete.

"No. He apparently takes after our dad. He's 6'3" and 170 pounds. If anything, he's a little underweight."

Curiouser and curiouser. If there was something with

the family dynamic where the mother, the father or both were unconsciously or subconsciously causing their children to overeat, the brother would probably also have a problem. Hallie knew one of the ways parents could screw up their children would be to put their own neuroticism about food on their kids. The father was a dedicated triathlete, and he might also be a guy who would weigh and measure every morsel of his food, which wasn't entirely healthy, either, since that type of eating pattern took the joy out of food. Or perhaps the mother, a former beauty queen, made young Pete feel bad about himself, like he would never measure up.

"Why do you ask these questions?" Pete asked Hallie. "Are you trying to find out why I overeat?"

"Well, I'm trying to get some information to figure out when the overeating began," Hallie admitted. "If there was something in your background or upbringing, that would be where I would begin my investigation, and it'll help me give you better counsel."

"You can rule out my parents screwing me up," Pete said. "They're both great. My mother always tried to steer me into making better choices, and when she packed my lunches for school, she always packed something healthy like a turkey sandwich, yogurt and fruit. But she let me go to my friends' homes, where they served pizza, cookies and candy. She let me go trick or treating, and while she made sure I didn't eat every piece of trick-or-treat candy in one night, she let me eat all my candy as long as I only ate one or two pieces at a time."

All of that sounded reasonable to Hallie. The mother encouraged healthy habits but didn't stop Pete from living a normal life with his friends.

"What about your dad?" Hallie asked. "He's a triathlete. What kind of relationship does he have with food?"

Pete shrugged. "Dad was fine, really. He might compete in triathlons, but he was never obsessive about food. He would go get pizza with us, ate the occasional In' n' Out burger and fries, and never tried to tell me what to eat."

So far, the family dynamic for Pete seemed healthy and reasonable.

"Did either of your parents make you get on the scale?"

Pete shook his head. "No. My mother tried to get me to lose weight, but she wasn't crazy about it. She simply made sure I had healthy choices for my lunch, and she made healthy things for dinner, usually chicken or fish, some kind of salad, and some kind of potato. She's actually a very good cook. I still see my mom and dad over Thanksgiving, and the meals are always healthy. She worries about me all the time, but she's not demanding. But she recommended this retreat. Her friend went through it and loved it. So, Mom told me about this place, and here I am."

"And when did you start to gain weight?"

Pete took a deep breath. "In the sixth grade. Before I was 11 years old, I was a normal kid. Normal weight." He swallowed hard as he walked along.

"Okay. What happened when you were in the sixth grade?" Hallie asked him. "Did you get sick somehow? Did something happen to damage your thyroid or hormones or something of the like?"

"No," he said. "Something happened when I was in sixth grade, though. I can't quite talk about that."

Hallie nodded. "I understand," she said. She would drop the topic for now. She'd try to draw him out but didn't want to push. "Look at those ducks," she said, pointing to a small pond filled with colorful mallards. "If only we could have such a peaceful existence, huh?"

Pete grimaced. "These ducks are peaceful, but most

aren't. They're prey. They might not know it as they're swimming along the pond, but they're naïve, those poor things. They'll find that out soon enough. They're protected here, but if they ever venture into a land where they're not, they'll get blasted out of the sky."

"Have you ever felt like the ducks?" Hallie asked Pete. "Unprotected. In danger. Out in the middle of the water, swimming along, unaware of what's around the corner?"

Pete shrugged. "Doesn't everybody?"

Hallie thought about it. He had a point. Everybody probably felt that way at least one time in their life. Hallie, herself, felt that way when she was married to Nate. She felt trapped in a toxic marriage she couldn't get out of. During her marriage, she was a bit like those ducks.

And there were other times when she felt vulnerable. And that's what those ducks were, really - vulnerable. Naked. Just waiting for a predator to swoop in.

"You're right," Hallie said. "Everybody feels vulnerable at various times in their lives. I'm vulnerable whenever I drive up here because the drivers behind me aren't so careful and want to tailgate me and make me go faster. I felt vulnerable once when I was in a coffee shop, and a man got irate and screamed at the top of his lungs that he would take everybody down. Thank God he didn't have a gun, but if he did…"

Hallie thought about that moment. Ultimately, it was just a case of a guy who was mad about something. And he really didn't have the motivation or wherewithal to shoot up the place. Nevertheless, it was a scary moment for Hallie, who knew mass shootings happened more frequently than she'd like to think about.

"Were those the only times you felt vulnerable?" Pete asked.

"Of course not," Hallie said. "I'm human, so things happen regularly that make me feel I'm not quite safe. The world is a crazy place sometimes. And it's not just our corner of the world, of course. Things happen in other countries where people really are unsafe every day. But I'm just wondering if something made you feel unsafe."

Pete just walked along and didn't say much more. And then he proceeded to change the subject. "What happens after this hike?" he asked Hallie.

"Some people will go to group therapy, while others will attend various exercise classes," Hallie said. "You're a man, so you probably want to lift some heavy weights. We have a personal trainer who can help you get started. Or, maybe you want to do yoga, Pilates, or join a spinning class."

Pete smiled. "I probably could use yoga. I've been doing a lot of research on yoga and stuff like that. I guess it's really good for strength and flexibility. I'm not all that interested in getting huge, anyhow. I don't think I could keep up with the roid-heads."

"Yes. Yoga is very good for strength and flexibility. Also, it emphasizes the mind-body connection. That's good for some people. For other people, not so much." Hallie couldn't quite tap into the mind-body connection when she did yoga. Her instructors always encouraged her to be quiet in the stillness and listen to herself. But she never really did. However, she found that, after doing regular yoga for the past few years, she was extremely flexible, much more than before, and very strong. She could carry cases of water now when she never could before.

She loved that she was stronger and fitter now than she ever had been. Even after her cancer, she could still get back into shape fairly easily, mainly because she never quit doing yoga, even when very sick.

The group hike came to an end. Everybody arrived simultaneously at the meeting room, and half the people followed counselors into different parts of the media center for group therapy. Hallie had seen the rooms where the group therapies took place, which were beautiful. They were far from the pedestrian meeting rooms Hallie knew about before, with fluorescent lighting, uncomfortable plastic chairs and cheap carpeting. No, these rooms were constructed for maximum beauty, relaxation, and comfort.

One of the meeting rooms was on the deck of the main house. Since the main house and the entire resort were situated on land that overlooked the Pacific Ocean and was landscaped with beautiful trees, flowers, and plants, the deck was a peaceful place to talk. The furniture on the deck was plush and comfortable, and most of the chairs and sofas were arranged around a fire ring.

Another of the meeting rooms had a view afforded by floor-to-ceiling windows that looked out on a lake. Inside the room were a waterfall and beautiful tropical plants, flowers and trees. The waterfall was peaceful and tranquil, and that room also benefited from the aromatherapy afforded by multiple soy-based candles. As with the room on the house's deck, the waterfall room furniture, as everybody referred to it, was extremely plush and comfortable.

Hallie was very impressed with the Feng Shui of it all. She'd studied a bit about Feng Shui, which was the art of making living space the most tranquil it could be. It all had to do with how the furniture was arranged in a room, what hung on the walls, and the color of those walls. The waterfall room was painted a color of soothing blue, which was the color that most interior decorators and Feng Shui experts say is the color that brings the most calm.

When everybody came back from the hike, Annie asked

the participants who wanted to go to group therapy and who wanted to go through exercise. Pete opted for group therapy, so Hallie went along.

She hoped Pete would open up enough to the group that he'd give a clue about what in his background caused him to feel unsafe. Because Hallie knew something had caused him to feel unsafe at one point in his life.

She just had to find out what it was.

Chapter Six

Hallie

Hallie arrived home feeling accomplished. She was almost on a little high because she thought she could help Pete, who seemed like such a nice man, even if he apparently had some issues that he was presently unwilling to discuss.

And it was just the high of helping somebody, in general, putting Hallie on cloud nine.

When she got home, she saw a note on the fridge that told her Conrad was at the art gallery, and he wanted her to meet him there because he wanted her to see some new works of art they were displaying. His note also said he wanted to take her to dinner.

Hallie got excited about going to the gallery like she always did. She loved that space. Morgan did a great job with it and did a fantastic job of finding different artists to be part of her cooperative. Hallie was so proud of her daughter, and she was proud of her roommate, too. And she wanted to support them, not just Morgan and Conrad, but all the other artists who were part of the cooperative.

However, before she could go to the cooperative, she got a phone call from Pete. "Hello," he said tentatively. "I hope I'm not bothering you."

"Of course, you're not," Hallie said quickly. She'd encouraged Pete to call her whenever he felt like talking. "What's on your mind?"

"Well, I'm just sitting in my room. I need somebody to talk to."

Hallie knew Pete was reaching out to her because she was the first person who'd taken an interest in him for quite a while. She got the feeling that most people in his life had counted him out and let him down. She was concerned that he didn't fit in with the other clients on the ranch. It didn't help that he was isolated and not rooming with others. At the same time, Hallie also knew most of the clients at this time were socializing in the main house. Every night, there were activities in the main house that everybody was free to attend or not. That night was game night. It was his choice if Pete was sitting isolated in his room, probably because he felt like an outsider.

"Thanks for taking my call," Pete said tentatively.

"You're welcome," Hallie said.

She waited for him to say more. She could've jumped in the silence and just plowed ahead because she was nervous that he wasn't talking that much. But she knew Pete had called her for a reason, and she wouldn't step on it.

"Anyhow, I just wanted you to know how much I appreciate your talking to me about my issues," he finally said after a long silence.

"Of course," Hallie said. "By the way, I know a game

night is going on tonight. I was wondering why you weren't participating in that."

"I don't know. I'm just hanging back right now. I'm tired because of all the exercise and everything. So I'm just in my room watching Netflix."

Hallie got the feeling Pete wanted her to keep him company. She wondered if he would participate with the others if she were there. Hallie was a bit concerned that he was looking at her as a kind of security blanket, but then again, it was difficult for some people to assimilate with others if they don't have somebody there to encourage them.

She took a deep breath. Conrad invited her to dinner that evening, and she was looking forward to going to the art gallery. At the same time, she really wanted to help Pete feel more comfortable at the ranch. But it was 6 o'clock and getting dark, as it was only January, so Hallie was slightly nervous about navigating the winding roads up to the ranch.

But she knew that she, like all counselors, could stay at the ranch overnight. There was a special part of the main house for the counselors who decided to hang out and stay. Some of the counselors did just that – several had decided to remain at the ranch all the time, even though they were technically off the clock after 5 PM every day. Mainly they were the ones who didn't have any family obligations and just really enjoyed the ranch atmosphere. So, it wouldn't be a problem for her to head back up to the ranch and stay all night, which she'd be doing if she had to drive back up there because she certainly wouldn't drive home when it was pitch black. She still didn't know all the twists and turns of those roads.

"You know, Pete, I think game night sounds really fun,"

Hallie said. "I'd enjoy playing games with everybody and getting to know everybody. I could head back up there and join in the fun. You could also come on out with everybody if I'm there."

Hallie wanted to put it that way because she knew he'd tell her to stay home if she came out and asked him if he wanted her to come to the ranch. He didn't want to put her out. That was plain. At the same time, because he was shyly talking to her on the phone, Hallie had an intuition that he really wanted her to be there with him, even if he didn't want to explicitly ask her.

"You'd like to come and join in the game night?" His voice sounded so hopeful that Hallie's heart went out to him. "They're playing my favorite game. Trivial Pursuit."

Hallie would be letting down Conrad. At the same time, it wasn't like she'd committed to going to dinner with him. And there was always the next night. Conrad had plenty of things to do at the art gallery. He didn't need to see her that night.

"That's my favorite game, too," Hallie said, closing her eyes. That was her favorite game, but she didn't want to go to the ranch because she didn't want to let her roommate down. Yet, she had the feeling Pete really needed her.

"I don't want to put you out or anything. I'm sure you have your own life."

"No, no. I actually wanted to join the others. Several other counselors will be there, and I'd like to know them better. Plus, those games are fun and I've always loved game night."

"If you're sure it's not a problem…" he said.

"Of course, it's not a problem," Hallie said. "I think it'll be a lot of fun." And, of course, Hallie wasn't lying about that. She really enjoyed game nights and wanted to get to know some of the other clients. And she sensed Pete really needed her. "I can be there in a half hour."

"Really? Then I'll be looking out for you. I'm really excited you're coming back. I wanted to play the game with the others, but I don't feel like I fit in yet. Having you around to help break the ice will be helpful."

Hallie knew this was really how Pete was feeling. She told herself that she could help him assimilate with the others and kick him out of the nest like a baby bird.

It made her sad that Pete had such low self-esteem and that people had overlooked him. Hallie was determined to turn it all around for him.

Hallie got into her car and called Conrad. "Conrad, I'm so sorry. I got the note on the fridge that you wanted me to go to the gallery and have dinner. But I have to go back up to the ranch. My client really wants me to accompany him on game night."

"Don't worry about it, lass," Conrad said. "It was just a suggestion. I thought it'd be fun for us to get pissed together. We don't see each other that much even though we live together. But I'm having a good time up here. I'll see you when I see you."

Hallie just nodded. "Well, I can't really stay on the phone," she said. She had a hands-free phone system in her car to talk to him while driving. But she wouldn't talk to him while driving the mountain roads because she needed to concentrate. "I just wanted to call you and let you know what I was doing."

"Okay. Have fun with your chap. I take it you'll be spending the night?"

"Yes. I should probably do that because I don't want to be driving on those roads at night."

"No, you probably wouldn't want to do that. So I'll be seeing you sometime."

Hallie hung up. Conrad was right – even though they lived together, they hardly saw one another. And Hallie wanted to really spend more time with her roommate. She was very fond of him. He always made her laugh and was madly talented, which Hallie admired. So, she was torn between her feelings for Conrad and her duty to her client.

But she would just have to put those misgivings away. Pete really needed her. That much was clear. So she would have to suck it up. That was the one thing Hallie was always somewhat missing in her life – somebody who needed her. Her daughter never seemed to need her, which wasn't necessarily bad. Morgan had always been very independent, a daughter who marched to the beat of her own drummer and didn't really want or need Hallie's guidance. Her ex-husband never needed her, of course. He didn't even really like her, and the feeling was mutual. Her best friends loved her, but they didn't need her either.

Hallie was starting to realize she wanted somebody to need her. She wanted to believe she could make a difference in somebody's life. So that was what was motivating her with Pete. He was filling that void she always wanted to fill.

She just didn't like taking away from Conrad in the process.

Chapter Seven

Hallie

Hallie arrived at the retreat and found Pete sitting on the bed. He was dressed up in a dress shirt and khaki pants and wearing cologne. He looked up at Hallie shyly. "I'm so happy you came up here." And then he looked at his hands.

Hallie sat next to him on the bed. "Of course. I'm thrilled to be up here."

"Are you going to be okay? It's really dark out, and I know you're very nervous about driving the mountain roads. I thought about that after I hung up with you. I'm sorry I didn't think about that before."

Hallie just smiled and put her hand on Pete's shoulder. "It's okay. I can just stay here overnight. I brought an overnight bag with me. Complete with face cream, toothbrush, toothpaste, soap, shampoo, and a change of clothes. So I'm all ready to go."

Pete nodded, but then continued to stare at his hands. "Still, I hope it didn't put you out."

"I told you, I love game night myself. So, let's go downstairs and join the others."

So, Pete and Hallie went downstairs, where the rest of the clients were busy in the middle of Trivial Pursuit. Hallie enjoyed playing Trivial Pursuit because she had a lot of knowledge. She had a feeling Pete would be much the same.

"Hey, everybody," Hallie said to everybody sitting around the large table. "Can we join in?"

To Hallie's relief, Selma, who was one of the clients and appeared to be a bit of a leader – she reminded Hallie of a popular girl from college or high school because people just flocked around her, like Ava's sister Sarah – smiled at Pete and patted the chair next to her. "Come and join my team. We need all the help we can get. Especially since we only have five people on our team instead of six, like everybody else."

Pete looked a little uneasy, but he sat down next to Selma. "Just so you know, I'm pretty good with the geography, history and science categories. Not so much literature, entertainment, and sports and leisure," he said.

Selma smiled and playfully punched Pete on the shoulder. "Well, it's good you're on our team because we need somebody good with the science and geography categories. As you can see, we've not gotten a pie piece yet in those categories, even though we've had many tries. Looks like you might be a good addition to the team."

Hallie felt a keen sense of relief. She watched Pete relax, and, over the next few hours, as Pete got one difficult and obscure question after another correct in his chosen categories, and even knew some literature and entertainment questions that nobody else knew, even though he said those were not his strong categories, Hallie saw Pete's confidence grow. Hallie knew she did the right thing in coming to the retreat that evening, if only to give Pete the confidence to join the others.

Hallie herself joined a team. The categories that she was the best in were definitely entertainment and literature. She had a minor in Russian literature from the University of Missouri and was very much up on popular culture, music and art. So she held her own for her team.

In the end, it was a very good night for both Hallie and Pete. Pete seemed to be positively glowing because he was making friends at long last. Everybody around the table was impressed with Pete. The ice was broken, and Hallie knew Pete would feel much more comfortable socializing with everybody from then on. At least, Hallie hoped that was the case.

Around 10 o'clock, everybody quit for the evening. There still wasn't a clear-cut winner of the game. Pete's team had all the pie pieces they needed, but still needed to answer the final question in the middle of the board.

"We all have to go to bed now," Pete said. "Because 7 o'clock in the morning comes very early."

"Yes, it does," Hallie said. "And it is so important that everybody gets enough sleep. That's one key to weight loss, really. When you don't get enough sleep, your hormones go awry, and when your hormones go awry, you eat a lot more." That was one thing Hallie learned through her online nutrition class, how hormones and weight loss or weight gain are related. Specifically, a lack of sleep causes the hunger hormone to go into overdrive. That was much of the reason people overeat.

Pete smiled. "Okay, then. I guess I'll be seeing you tomorrow morning."

Hallie went to her room and tried to fall asleep. Because she was having an issue with menopause, sometimes she could not fall asleep. Or, worse yet, she'd wake up about midnight and be unable to go back to sleep. The acupuncture treatments she took from her friend Willow helped tremendously with that. But Willow was no longer doing the spa thing. She was now writing screenplays and looking forward to the birth of her first child with Jackson. She had abandoned her spa on Nantucket and sold the place because she wanted more flexibility and time for her newborn. Writing screenplays allowed her to have this kind of flexibility. Willow still did tarot readings, though. She even had a new partner named Greer Davidson.

But Willow was no longer doing acupuncture, and Hallie had yet to find a new acupuncturist she trusted in California. She was slipping back into her old habits. That meant she had trouble falling or staying asleep once a week. And tonight, she was having trouble.

She realized she might've been having a little problem with Conrad. She really wanted to join him for dinner that night. But she wondered if she had a problem because she didn't know how Conrad felt about her. So far, they were housemates and nothing more. But there were a couple of times when Hallie realized Conrad was looking at her differently. They'd be having dinner with Ava and everybody, and Hallie would notice Conrad staring at her from across the table. One night, when the two of them had a few too many glasses of wine, they'd gotten close to kissing. But, so far, they hadn't actually locked lips.

So far, the only person in Hallie's intimate group of friends – Ava, Sarah, and Quinn – only Quinn had found a serious relationship. Quinn had been dating Mia for the past month or so, and they seemed very happy together. Willow would say they were both old souls who found each other in this life because they had such an easy rapport. They finished each other's sentences, got each other's jokes, and just seemed to click. Hallie was thrilled for her friend, who seemed to find her soulmate. And a part of Hallie thought that maybe Conrad was her soulmate. But maybe not. If he was her soulmate, they wouldn't have so many problems getting together, would they?

Hallie rearranged her pillows and lay on her side. She did this when she couldn't sleep – she'd try to lie on one side and then the other. She would trade one pillow for another. She would stare at the clock, paranoid that she would fall asleep the next day instead of being at her best for her client. She would do anything to fall asleep but knew she would have issues. And all the advice she found on the Internet about insomnia said it was not good to lie in bed obsessing about sleep or lack thereof. It was better to get out of bed and do something else, anything else, until you felt sleepy. The last thing you're supposed to do is train your brain that the bed is associated with not sleeping. That happens when you lay in bed staring at the clock and obsessing – your brain thinks the bed is a place of stress and insomnia.

Hallie got out of bed, tiptoed through the main house, where her room was, and went out the front door. It was late January, so there was a chill in the air. Hallie went back into the house, grabbed a sweater, and came back out again. She could hear owls in the trees and crickets galore. The grass smelled of recent rain, and the ground was wet beneath her bare feet.

She loved this place so much. It was in the middle of a veritable sanctuary, a quiet place where you could hear only the sounds of nature. She walked a little further and came upon a stream. She put her feet into the water and closed her eyes. She was alone with her thoughts and could think more clearly than in a long time.

She wondered why she had this burning need to feel useful to another person. When she was married, her husband Nate always virtually ignored her. And sometimes, it wasn't even virtually ignoring her – he actively ignored her too. She wasted so many years in a dead marriage where the two people didn't like one another, let alone love one another. So she wanted to be useful to her daughter, Morgan. And she went overboard with Morgan. She smothered her daughter by trying to live Morgan's life for her. She intruded on Morgan's life by going to bars where Morgan was with her friends, going to Morgan's art gallery in New York City, where her daughter was a curator, and trying to get the gallery director to take Hallie's recommendations. Whenever Morgan couldn't make enough time for her, she would become a martyr and whine about how she never got to see her daughter. She was too clingy with Morgan, which drove a wedge between mother and daughter.

But things were going really well between Morgan and Hallie now. Hallie had learned to back off and let Morgan live her life and blossom. She was certainly doing this as she had a cooperative of artists who had opened up a gallery on Gallery Row, which referred to an area in Downtown Los Angeles that hosted over 50 art galleries in a few block radius. Conrad and Morgan were two of those artists, and there were several more from different genres and mediums. They were wildly talented artists and had had several successful shows and exhibits. And Hallie was content to let her daughter get these exhibits and shows together without her meddling.

To her surprise, she heard footsteps just behind her. Pete stood about 100 feet from her, his hands in his pockets. He was staring into the distance. He didn't seem to know she was there, and he probably didn't.

She walked over to him, and he almost jumped out of his skin. "Oh, Hallie. I didn't know you were there."

Hallie smiled. "It's 2 o'clock in the morning. I guess you couldn't sleep either."

He shook his head. "Sleeping has been a problem with me for quite a long time." Then he took a deep breath through his nose and let it out through his mouth. "The darkness is not always comforting for me."

Hallie narrowed her eyes. There was something about the darkness that frightened Pete. And he also talked about the ducks being prey and how humans could also be prey. They just didn't know there was danger around every corner. There was something in Pete's background that was causing a lot of mental anguish. And she understood that had to do with feeling unsafe and like the darkness was not his friend.

"That's too bad. Because all the advice I've ever seen about insomnia suggests that having a pitch-dark room is very important. Because light, any kind of light, apparently signals your brain that it's not time to fall asleep."

"I know. And that's been my problem ever since I was 11 years old. Darkness has always been frightening. Well not always, but ever since that time." He visibly shuddered.

"Pete, what happened when you were 11? Can you tell me about it?"

Pete shrugged. "I'm not really sure. But I remember being in darkness for a few weeks. It's all very hazy."

"And you remember little else besides darkness for a few weeks?"

Pete shook his head. "No. That's really all I remember. But I know that darkness was something bad."

"Do you think hypnosis would help you?" Hallie asked. Willow was very good at hypnosis. She offered that service at her old spa, along with acupuncture and metaphysical things like tarot and astrology readings. If Pete was open to being hypnotized, he could figure out what happened to him when he was 11 years old and get past it. Willow wasn't actively looking for clients anymore, but she still would help a friend of Hallie's. So, she probably could help Pete. If he would let her.

Pete just stood there, looking into the distance for a few minutes. Then he looked at Hallie. "I really don't know. I'd like to think hypnosis could help, but I don't know if I can be hypnotized. Not everybody can be hypnotized, you know. I've even gone to Vegas shows where they tried hypnotizing me on stage, but it doesn't work for me, even with the magicians."

Hallie smiled. "You were a volunteer at a Vegas show? How did you get chosen?"

Pete smiled back. He had a sweet smile, very shy, yet somehow knowing. "I don't know how I got chosen. All I know is I was, and I came on stage, and I think everybody was very disappointed that I didn't fall into a trance and do crazy things like a lot of other people did. The magician was very talented but couldn't put me under."

That was too bad. Still, she wondered if Willow could help Pete anyway. If nothing else, Willow had an uncanny ability to see somebody and know their problem. She did it with Hallie, and she did it with Ava's mother, Colleen. She could see Colleen, meet her, and know immediately that Colleen was hiding two enormous secrets from Ava. One secret was that Colleen was gay and had a female lover for many years. The other secret was that Ava's father was not who she thought. Ava's actual father was James Bloch, who willed Ava his house on Nantucket.

Maybe Willow could do the same for Pete. However, Willow said she could only sometimes get a read on people. If the person had some kind of energy blocking Willow, then she couldn't work her magic and figure out traumas and secrets the person had buried. Willow even told Hallie that she couldn't get a read on Jackson, who was now Willow's significant other and the father of her impending child. Apparently, Jackson had energy that blocked Willow from reading him, which was good because Willow wanted to have some kind of surprise with her extremely handsome boyfriend.

"Well, I know somebody who might help," Hallie said. "That is if you want help." Hallie understood that people dealing with trauma are often helped by hypnosis if they didn't quite remember the source of their injury. Because that was one thing about trauma - you need to deal with it. But you can't if you don't know what's causing the problem.

That was the case with Jessica Bloch, who stayed with Ava and was Ava's niece from the side of the family that Ava didn't even know existed until just recently. Jessica was dealing with addiction and trauma because she didn't remember that her mother was killed right in front of her. Her mother had stepped in front of a bullet meant for Jessica's friend, Andrew. Andrew later became an international super popular popstar, landing on Nantucket for some rest and relaxation and songwriting. Jessica and Andrew became fast friends because neither had remembered that they were each other's childhood best friends, but they knew they had an instant connection. They fell in love, and when Andrew moved to Los Angeles, he asked Jessica to go with him, and she eagerly accepted the offer. Now they were engaged.

"Yes, I definitely want help. Something happened when I was 11, but I don't remember what it was. My parents are great people, but they've always treated me like, I don't know, I could disappear at any moment. They've never treated my brother Brad the same way. Only me."

Hallie stared at the rushing water and listened to the crickets. "You said your parents are wealthy. What does your father do?"

"He's a CEO of a pharmaceutical company. It's not a large pharmaceutical company, only about 200 employees, but it does quite well. It's on the cutting edge of biotech. So, while he's not a gazillionaire like CEOs of large pharmaceutical companies are, he does well for himself. Why do you ask?"

There was something there. Something about his father that was teasing at the edges of Hallie's brain. She couldn't quite put her finger on it, but it was something. Something she'd heard years ago. About 40 or so years ago, there was something in the news. But what was it?

Pete was currently 51 years old. So 40 years ago, he would've been only 11.

Hallie just shook her head. "I don't know. But maybe I can bring Willow up here. I'll have to ask permission from Annie, but if you're open to it, I'd like to bring her up here."

"What does Willow do?" Pete asked.

"Well, she was an acupuncturist, and she is a psychic. But right now, she writes screenplays. But she's very good at pinpointing people's issues. That is, if they don't have a protective veil around them like many people do." Hallie wondered if Pete had that protective veil around his own energy. If he did, Willow might not help him.

"I'd love for her to help. I'd do anything to sleep at night and stop eating my life away."

Pete stood silently and listened to the rushing water for a few more minutes.

"I remember when I was a young boy," he finally said. "I was so happy. I really had no cares in my world. I went to a private school in San Francisco, and I had a lot of great friends in elementary school. There was always something going on around my house – my house was where my friends came to visit because my mom stayed at home, and she was a great mom and always had things for us to do. When you have a group of friends, there is always one house where everybody gathers more than any other house, and that was my house. My mom always had great snacks and video games for us, even though the video games back then were not exactly fantastic. It was just things like space invaders, Tetris, and very rudimentary Pac-Man games. We also watched MTV for hours on end. That was back when MTV actually played music."

Hallie smiled. She remembered those days when MTV was the place to discover new bands and songs. So many great acts broke through back then because they had a great video played on heavy rotation on MTV. It was such a revelation to hear all those wonderful songs and music, and the videos were so creative and artistic. Once in a while, Hallie got nostalgic for those days when life seemed so much simpler. Then again, if she was given the choice to live her entire life over again, on the condition that she could not change a single thing along the way, she wouldn't take that deal for anything. There were just too many painful moments when she didn't know much better. She would not want to live those moments again.

"But things just came to a halt when you were only 11?"

"Yeah. I blocked it all out. And I've tried to ask my parents about it, but they won't talk to me. My mom talked about possibly getting professional help, but my father was against it. I heard them talking one day, and my dad said I apparently had forgotten what had happened to me, and he thought it best to put it behind me. He didn't want therapy to bring it out."

It sounded like Pete's father meant well. And that was perhaps understandable. Parents in the early 1980s, when Pete would have been 11 years old, didn't quite know about psychology and child rearing and trauma, at least not as much as parents of today might know. If Pete's father was just relieved that whatever happened to Pete was blocked out of his mind, therefore he didn't want Pete to get therapy for his trauma, his father couldn't be blamed for thinking that. He couldn't possibly know how much unresolved trauma can come out in harmful ways.

Hallie put her hand on Pete's shoulder and squeezed. "I'm really happy you're here. I think you're right where you need to be. You want to change your life; this is the best place to start. And I saw you playing the game last night, and you really seemed to have a good time. You seemed to make some friends."

He smiled. "That was because of you. If you didn't come back, I don't know if I would've joined everybody. I had it in my head that nobody really wanted me around. But you came back, and maybe I realized somebody cares about me. I mean, my family cares about me. They love me. But I've had trouble making friends and socializing for quite a few years. But you're right, when I was playing that game, I felt like, I don't know, my teammates seemed impressed."

Hallie raised her eyebrows. "And Selma seemed friendly. That's a good thing. She's a natural leader, and people flock to her. She would be a great ally for you."

Pete nodded his head. "I thought that, too. Selma is like

a lot of popular girls in my high school. Natural leaders, outgoing, confident. Everything I wish I could be."

Hallie realized she and Pete had a lot in common. They both felt like outsiders. Maybe that was why she felt such an invisible connection to Pete. She felt this invisible thread between them, but that might've just been because of the outsider status they both felt. "I know. I think the same thing about myself. I never quite felt I fit in. But I have some good friends who always make me feel loved and cherished. And that's all I really need in my life. Just a few good people who always have your back and a wonderful daughter."

"I have that with my family," Pete said. "They've always had my back. But I really would like to find my person. You know?"

Hallie knew what he was saying. She was still searching for her person. The person who would romantically love her. She had not experienced that ever in her life, mainly because she had been in a toxic relationship and marriage with Nate since she was in her early 20s. So she really didn't find that true love. So many years she had wasted in a bad marriage with a man who didn't understand her and didn't care to do so...And that was the rub. It was one thing to be with a partner or husband who didn't understand you but really wanted to, so he tried. It was quite another to be with somebody who didn't understand you and had no desire to do so. And that was the case with Nate.

Hallie suddenly realized that she was, at long last, feeling sleepy. It was now past 3 o'clock in the morning, and everybody had to be at the breakfast table at 7 o'clock in the morning, so she would be functioning on four hours of sleep as it was. And so was Pete.

"I'm going back into the house. You can either come back in the house too or stay out here. I'm not your mother.

You should get some sleep because sleep is so important. But if you can't sleep, then you can't sleep. Incidentally, how often do you have a sleepless night?"

Pete shrugged. "Once or twice a week, I can't sleep at all. I hate it when that happens, though. The next day, I feel like I'm hungover. My body aches, and all I want to do is take a nap. And I'm having trouble sleeping tonight because I'm in a different place. I sometimes need help sleeping if I'm not in my bed. Hopefully, that'll work itself out the more I get used to being here."

"Yes, I hope so, too," Hallie said. There was another clue there. Pete was having trouble sleeping because he wasn't in his own bed. Damn, there was something teasing her brain about Pete's situation. But she just couldn't put her finger on it. "Anyhow, night night," she said with a smile.

"Night night," he said back. He also was smiling. "My mom always said night night," he said. "I'll go back with you. Maybe I can sleep."

So, Hallie and Pete walked back into the house together. There was a part of Hallie that wanted to grab Pete's hand, to tell him it all would be okay.

But she was hesitant. She was having confusing feelings for Pete.

What would Conrad think?

Chapter Eight

Hallie

Hallie woke up at 7 o'clock in the morning, just like everybody else did at the retreat. Everybody was supposed to have breakfast together, after which would be the morning hike. Pete was not at the table yet, so Hallie went to his room and knocked on his door.

"Come in," Pete said.

Hallie opened the door and saw Pete sitting at his desk. But his head was hanging down, and he was staring at his hands. Hallie wondered what was going on with him.

"Pete, everybody has been looking for you at breakfast."

"I doubt it."

Hallie sat down, feeling very concerned about Pete. "What's going on?"

He took a deep breath. "I'm not sure. Being here has stirred up something. I'm starting to remember what happened to me when I was 11, and it's just a little scary. That's all."

"What do you remember?"

"A walk-in closet. I remember the smell of mothballs. It seems like I was in the closet for a long time. And, no, it's not a metaphor. It was an actual closet."

"I don't understand."

"Neither do I. That's the whole thing. I came here because I wanted to become healthier. I know that my extra weight and poor eating habits make me feel unhealthy and like my life will end prematurely. But I understand that I need to get to the heart of my issues, and that's what's happening. I just don't really know what's in there. What darkness is there."

"What can I do to help?" Hallie asked.

"I'm not real sure. I couldn't sleep last night, so I started to journal. That's something I haven't done in a long time. And I realized there's a specific reason why I want to become healthier. I haven't done things in my life I want to do. It's not just finding my person, which is what I want in my life. But it's... I don't feel like I've lived. I feel like I've been sleepwalking for so many years. The world is going on around me, but I'm not a part of it. And I have to stop feeling like that."

Hallie nodded. She had a lot in common with Pete because how he described the way he felt was how she always felt about her own self. Sleepwalking, feeling like the world was revolving around her without actually carrying her along with it. She definitely felt like that.

"Did you think any more about my bringing my friend Willow up here? I know she's not a psychiatrist or psychologist, but she is very good at pinpointing problems."

"Yes, I think that would be a good idea. I don't mind the idea of a psychic. It's not like I disbelieve psychics or people with some kind of second sight. I don't believe either, but I always have an open mind about everything. If you think she could help, I'd love to talk to her."

Hallie made a note to herself to speak to Willow and ask if she minded coming to the retreat. "Okay. In the meantime, maybe you'd like to go downstairs and join everybody at the breakfast table."

Hallie and Pete then went down to the breakfast table and joined everybody there. Pete was much more comfortable around the clients, and they were also friendlier with him. And when they went on their hike that day, Pete was talking to other clients all along the way.

Hallie hung back and let Pete socialize. She talked to Annie while everybody walked along. "How are things going?" Annie asked Hallie. "With Pete?"

"Well, I think. He's good at Trivial Pursuit and seems very smart, which broke the ice with everybody last night."

"That's why we have game night. I've often found that game night is the perfect way for everybody to get to know each other. Much better than movie night because everybody talks and bonds over games. So, I guess it was a success."

"Yes." Then Hallie took a deep breath. "What do you know about Pete?"

"Nothing much. He's just like the other clients, sick and tired of being sick and tired and has the money and the time to do something about it with us. Why do you ask?"

"Well, you know, sometimes people eat their feelings. And I think that's what Pete was doing. Maybe that's what he's still doing. I just think there's some kind of trauma. No, in fact, I know there is. I just didn't know if you had any clue what happened to him in his childhood."

Annie shook her head. "If there is, I'm not aware of it."

They walked along, watching a flock of turkeys gobbling into the woods. When they got to the lake, Hallie saw three ducks together that she considered to be "her ducks." These three ducks were always together. One was big and brown, with a black bill. The second one was big and white with an orange bill. The third was a kind of hybrid duck, part mallard and part white, for he had a green head and white chest. Hallie fed them by hand whenever she saw them, and she had some pellet duck food in her hand. She went over to the waterfowl and sat down and let them peck at the pellets.

Annie smiled. "You should have some pet ducks at your house. Have you thought of that?"

"No, but I wish I could. But I don't have much of a yard. And I don't think my housemate Conrad would be too happy about having ducks around. They're messy, and they make a lot of noise. I'm perfectly happy with these three adopted ducks."

"You're going to get a pet, though, right?"

"Maybe. I'd like to get a dog. I need to talk to Conrad about that."

"You're very good with animals," Annie observed. "It would be a shame if you didn't have a pet at home."

Hallie stood up, her duck pellets completely eaten up by the three. "Yes. I agree, and I might talk to Conrad about getting a dog soon. Conrad works from home, so he'll be around to watch the dog if we get one. That's always a problem when people work outside the home and leave the dog alone all day. But that won't be a problem with us."

They walked a few more miles into the woods and then circled around back to the house. And then Hallie, after several more hours of working with Pete through group therapy and through exercising with him, went home.

She was looking forward to seeing Conrad. It had been a few days since she had been home. She was surprised at how anxious she was to see him.

But, when she got home and Conrad was nowhere to be seen, Hallie was surprised that she was thinking about Pete.

Chapter Nine

Morgan

Morgan Gleason looked around her art gallery, feeling nervous yet accomplished. She had always dreamed of owning her own art gallery, and she had finally accomplished it. She formerly had a gallery in San Francisco, but this was the first time she put together a real cooperative with different artists, and this gallery was much more successful than the one she had in San Francisco.

She had just brought a brand-new artist in, Nicole Woodruff. Nicole was a photographer and a pop artist who painted portraits of famous people and celebrities in vibrant colors. The problem was that it seemed that Nicole had an eye for Conrad. And Morgan dearly hoped that Conrad did not return the ardor. Morgan knew how her mother felt about Conrad, and it was Morgan's hope that Conrad and her mother would just admit their feelings for one another and become the solid couple they should be.

But it made Morgan feel uncomfortable whenever she

saw Conrad and Nicole together. There was a part of Morgan that really wanted to shake her mother and tell Hallie that she needed to be bolder, grab the bull by the horns and just tell Conrad how she felt. That was always a problem with Hallie. Morgan saw how her father, Nate, treated her mother throughout their marriage. Hallie was nothing but a doormat for her father.

What's more, Hallie let herself be a doormat for her father for all those years. So, Morgan understood that Hallie was beaten down, her self-esteem just about zero. Hallie got better when she was on Nantucket because she was working with Willow, who was opening up Hallie's energy centers with acupuncture and that helped Hallie to blossom.

But that didn't mean that her mother was any more likely to grab happiness than she was before. Morgan got the feeling that Hallie still felt entitled to only scraps in life, and that made Morgan sad. And Morgan wasn't close with her father at all. She hated how her father treated her mother and wanted nothing to do with him. It wasn't like she was not returning his phone calls, either. Her father never called her, so there were no calls to return. This was just fine with Morgan because she had nothing to say to him.

Conrad came in the front door. He had been working hard on some paintings and brought them in to display in his part of the gallery. Nicole was already in the gallery as well, working on her part, and she immediately went into the main part of the gallery when she heard Conrad come in.

"Conrad," Nicole said a little too eagerly. "Come and see some of my new work. I've been waiting for you because I want your feedback."

Conrad was carrying both his paintings and a cup of

coffee. He wore a newsboy cap, a scarf around his neck, and a tweed coat. He was very fashionable in a British way, and he also had a certain British charm.

"Hold your horses," Conrad said to Nicole. "I just got in the door. And I need to hang up my own paintings. But I'll be in your corner in two shakes."

Conrad shook his head and went back to his part of the gallery. Morgan followed him because she wanted to see his new paintings and maybe subtly talk to him about Nicole.

Conrad's new paintings were stunning and not quite his style. When he was on Nantucket, his artwork was angry, searing, a protest against injustice and what he saw in the world. He commented on injustice playfully, however, which was more like a Dada way of using satire to point out major problems in the world.

Lately, however, Conrad's artwork was more visceral yet somehow happier. He had turned his artistic eye towards the everyday, away from angry symbolism and searing satire. And this picture he'd painted was colorful, soft, and emotional. It was a woman next to the raging surf, her toes in the water, her posture perfectly straight, her face and body a mélange of colors. Her back was turned, but her hair was dark, her frame slight.

It was almost a portrait of her mother. Or, rather, it could be. It was hard to tell because the only thing shown was her back. And that was just one of the pictures that featured this same woman. One of the pictures was a painting of the woman against the backdrop of colorful purple mountains, her back arched, and a cape in her hands billowing out behind her. Another featured her in a chair, her face obscured, and she looked to the floor. Whoever this woman was, Conrad had painted her very elegantly, almost regal.

These weren't the only paintings he had created. There were more pictures of rocks, surf, mountains, flowers, and city life. Each painting was signature in a way, as Conrad really liked to paint with various colors, so everything looked whimsical.

"Conrad, these paintings are amazing," Morgan said. "And they're so different from what you used to paint."

"Oh, I know, I've gotten soft. I've been much more chuffed living out here than I used to be. Before, I used to only see problems. Only the sadness in the world. But now, I see a lot more light." He shook his head. "Living in Southern California has made me a bit of a beach boy, if you will. Has something to do with the weather."

Morgan helped Conrad hang the paintings in his space and then sat in a chair. "Conrad, is something else possibly making you happy these days?"

He raised an eyebrow. "Whatever do you mean?"

"It's just that these new paintings are emotional and very human, but they're also quite romantic. This woman you painted so many times looks almost idealized. Don't get me wrong. I love them. They draw my eye, and you can sell them quite easily. But I can see a different perspective in them, and I wanted to know if you had your eye on somebody."

Conrad waved his hand dismissively. "If you're talking about Nicole, you're daft. She's attractive, but she's kind of a harpy. Or she tends to be. You just haven't seen that side of her, but I have, and it's not pretty."

Morgan took a deep breath. She didn't want to push the issue of Conrad and her mother. And she found it somewhat disheartening that Conrad didn't immediately pick up on her subtext. She was trying to find out if Conrad was happy because he was living with Hallie, but he didn't immediately come out and say that, so Morgan wondered if she was barking up the wrong tree.

"No, I wasn't talking about Nicole. Although I'm glad to hear that you're not interested in her because it's plain she's interested in you."

"She's not interested in me. She wants a free trip to London when I visit my sister Ruth. But she doesn't know that I'm not going to visit Ruth anytime soon, so the jokes on her, as it were."

Morgan didn't really believe that. She believed that Nicole actually liked Conrad, but it seemed that Conrad wouldn't address that. Or, at least, he wouldn't address it in any kind of serious way.

"Okay." Morgan looked around at Conrad's paintings and was amazed at how different they were. His earlier work was surreal and satirical and had something to say. His new work also had something to say, but the message differed greatly. And, no matter what Conrad tried to say, Morgan knew something was in his heart. Something that he was not ready to share with the world. Conrad did have a love. That much was plain. It was probably unrequited, as, to Morgan's knowledge, Conrad was not seeing anybody.

Then again, it might have been unrequited because Conrad wasn't ready to tell the world how he felt about one person.

Morgan hoped that person was her mother.

Chapter Ten

Hallie

Conrad got home around 10 o'clock that night. He'd been drinking, and, to Hallie's dismay, Nicole Woodruff, a new artist at the gallery, was with him. The two of them were giggling as they walked in the door.

"Hallie, my dear, are you making a guest appearance tonight?" Conrad asked in a jolly manner.

"I know, I haven't been around very much lately. And I'm really sorry about last night. I really would've liked to have gone to dinner with you."

"Oh, it's okay. You know Nicole, don't you?"

Hallie nodded. "Nicole," she said. "Of course, I know her."

Hallie felt threatened by Nicole, who was wildly talented, completely free-spirited, and obviously had a thing for Conrad. Nicole was the kind of person who Hallie always wanted to be. She was confident, brash, and colorful, literally and figuratively. She was colorful literally because she favored loud clothing colors, and her hair was streaked with pink, green, and blue. She was tall and thin, with magnetic blue eyes, a thin dainty nose, and disturbingly full lips.

Nicole smiled at Hallie. "Hallie," Nicole said, extending her hand to Hallie. "Enchanté." And then she started speaking in French, which Conrad also knew because he started laughing at what she said.

Nicole went to the chair and sat down with her legs spread over the side. "Conrad, you got a bottle of tequila in there?" she asked. "We're celebrating."

Hallie felt her face flush. "What are you celebrating?"

"Life. The fact that we're on this side of the ground. Every day is a day to celebrate not pushing daisies as it were."

Conrad brought out two rocks glasses that were filled with tequila and ice. Hallie shuddered, looking at all that tequila. That was one liquor she could not hold, making her sick. There was more than one occasion when she would start drinking tequila and end up on the floor, puking everywhere. The last time she had tequila, she had no knowledge of what had happened the night before. All she knew was she woke up in the basement at a friend's house, lying on a shower curtain. Apparently, she was puking and had to sleep on the shower curtain. There were two dogs right next to her. Dogs were really good when people were sick. They liked caring for their humans and ensuring their master was okay. It was probably in their DNA. They had to protect members of their pack and care for one another when they were sick. Since the humans in their life were a part of their pack in a way, dogs carried that instinct to the people who care for them.

"Hallie, why don't you have a drink with us? I can get you a glass of wine if you like."

Hallie really didn't feel like drinking that night. She liked to gather and drink wine with her best friends - Ava, Sarah, Quinn, and now Mia, who was always with Quinn. Hallie positively adored Mia, as did everybody else, including Sarah's daughter Julia and Quinn's daughter Emerson. Mia was working with the two girls, Julia and Emerson, helping them craft songs. Julia was the poet and the lyricist, and Emerson was the musical genius who could seemingly play any instrument and was a prodigy. While she loved their Wednesday night standing date, where she and her friends gathered at Ava's home, which was also the home of Sarah and Quinn until their home was renovated, she was less thrilled about drinking alcohol around Conrad.

She knew why. She feared that if she drank around Conrad, she might get carried away and admit how she felt to him. And that simply wouldn't do because they were living together, so if Hallie admitted to Conrad that she had romantic feelings for him, it would make things awkward in the house. And that was one thing she didn't want. She could imagine herself admitting to Conrad that she wanted to be with him. And then she could imagine him not knowing what to say and then coming out with a rejection, and then Hallie's heart would be broken, and she would be completely embarrassed and humiliated.

"No, thank you," Hallie said. "I'm pretty tired. I think I need to go to my room, read a book and fall asleep. But you guys have fun."

Conrad looked disappointed. "Oh, come on, my lass. We never see each other." Then he looked at Nicole with a side-eye. His look was unmistakable. He was telling Hallie with his eyes that he didn't want to be alone with Nicole. Or, at least, Hallie thought she saw that in his expression.

Hallie nodded. "Okay. One drink."

Conrad got up. "I'll help you in the kitchen. We need some refreshments. I think we have some crisps in the house."

"I can get the potato chips," Hallie said.

"Well, I think I have some crisps put by in a place you don't know about. Some special crisps."

"Okay," Hallie said. "Let's go in the kitchen, then."

"I miss you already," Nicole said, drinking her tequila on ice. "Be back soon with some Kettle Chips if you got them. I'm craving salt like crazy for some reason."

Hallie and Conrad went into the kitchen. Hallie found the bottle of wine and Conrad grabbed her arm.

"I wanted to talk to you," he said. "That's why I followed you in here."

"Oh," Hallie said. He was so close to her. She felt butterflies turn around in her stomach as she looked at him. *Stop, Hallie, stop. He's your housemate. You guys can't hook up unless you both want the same thing.* And what Hallie wanted from Conrad was everything. A relationship, a marriage, sharing their lives together. It wouldn't do for Hallie to break down, maybe share Conrad's bed during a drunken interlude, and then have Conrad treat the whole thing casually. It would break her heart to see Conrad with another woman after giving into him sexually, which would happen if the two of them started some kind of casual, I'm-lonely-you're-lonely-so-why-not kind of relationship. "Go ahead."

She closed her eyes as he got closer to her. She felt his lips on hers. At last. She didn't know how she'd ever react once they kissed. Would she feel it to her toes? Would his kiss fill her with electricity and light her up from within?

As his gentle kiss became more urgent, all her wonderings were answered. Yes. Yes, she felt it to her toes. Yes, her body lit up from within. Yes, there was electricity running through every cell in her body. He was an amazing kisser, gentle yet firm, even if he smelled like tequila. It was apparently good tequila, maybe Patrón or some kind of specialty mezcal.

Hallie sighed as Conrad broke away from her. "I'm sorry," he said. "That won't happen again. But I wanted to tell you that I don't want to be alone with Nicole. That's the reason why I came back here with you. That kiss was just something I've been dying to do for longer than I can remember and I just couldn't stop myself. I'm sorry about that, though."

Hallie still had her eyes closed. She still felt his lips on hers, and she touched her mouth longingly. When she opened her eyes, she focused on Conrad's lips, thinking she'd never been kissed like that before, and she'd never felt this way in her life. What had she been missing all these years in a dead marriage with Nate? This. She'd been missing this. The butterflies, the magnetic attraction, the desire.

"Why?"

"Why what?"

"Why won't that kiss happen again?"

He smiled. "We're housemates, Hallie. We can't make love. We can't even shag. Not unless we're ready to take this to the next level. So, I guess we'll just have to live together with the sexual tension."

Hallie wanted to confess to him that she wanted to take it to the next level. That she suddenly saw the two of them on the beach, holding hands and taking vows in front of all her closest friends and family. That she imagined them making love and shagging and everything in between. That she dreamed of finally being in love for real. And being loved back.

She just nodded and opened the bottle of wine with shaking hands. "Well, we probably should get back out there. Nicole is no doubt wondering what happened to us and will soon send out a search party."

They went back into the living room, where Nicole was still sitting in the chair with her legs slung over one side. "I hope you guys don't mind, but I invited some divine people to come over for a spontaneous soirée."

The doorbell rang, and, just like that, some 20 people were coming through the door. They were all artist types, some around Hallie's age, some quite a bit younger, all who seemed ready for a good time.

Hallie sighed. She was looking forward to a quiet evening and some decent sleep, not having slept well the night before. But it seemed that wouldn't be the case that night.

Still, she looked over at Conrad, who didn't seem angry about the intrusion. "I'm going to beg off," she said. "I need to be at the retreat early." She usually left the house at 6:30 or even earlier, so there was no way she could stay up all night with the partying artist-types.

Conrad could stay up with them. He didn't have a set schedule and could sleep until noon if he wanted to. He tended to be a night owl, so he was no doubt in his element with these new people.

Conrad nodded and then held court with the partying people.

But as Hallie lay in bed with ear plugs to block out the sound below, she thought about Conrad's kiss.

And she wanted him in her bed right at that moment.
And every other night to come.

What had she gotten herself into?

Chapter Eleven

Greer

Greer Davidson had just finished a tarot reading when she got the call from her attorney, Scott Osborne. She had been living in the Pacific Palisades for the past six months, having lived in West Hollywood for most of her married life. Her husband was killed in a boating accident, and his will was most peculiar. He had left a small cottage in the Santa Monica Mountains and his bookstore to their firstborn. The only problem was that their firstborn had long since been given up for adoption.

So Greer knew she'd have to find her firstborn daughter. At first, she was apprehensive about doing so. The circumstances of her firstborn's birth were tragic, to say the least. And she didn't like to think about that period of her life anymore. Meeting her daughter was bound to bring up emotions she had not acknowledged for way too long. Yet, at the same time, she was so anxious to find out who her daughter was. What had become of her? Was she happy? Did she become successful? Was she loved?

Scott Osborne answered all her questions. And it turned out that at least one concern was addressed - her daughter was successful. Very successful. Whether or not she was happy or loved, Greer didn't know. But she knew that success had blessed her firstborn, which made her happy.

Just then, her business partner, Willow Killeen, walked in the door, bearing two iced coffees from the coffee shop down the boardwalk. "Hey dude," Willow said. "Any word on your kid?" Then Willow smiled, and Greer nodded. Willow knew Greer would get in touch with her firstborn daughter and knew her firstborn was somebody special. Willow had told Greer when Greer first started this endeavor that her firstborn daughter was somebody wealthy and famous.

"I just got a call from Scott," Greer said. "And you were right. My daughter is Fiona Kennedy."

Willow just started laughing. "I told you she was somebody famous. But good on you. Your daughter is the hottest ticket in this town. Your genes must be amazing."

Greer had met Willow by chance in a coffee shop where Willow was working on a screenplay. Something about the young woman's energy drew Greer in and enveloped her like a warm blanket. When she saw Willow working in that coffee shop that day, she knew that Willow was a kindred soul. So she boldly went over to Willow and asked if she could join her. She bought Willow a coffee, the two got to talking, and Greer knew that her instincts were right on the money. Willow, like Greer, was a psychic, astrologist and tarot reader. She also owned a spa on Nantucket until just recently and was looking to get out of the acupuncture business and concentrate her efforts on tarot, astrology, and psychic readings and writing screen-plays on the side.

It was perfect! Greer was newly widowed, was grieving, and needed a focus and a source of income. She loved doing tarot and astrology readings. And she had a small nest egg because her husband Ewan had left her about $250,000 through his life insurance. So, by the end of the day, Willow and Greer had decided to open a psychic services storefront on Venice Beach, facing the boardwalk. It was like heaven for Greer to go to work every single day. It wasn't just that she loved giving readings, but having a store on the beach was comforting. She was a Pisces and truly a water person, so she loved leaving her storefront, getting on the board-walk, and walking to the beach and listening to the waves.

"Yes, I guess I have good genes," Greer said. "Creative ones, anyhow. But I wonder if Fiona is gifted like I am."

"She probably is, even if she doesn't know it," Willow said. "These things run in the family. When will you meet her?"

"I don't know yet," Greer said. "I threw the cards on it, but they were hazy. But I strongly believe I'll be seeing her soon."

Willow nodded. "You'll be meeting her soon. Of that, I'm sure. Take that to the bank."

Greer knew Willow was right. She was excited about the prospect yet nervous all the same. How would Fiona be with herself and her daughter, Cora? Would Fiona think she was too good for her birth family? Greer read somewhere that Fiona had gotten married to another wealthy actor. The wedding was in Malibu, and Willow's future sister-in-law, Samantha, made the cake for the shindig. Jackson Flynn was Willow's boyfriend and hopefully future husband - Jackson was dying to get Willow down the aisle, but Willow was resistant for some reason - and Samantha was Jackson's sister. So, Fiona was a newlywed, and her husband was another famous actor. What were the chances that two world-famous actors would accept Greer Davidson, kooky tarot reader and astrologist, and her daughter Cora as a part of their new family? Especially since she and Cora lived in a trailer park on the beach in the Pacific Palisades?

Willow shook her head. "Relax, Greer," she said. "Fiona won't be stuck-up. I've heard she's really cool. Very down-to-earth. That's what Jackson told me, anyhow."

Jackson was an actor in Hollywood, very up-and-coming. His first big movie was due to release in the spring, a biopic on F. Scott Fitzgerald and his wife Zelda. So far, everyone who had seen the dailies had raved about Jackson, so it seemed he would soon be A-List himself.

"How does Jackson know her?"

"He doesn't. But he knows people who do. Industry parties," Willow said. "Everyone knows everyone in the movie business."

Greer wished she could psychically foretell the future with Fiona, but Greer had found that her psychic powers didn't extend to events in her own life, unfortunately. She had second sight when it came to events and people around her, but as for her own future, it was as mystifying to her as it was to everyone else.

She decided to do another spread about the situation. Hopefully, she could get better answers this time.

After doing another tarot spread, she had her answer.

Fiona would see her and Cora.

And she was going to be perfectly lovely.

Chapter Twelve

Fiona

Fiona's phone rang at 8 in the morning.

"Hello?" Fiona said sleepily into the phone. After Fiona skipped the wrap party, she couldn't sleep, so she started to re-read her favorite novel, *Anna Karenina*, even though the subject was rather depressing yet completely engrossing. And she needed to be engrossed in something, even the life of a suicidal woman in 1870s Russia.

"Yes, Fiona Kennedy?" a voice said.

"Yes. This is she."

"Of course, of course," said the voice. "My name is Scott Osborne. I'm an attorney here in LA."

"Okay," Fiona said. She racked her brain to figure out why a lawyer was calling her at 8 in the morning. Was she being sued for something? No, she'd broken no contracts. She was dutiful in fulfilling every term of every contract, reading every word of these documents, even the boilerplate terms. One never knew when an errant term would slip in unnoticed.

An uncomfortable silence followed. Fiona was still sleepy and felt like she was at the bottom of a dark pit. She wasn't in the mood to fill the silence with this stranger on the other end of the line.

Scott Osborne cleared his throat. "I apologize. I'm very nervous. My boss told me who I was calling, and I'm so sorry. I live in Los Angeles but am not used to talking to a celebrity."

Fiona raised her eyebrows. No matter how often it happened, she couldn't get used to people treating her like royalty. And this was an attorney. She thought attorneys weren't supposed to be star-struck, but this one apparently was.

"I can assure you, Mr. Osborne, I put my pant legs on the same way you do every morning. I do my grocery shopping and clean my own house." That was a bit of a lie. Lately, she had her groceries delivered by Instacart because she didn't want to deal with the stares. She also didn't tell him that whenever she left the house, she had to ensure she had full makeup on and perfectly combed hair. Otherwise, there would be an unflattering pose of her on the cover of some tabloid because, sans makeup, her eyelashes and eyebrows completely disappeared. She was a redhead with translucently white skin and no eyelashes to speak of.

"I understand. But what I'm going to tell you might shock you. I'm intimidated because I'm giving you this news."

Fiona didn't like the sound of this. She would be shocked? She hoped to be shocked in a good way, not a bad one.

"I'm intrigued."

Scott took a deep breath on the other end of the line. "I've been hired by a close friend with relatives who live in the Pacific Palisades."

Fiona's head started hurting, and she wondered if she was dehydrated. She needed help remembering to drink enough water. She was losing patience with this entire conversation.

"Okay. Go on."

"Well, there's a woman named Greer Davidson. She hired me to find her daughter. She gave a child up for adoption about 28 years ago or so, and she wanted to track her down."

Fiona closed her eyes. "Okay. And what does this have to do with me?" She couldn't imagine what this guy was getting at. She only knew her head was pounding and she was completely out of aspirin or any other painkiller. She'd have to order something from the Instacart guy, which she usually did when she ran out of stuff. She usually had the Instacart people leave the stuff at the door because she didn't want to deal with the usual gaga stuff.

"Well, that's what will be such a shock to you. You are her daughter."

Chapter Thirteen

Cora

Cora Morrison was at the end of her rope. She always imagined motherhood would be this glorious thing. When she married Alistair, they decided to have a brood of children, and she was so excited about all of it. She imagined a beautiful little boy or girl who would have her clear green eyes and Alastair's jet-black hair, with curls and dimples and smiles. She knew any baby she and Alastair would produce would be so beautiful that people would stop them on the sidewalk to tell them how lovely the child was, and the child would also be wildly talented and intelligent and set the world on fire.

That could still happen. Cora didn't know. What she knew was that this baby, Daisy, was nothing like Cora imagined she'd be. Cora felt absolutely nothing for this child but contempt. All she could think about daily was what would happen if she gave little Daisy to somebody else to raise. She knew Alistair would rightfully leave her if she did that, yet that was all she thought about. She felt completely trapped by her decision to have a baby with Alistair, and there had to be a way to undo all of it. Daisy was only four months old, and surely she'd adapt to a different household if it came to that.

And then, whenever she thought this way, she'd feel so guilty that she'd feel like harming herself. That was her other obsessive thought - Daisy deserved a mother better than her. She imagined drowning herself in the ocean, which raged just outside her trailer door. She lived in a mobile home park that was right on the beach in the Pacific Palisades. She loved living in her single-wide trailer home because she could hear the surf come in when she sat on her porch, and she loved her neighbors, too. But, lately, nothing made her happy, not even living on the beach.

About six months after she moved to this mobile home park, when she was about 8 months pregnant, her father died in a boating accident. Her mother was alone, so Cora invited her to buy a trailer and live close by, so Cora could keep an eye on her. Not that anybody had to keep an eye on Greer Davidson, who was only 55 years old and had been living a very active life in West Hollywood before her husband, Cora's father, Ewan Davidson, ventured out onto a speedboat, three sheets to the wind as he usually was, and ran into a pontoon, killing him instantly. Yet Cora felt it was her duty to ensure her mother was looked after, and Greer was ready to get out of the big city life anyhow, so Greer readily agreed to buy a trailer and live on the beach in the Pacific Palisades Bowl Mobile Estates.

So, Cora had some help with little Daisy because her mother did the tarot and astrology readings but she co-owned the psychic business, so she was flexible and could help out with Daisy. She was quite good at her readings and had made a name for herself, with women coming from all to ask for advice about love, business, and life. She had a business partner, Willow Killeen, and the two of them did quite well with their tarot business. Willow was also a screenwriter in her spare time and was due to give birth to her first child in a matter of months, so Willow had a lot on her plate.

So, ironically, Cora's mother was living her best life while Cora was drowning. And she couldn't tell anybody how she felt about Daisy. Nobody would understand how desperately Cora wanted to hand Daisy over to the next random person and take her daughter away so Cora would never have to see her baby again. She couldn't possibly take care of the baby. She wanted to tell her mother how she was feeling about little Daisy, and she knew her mother would understand because her mother was like that – if there was one thing that Greer could relate to, it was weirdo thoughts. That was what Greer was all about, after all.

Yet something stopped Cora from confiding to her mother about how she felt about her baby daughter. So, whenever Greer would come over to visit her granddaughter and her daughter, Cora would plaster on a fake smile, offer some tea to her mother, and manufacture the proper emotions when watching Greer and Daisy interact.

Cora knew she was supposed to laugh when Greer would lift Daisy's little shirt and blow raspberries on her tummy, so she did. She knew she was supposed to tear up a little when she saw her mother read Daisy the books Cora loved as a child – Aesop's fables, *The Little Mermaid* (the Hans Christian Andersen version where the prince married somebody else and The Little Mermaid ends up killing herself, not the sanitized Disney version), and *Beauty and the Beast* (again, her mother would always read her the original fairytale which was much darker than the Disney version, which was usually the case, even though Beauty in this tale lived happily ever after with her prince). Even though little Daisy was only four months old and couldn't understand the words coming out of Greer's mouth when she was reading the fairytales, that didn't really matter. It was still a touching scene, so Cora pretended to be touched by it.

She couldn't admit to her mother that she felt nothing when she saw her mother with her baby. She felt no joy in her life at all. This wasn't how it was supposed to be, yet this was her life. And she didn't feel she could tell anybody the truth.

It didn't help that Alistair was gone for months at a time. He was part of a fishing crew that had to go further and further out to get the same catch they used to get closer to shore. Because the ocean was warming, and the fish closer to shore were being depleted, the best catch could only be had much further out in the Pacific. So he'd go on these long trips and leave Cora alone with Daisy. This made her feel even more hopeless and alone.

She looked out the window and saw her mother coming up the steps. She didn't know why her mother was there. Cora hadn't invited her over that day, although most days, Cora invited her mother to come over because she wanted some company and was desperate for help with Daisy.

She smiled her plastic smile. "Mom, hello. How are things?"

Greer raised her arms and enfolded Cora in a large hug. "My dear, I have some news." Her mother had tears in her eyes, which was unusual because Greer rarely cried.

"What kind of news?"

"I found my firstborn." Greer had been searching for her firstborn daughter for two reasons. One, she wanted to get to know the girl. Cora knew her mother had always regretted giving up her baby. The other reason was that her father had put into his will that two things he owned before he married Greer – a run-down cottage in the middle of a dense forest in the Santa Monica mountains and a defunct bookstore on Venice Beach - were left to the unnamed child. Cora figured her father wisely thought nobody in the family would want those two white elephants, so he'd dump them on somebody who technically didn't even exist in the Davidson family.

Cora sat down at the tiny breakfast nook she'd fashioned in her kitchen. It was nothing really, just a small table with two wrought-iron chairs painted white with colorful cushions Cora had sewn onto them. The cushions were bright red with tiny tea kettles and teacups printed on them. Cora liked whimsical, and Alistair didn't care, so she tried to inject a note of whimsy wherever appropriate. The curtains in the tiny kitchen matched the cushions because Cora sewed the curtains in the same material she used for the cushions. Elsewhere in the two-bedroom trailer were throw rugs that reflected Cora's same sense of the whimsical, as she found a multicolored rug that was mainly fuchsia, but it had many other colors woven in the fabric, including yellow, black, and teal. The thing looked like a Jackson Pollock painting, which attracted Cora. She often wondered if Alistair minded the loud rug and didn't say anything or if he didn't care. At any rate, he never said a word about any of it.

"Have a seat, Mom," Cora said. "Now, tell me about my half-sister."

Greer raised her eyebrows. "Actually, she's more than your half-sister. She has your same mother and father."

Well, that was a new one. "Oh. I've always assumed the

baby had a different dad. I thought you got knocked up out of nowhere. But you were married to our father when you gave birth to my sister."

"Yes. That was a very different time in our life. One day, I'll tell you about it. But it wasn't a good situation, to say the very least."

Huh. Cora's parents had a good marriage. They had their share of fights, where one or the other would leave the house and not come back for several hours, but who didn't? That was part of marriage. Thankfully, Cora and Alistair didn't have those kinds of fights, mainly because Alistair was gone for much of the year, several months at a time, so when he was home, they were glad to see one another. They got a break from one another quite a lot, so that was probably the secret sauce to why they always got along.

"Okay, so you weren't getting along with Dad when my sister was born. By the way, what's the name of my sister?"

"No, your father and I were getting along fine when your sister was born. That wasn't why she was put up for adoption. And your sister's name is, and I'm glad you're sitting down for this, but it's Fiona Kennedy."

Huh. That was strange. So, thought Cora, her mom was getting along fine with her dad when her sister was born. So why, pray tell, was the poor baby given away? A mystery, that was for sure, but it seemed her mother still wouldn't explain it.

"Okay," Cora said. "I don't know why I must be sitting down to hear my sister's name is Fiona Kennedy."

"Fiona Kennedy. *The* Fiona Kennedy."

"What do you mean 'The Fiona Kennedy?'"

"I mean, your sister is an Oscar-winning actress who's known around the globe. That's what I mean."

Cora blinked. "Mom, you're crazy. That's impossible."

"Why is it impossible?"

Cora opened her mouth and shut it again. "Because she's famous for being this orphan shuffled around foster homes and somehow became this fantastic A-list actress. She never mentioned in any of the interviews that she was adopted."

Greer just shrugged. "I don't know why she never said she was adopted. Maybe she didn't know."

"What do you mean she didn't know? Who does that, just not tell the child she was adopted?"

"Dear, I don't know what to say. I hired a private detective to track down my daughter, and Fiona Kennedy is her name. It'll be easy to prove if she meets us. She'll take a DNA test, and that will be that."

Wow. Fiona Kennedy, *the* Fiona Kennedy, was possibly her sister. Cora tried to process this. She'd always loved Fiona Kennedy movies. Fiona was a great actress. She had a certain charm and charisma on the screen that made audiences fall in love with her and feel they knew her. Fiona was one of those people everybody wanted to have a drink with, like Sandra Bullock or Jennifer Lawrence, two of Cora's other favorite actresses. She seemed so down to earth yet beautiful, accessible and luminous all at the same time.

And Fiona was maybe her flesh and blood? That wasn't on Cora's bingo card. She supported her mother's quest to find her firstborn, even if she secretly thought it would end in heartbreak. What were the chances the child Greer was searching for would want anything to do with any of them? Cora knew that was probably the case with Fiona. Just because they were blood relations didn't mean Fiona would even decide to visit them. Cora couldn't imagine such a star as Fiona wanting to get to know herself and her mother, two trailer-park ladies without a pot to piss in.

"Mom," Cora said as gently as she could. "That's great you found your daughter. And I must admit, it's overwhelming that, if it turns out to be true, your firstborn became such a household name. But I don't want you to be disappointed if Fiona wants nothing to do with us. We have to face facts. We would be her dirt-poor relations. I don't think she'll want to visit us."

Greer shook her head. "You of little faith. I've already done the cards on this, and I'm 100% sure she'll visit us." Greer clapped her hands. "The tarot spread had both The Sun and The Ten of Cups. The Sun means optimism and positivity. The Ten of Cups means strong and happy family ties. So not only will she visit, but it'll be a joyful reunion."

"Well. That settles it, then. If the tarot cards say she's coming, I guess she's coming."

Cora was being sarcastic, of course, because she didn't believe in the tarot. No matter how often she talked to women who gushed about how wonderful Greer was with the cards and how accurate her readings were, Cora never believed. It was like believing in Santa Claus, a belief Cora was disabused of when she was quite small. It still made her angry when she thought about finding Santa Claus wasn't real. As far as Cora was concerned, the tarot had as much reality as Santa Claus or the Easter Bunny.

Greer put her arm around Cora. "That's the spirit. I know you didn't mean it when you said you thought she'd come because the cards say so, but you'll be proven wrong. Fiona is my daughter, your sister, and I know she'll visit. Mark my words."

"Okay, Mom," Cora said. At that, Daisy apparently woke up because Cora heard her stirring in her crib. Cora closed her eyes, knowing she'd have to go in there and change Daisy's diapers and maybe nurse her. She dreaded all of it. She never thought she'd feel so overwhelmed. How could one tiny creature make somebody feel so inadequate?

Cora went into Daisy's room. The tiny baby's green eyes were wide open, but she wasn't crying. She rarely cried, which was a saving grace. Daisy had the trademark Davidson copper hair. Daisy's hair was naturally curly, while Cora's was straight. Cora wanted the baby to have Alistair's coloring, for he had black hair and skin that was not translucently white like Cora's family. Not that Cora minded having milky white skin, but it was a hassle always having to worry about slathering on a ton of sunscreen whenever she went outdoors. She had a few serious sunburns when she was a child, and she wanted to avoid that, so a good sunscreen was a must.

Cora cocked her head. Daisy was a pretty and sweet child. Cora wanted to feel blinding love. She wanted to wake up one day and feel the bonding she was supposed to feel for her only child. She hated the nothingness she felt when the child suckled her breast or when she picked up the child and rocked her to sleep.

Cora picked up her daughter and nursed her after changing her diapers. Greer came in and watched the two of them together. Cora smiled because she was supposed to have a happy expression when her child was nursed.

"The two of you are so lovely together," Greer said. "It reminds me of when you were a tiny baby. You need to cherish these days with your Daisy because you'll blink and find she's in her 20s, married and no longer needs you."

"Mom, don't say things like that. I need you. I'll always need you. So don't be crazy and say things like I no longer need you."

"You know what I'm saying. Yes, you need me. But what I wouldn't give to experience the quiet moments I experienced with you when you were a baby." And then Greer looked sad. "And I never got to experience that with your sister, much to my eternal regret."

"Mom, here's the thing. Whatever happened was supposed to happen. If Fiona Kennedy turns out to be your birth daughter, imagine what would've happened if you'd raised her as your own. She probably would've never become the movie star she is. So, look at it that way. She became who she was because of your sacrifice to give her a better life."

Greer smiled. "How did you become so smart?"

"I guess I just inherited my brains from you."

Chapter Fourteen

Fiona

"Daughter? I don't understand," Fiona said to the disembodied voice that had just informed her she was adopted.

How could she have been adopted and never knew it? It was always a small issue because her parents looked nothing like her. Her mother was half-Filipino, with dark hair, eyes, and skin. Her father was pale but had jet-black hair and blue eyes. Fiona was a pale redhead with green eyes and lots of freckles. When she went out with her mother to the grocery store when she was very small, the cashiers would playfully ask her where she got her red hair. She, being a child, took the question quite literally and would matter-of-factly answer, "I was born with it." And, for some reason, the cashiers would think that response was *just the cutest thing*. She didn't know why she was so cute when she would say those things, and she thought the cashiers were just weird for asking her the question.

But she didn't think about why she looked nothing like her parents because her mother was only half Asian. Her mother's other half was pale European stock. Her maternal grandmother Pearl had pale blonde hair and pale skin. And her father apparently also came from pale European stock. Allegedly, one of her father's ancestors had come over on the Mayflower. And it was Fiona's understanding that her great-grandmother Rosemarie had bright red hair, so she always figured that was where her coloring came from.

Now, suddenly, there was a possibility that her parents weren't her birth parents. She was only eight when they were killed in a car accident. Usually, parents wait a while to tell their child he or she was adopted. Fiona was sure her parents probably thought eight years old was too young to understand what the word "adoption" meant. So, she might have had different birth parents from the ones who'd raised her. Nonetheless, she was shocked to hear that was even a possibility.

"Yes. You are the biological daughter of Greer Davidson."

Fiona closed her eyes. "I'm sorry, this is… a great shock."

"There's more."

"More?"

"Yes. Your biological father, Ewan Davidson, was killed in a boating accident a few months ago. His will included you in it. Specifically, he identified you as his biological first-born who was put up for adoption. He had some property that was his separate property to dole out as he wished because he bought this property before marrying your mother. It's a small cottage in the Santa Monica mountains and a beach bookstore that has not been a going concern since his death."

Fiona cocked her head. A bookstore? Suddenly, for the first time in a long time, Fiona felt excited. She was always a bookworm, especially after the accident. Books were her way of escaping her situation as an orphan living with random families. She could still remember sitting in her room and reading *The Secret Garden* repeatedly, wishing she had a healing garden that could bring her hope and peace. Growing up, she didn't have such a garden because her first foster family lived in an old rickety house with only weeds in the yards. *Anne of Green Gables* was a heroine who Fiona identified with, as Anne, like Fiona, was a red-headed orphan who hated her red hair, pale skin and freckles. Anne became Fiona's ideal, as the headstrong Anne made the best of her situation, earning a scholarship as a top student and doing the selfless act of giving up her scholarship to help her adoptive mother after her adoptive father died, all while bringing joy to the joyless siblings who adopted her.

Those were her favorite childhood books, along with the adventures of Pippi Longstocking, the plucky Swedish heroine with superhuman strength who was also a pale redhead, and *The Chronicles of Narnia*. And as she got older, she still loved books, even if her tastes changed. She read the classics - Jane Austen, the Brontë sisters, Dostoyevsky, Kate Chopin - and the bestsellers. Danielle Steele, Robin Cook, Dean Koontz and Colleen McCullough were some authors she devoured when she was around 12 to 13 years old.

Even now, she sought escape in the pages of a book whenever she felt stressed. It was perfect that she apparently was willed a bookstore.

"Tell me about the cottage," Fiona said to Scott.

"It's very small. Only one bedroom, about 600 square

feet. It's in the middle of the woods, in the heart of a small forest in the Santa Monica mountains. The Sycamore trees in that area are 60 feet tall and are so wide that they form a roof for that area and block out the sun. It's only accessible by an all-terrain vehicle."

Fiona closed her eyes. She was willed a Thomas Kinkade cottage? This all sounded perfect to her. She could have a house in the woods where she could isolate, decompress, and try to get back to who she really was. All while living in the middle of a nature preserve, where she could literally go out her door and walk in the woods. She imagined herself walking barefoot through the forest, listening for the birds, frogs, and other wildlife, spotting deer and wild turkeys and the occasional skunk or two.

"And the bookstore?"

"The bookstore is on Venice Beach, facing the boardwalk. It has a loft area, a fireplace and a nook. Before it closed, it was a very popular spot for the locals. It even attracted nationally-known authors to do readings. They used to do poetry readings, children's hour and hold weekly book clubs. It was quite the social hub, from what I understand."

"*Was* quite the social hub?"

"Yes. After Ewan Davidson passed away, nobody took over the bookstore, and it's died off. But I daresay there's still a hunger for the place. If you decide to take over the bookstore, you can bring it all back."

Fiona wondered if she could ever escape her fame. The prospect of living a normal life, just another bookstore owner, appealed. She would've loved it more if the bookstore and cottage were someplace else, maybe on the moon, but Fiona couldn't get everything she wanted. More than anything else, she wanted to escape Hollywood and all that went with it. She was tired of the fakeness of the movie-star lifestyle, the plastic people and their plastic-surgically-enhanced perfection.

Scott cleared his throat. "I know you have this great film career, so you probably don't want to bother with running a bookstore. But I wanted you to know you've inherited this property, so you can do with it what you want."

"Yes. If I take this bequest, I'll probably leave my life behind." Boy, did that sound like heaven!

"Of course. I know you've worked hard to get where you are. And you're at the very top of your game. So, I don't blame you if you decide to sell the property sight unseen. You probably have more movies coming up."

"Actually, I have a very free schedule right now. The timing of this couldn't be better."

Fiona made an appointment to meet with Scott to get the information about her bequest. In the meantime, she had to call her agent and break the news. She decided then and there to retire and live a quiet life running this bookstore.

This phone call did not go well, to say the very least.

"You can't do this," Michael screamed over the phone. "You have every big director wanting to work with you. Spielberg, Scorsese, Nolan, Tarantino, everyone is lining up. I've been looking at scripts that are perfect for you. Several of them have Second Oscar written all over them. You can't walk away. You can't even take a break. Audiences will forget about you."

"Don't threaten me with a good time," Fiona said. The prospect of audiences completely forgetting about her sounded heavenly. Oh, what she wouldn't give for the days when she could just walk out her door anonymously.

"This isn't funny. And what's this about you finding your family? Your story was always that you're the orphan who made good. What will the media think about your suddenly having a live mother?"

"And a sister," Fiona said calmly. "I have a mother and a sister who are alive and breathing. That's supposed to be a bad thing?"

"Yes. That's a very bad thing when your brand is built on your hard-luck story."

"That's funny. I always thought my brand was built because I'm a halfway-decent actress who works very hard. You seem to think my brand is built on personal tragedy. You can't even put this good news into the right context. And that context is that I have a family for the first time since I was a little girl. I can finally be happy."

"You're not happy now?"

"No. I'm not happy now. I haven't been happy for a long, long time. I haven't been happy since my parents died in that car accident when I was in the backseat. I saw them die. Do you know what that does to a person? Do you know how that affects a small child? It haunts her for the rest of her life. So I've been living this unreal life all these years, trying to become other people because I've had difficulty living with myself. I can now find my heart. And you're begrudging me this. I won't forget that, Michael."

Michael took a large breath, and Fiona knew he was trying to calm himself down. He was completely blowing this, and he knew it.

"I'm sorry," he finally said. "Everything I said came out wrong. I don't want you to make a mistake. Millions of young girls would love to be in your position. They all dream of seeing their faces on the big screen. They dream of being loved around the world. They'd do anything for just a smidgen of your popularity. And you're throwing it away. I just want you to think twice about what you're giving up, that's all."

"I know what I'm giving up. And it's not the life I want. It might be the dream of millions of other girls, but it's not mine. It never was. My dream was always to have a family. And now I can have that. You should wish me luck instead of berating me."

"What about Luke?" Michael demanded. He went for her sore spot, but that was fair.

"What about him?"

"You know what about him. He's one-half of a power couple. He won't want you to retire."

"So what? You want me to make life decisions according to what my publicist might want?"

"Yes. Everything you do conforms to what your publicist might want. Think about that."

"Listen, I only know I have a family. I have roots. I've never had that, and I've always wanted it. I've always wanted to belong to somebody. That's why I married Luke, a man who-" Fiona stopped. She wanted to say Luke was a man she didn't love, but that was none of Michael's business. Besides, the man was a gossip. He probably would go behind her back and announce to the tabloids that she, Fiona Kennedy, didn't love her new husband.

"A man who what?" Michael asked.

"A man who loves me," Fiona said.

Thankfully, Michael seemed to accept that this was what Fiona was about to say. "Yes, he does," he said. "And you're shitting on him."

"I know," Fiona said. "I know. But, Michael, I've wanted a family since I lost mine when I was 8. I won't let this opportunity go. Every cell in my body, every fiber in my being, tells me this bookstore and new family is the answer to my lifelong dream. You can't understand that. You know your family, so you don't know what it's like not to."

Michael was finally quiet. "Promise me this. Promise me your mind isn't made up about retiring. Promise me that you'll return to your movie career if this new life isn't for you. You're popular enough to take a little break and return bigger and better than ever. In fact, this break might be good for you. Give audiences a chance to miss you."

Fiona started to laugh. "Oh? What happened to 'if I take a break, audiences will just forget about me?' Were those just words?"

"Well, I might've gotten carried away. The more I think about it, the more I think it's a good idea. Look at Adele. She went away for six whole years. When she came back, audiences were dying for her."

"Adele's a singer, but I take your point."

When Michael spoke next, he obviously felt just a little relief. "Okay. So that's the plan. Go away, find your family and your roots, sell your bookstore and cottage, and come back rested and better than ever. Return to your career and your new husband."

Fiona sighed. She didn't want to break his heart; besides, she might hate running that bookstore.

At any rate, she needed a break. That was obvious.

"Okay. I promise to keep an open mind. I won't just automatically say this is the place for me, even if I'm unhappy. Okay? That's all I can promise."

"Yes." Michael's voice sounded too eager. "I predict you'll be back in front of the camera within a month or two. And I'm happy you have a family you didn't know about."

Fiona and Michael chatted for a few more minutes, and

then Fiona begged off. She was anxious to get off the phone to start researching her hopeful new life.

She promised Michael she wouldn't make rash decisions about retiring and running the bookstore. But, inside, she hoped she could make a new life.

She might finally call a place home.

Chapter Fifteen

Hallie

After Hallie and Conrad shared their very first romantic kiss, Hallie was confused to say the very least. She and Conrad had not really spoken of it even though a few days had passed. Hallie just told herself that the kiss meant nothing to Conrad. Maybe he didn't even remember it happened. Maybe he was drunker on the tequila than she realized that night, and nothing would ever come of it.

Who did seem to appreciate her was Pete. Pete was doing much better at the retreat. He was making friends and gaining confidence, and he told Hallie that it was all due to her. "If you weren't in my corner, if you didn't come back on game night, I don't think I'd be hanging out with everybody and making so many new friends."

Hallie was happy that Pete seemed to be doing well. He was following along with the dietary restrictions, and he was enthusiastically taken part in group therapy, hikes, and all the workouts. He even told Hallie was physically feeling better than he'd felt in years. Not that Hallie was surprised about that. It was her experience that once people detoxed from junk food and a sedentary lifestyle, they started feeling much better inside. More energy, sleeping better, just feeling healthier.

Not only that, Pete had already lost about 10 pounds. He had about 40 more pounds to lose, but he felt like he was well on his way. Hallie knew that the first 10 pounds comes off fairly quickly when people came to the retreat. It was mainly water weight, and men tended to lose it faster than women. It was after the initial weight loss that things became more difficult as far as taking off the rest of the weight. But Pete was well on his way, and if he could stay with his healthy habits, he might lose the weight and hopefully keep it off. Pete already told Hallie of his plans to stay at the retreat past the first 30 days. He was already booked for 60 days after the initial 30, or 90 days total. He figured that would be enough time for him to lose the rest of the weight. Hallie knew that probably was true, as long as he was faithful to the program and didn't somehow cheat. He only had another 40 pounds to lose, so, assuming he could lose around 4 pounds per week, which was definitely doable, especially considering he was a man, he could lose all his extra weight by the time he left the retreat for good.

But Hallie was still worried about him not acknowledging the core of why he was overeating in the first place. So she asked Willow to meet Pete, and Willow agreed to do so. Hallie arranged for Pete to go to Willow's new storefront on Venice Beach. Pete needed to get special permission to leave the retreat, as, generally, the participants at the retreat weren't allowed to just leave at any time. Of course, Annie allowed Pete to leave the retreat for the afternoon. Pete and

Hallie would go to Willow's storefront that Friday afternoon.

In the meantime, Hallie looked forward to her Wednesday evening pow-wow with the girls. As usual, everybody was meeting at Ava's place. Sarah and Quinn were still staying with Ava, because their house in Venice Beach was still being renovated. Mia, Quinn's girlfriend, would be there of course. Mia was around all the time, and everybody loved her, so she fit right in with the group.

Hallie really wanted to tell everybody about her kiss with Conrad and her confusion with Pete. Conrad and Pete really fulfilled two different sides for Hallie. She felt connected to Pete because he seemed to need her and she recognized his wounds. The feeling of being an outsider, the desire to fit in but not quite fitting in – Hallie felt the same way about herself. Conrad was different. He was the free spirited, creative genius, and Hallie really admired and envied him. Conrad just, in general, didn't give a crap about what people thought about him. He cared very much about what people thought about his art, but if people didn't like him for whatever reason, he just let it roll off his back.

"Some people love vanilla ice cream, some people love spicy garlic ice cream," Conrad said. "I appeal to the people who love spicy garlic ice cream, not vanilla, and that's fine with me." Conrad knew the truism that not everybody would take to you, and as long as your tribe loved you, that was all that mattered. Conrad didn't seem to take micro aggressions and slights personally the way Hallie always did. Hallie always wanted to be more like that, so Conrad appealed to her aspirational side.

Of course, so far, Pete showed no interest in Hallie romantically. So, Hallie's attraction to Pete probably wasn't reciprocated. But that didn't stop her from thinking that maybe Pete was somebody who she should be with. Even though she had fantasies about marrying Conrad, there was a part of her that realized that that fantasy was probably not to be. Conrad had never been married, even though he was now in his mid-50s, so there was no indication he would ever settle down with somebody. Pete had been married, so that spoke well for him in Hallie's eyes. It showed he was willing to make a commitment, even if that commitment to his ex-wife was not reciprocated.

Hallie was looking forward to telling the girls about her kiss with Conrad and her nascent feelings for Pete.

She arrived at Ava's that Wednesday. The plan was to order in some sushi from Uber Eats, pop open a few bottles of wine from Ava and Sarah's winery, and gossip like they usually do.

When she got there, everybody was already there, of course, since they lived there. Everybody gave one another hugs, and Hallie sat down and indulged in sushi and wine with her tribe.

"I have some news," Ava said. She looked absolutely delighted for some reason. Hallie was anxious to learn Ava's news, as were everybody else.

"What's your news, sugar?" Quinn asked.

Ava raised her eyebrows. "Well, you all know how much I love Fiona Kennedy movies. How much I have a girl-crush on her."

Hallie smiled. That was an understatement, that Ava adored Fiona Kennedy movies. She was definitely a fan girl, as much as one can be a fan girl at the age of 55. "Of course," Hallie said. "We've all watched all her movies right along with you. Whenever she has a new one out, you're first in line, right along with the rest of us."

Ava and the rest of the girls didn't go to the movies that often. They tended to wait until the movies came to a streaming service. Between all of them, they had subscriptions to many of the big streaming services – Disney +, Netflix, Paramount, Peacock, Max, and Hulu. So, there really wasn't a reason to go to the movies. But Ava always made an exception for any Fiona Kennedy movie. If there was a Fiona Kennedy movie coming out, the girls were in the theater on opening night.

Ava nodded. "Well, here's my news. Greer, who's Willow's new business partner, is Fiona Kennedy's birth mother. That means I'll surely be able to meet her."

"Oh my God, Ava, that's amazing," Sarah said. "Maybe we all could meet her."

"I hope so. But isn't that wild? I guess Fiona never even knew she was adopted. At least she didn't know until recently. So I guess it's probably kind of a stunner for her."

"Yeah, I thought she was an orphan," Mia said. "How head spinning would that be? Everything you always thought about your family is one big lie."

Hallie saw Ava's face turn red. Mia probably didn't know the story of Ava's father, how Ava didn't know until the past year or so that her birth dad was not who she thought. The man who raised Ava until she was five years old, before dying of cancer, the man who Ava always believed was her father, really wasn't. Everything she always thought about her father turned out to be one big lie, in other words. So, Ava *did* know something about what Fiona was feeling. Disoriented, confused, and maybe, in Fiona's case, elated. She didn't have a family before, after all.

"Oh, I think I can imagine what that feels like," Ava said. "Long story."

Mia looked confused, so Ava went ahead and told her the story about her father.

"Crap, Ava, that sucks," Mia said after Ava told her that her actual father was somebody other than Kenny Flynn, the man who Ava always thought was her father. "I have no idea what I would've done if I would've found out the same thing about my dad."

"It's fine," Ava said. "I've forgiven my mother for lying to me all these years about the real identity of my father. And it's brought us closer together, having everything out in the open. So, you know, silver linings and all that."

Hallie sat quietly while everybody talked. She was still in her head about Conrad and Pete. While everybody knew how she felt about Conrad, because she had long since told her best friends her feelings about her housemate, she hadn't yet said anything about Pete. And that was because she didn't really know how she felt about Pete after all. At any rate, she couldn't explore her feelings for the man until after he left the retreat for good. And if he was going to actually stay at the retreat for an extra 60 days after the initial 30, Hallie wouldn't be able to explore her feelings for at least the next few months.

Everybody else gave updates on what was going on in their lives. Quinn talked about Emerson, and how she was getting along in her new performing arts school, and Sarah talked about Julia, her step-daughter, and how Julia was slowly mending fences with her Aunt Hannah, after Hannah got custody of her against Julia's and Sarah's wishes for her own selfish reasons. But Hannah did the right thing in the end and brought Julia back to Sarah on Christmas Eve. So, even though there was still a bit of strain between Julia and Hannah, the two were becoming closer and there was a potential for a genuine understanding and love between them for the first time in their lives.

In other words, things were going pretty well for her best friends. And Hallie was very happy for all of them. When it came time for her to give a little update on her life, she told them all about Pete. And her confusion about her feelings.

"Sugar," Quinn said when Hallie confessed her nascent feelings for Pete. "What do you suppose his secret is?"

"I don't know. There's something that has been rolling around in my brain, but I don't know what it is. I hope Willow can figure it out."

Sarah put her hand on Hallie's hand. "I hope you can figure out what's going on with Pete. And I hope you can figure out what's going on with your feelings for him. We all want to feel needed. We're women. We're caretakers. But I hope you don't mind me saying that we all know that Conrad is really your main interest. Don't settle. Figure out what's going on with Conrad before you decide to throw in the towel."

Hallie knew Sarah was right about that. But she also knew it was much more complicated because she lived with the guy. If they tried to take the relationship to a different level, and it didn't work out, one of them would have to move out. She told the girls that, and Ava just smiled. "You could always just move in here," Ava said. "Sarah and Quinn's house renovation is almost completed, and I have to confess, I'm not looking forward to an empty house. I wish I could open up a bed and breakfast here like I had on Nantucket. There was something about having people around all the time that was comforting for me."

Hallie knew how much Ava struggled with her empty nest after her three kids moved out. And she was like Hallie in a way - she didn't like the feeling that her kids didn't need her as much as they did growing up. Those kids gave Ava purpose. Even though they continued to need Ava, especially Samantha, who, until fairly recently, was a complete flake without a direction in her life, it wasn't the same as when they were very young and needed Ava much more. It was difficult for Ava to accept her kids had their own lives that didn't necessarily involve her.

Hallie just laughed. "Ava, I appreciate that. But I'd like to not have to uproot my life. So, I don't think there's any way that we could take it to the next level unless both of us want the same thing. Which I don't think he does."

"Well, just see what happens after Willow meets Pete and assesses him," Sarah said. "And, maybe in a couple of months, which is when you can pursue a relationship with Pete if you want and he wants, things might be more clear for you."

Hallie nodded. She knew the girls were right. She probably shouldn't push it. There was nothing worse than pushing something that wasn't meant to be and could never be meant to be. And Hallie didn't know exactly why she was suddenly feeling so restless and impatient about her romantic situation. She only knew she was. She was anxious to get out of her rut and find the person who she was supposed to be with.

She only hoped he could become clear, just like Sarah said.

But nothing is ever that easy.

Chapter Sixteen

Fiona

Fiona needed to tell Luke about her plans. She met him over dinner to tell him the news and dreaded doing so.

There was nothing wrong with Luke. She liked him fine, and he was a sweetheart. She felt bad to be dropping a bomb on him. Yet, her heart was pulling her to retire and run that bookstore. And leave him.

She stood up when she saw him. He kissed her on the cheek and sat down, and put his napkin on his lap because it was that kind of restaurant – the high-dollar restaurant where people go to see and be seen, where courses ranged from $50 on up, with everything à la carte, which meant that the potatoes were extra, as were the vegetables and the salad. The check often came to around $300 for two people, even if each person only had a couple of drinks apiece.

She smiled and took a sip of her wine. She was nervous. She would leave the movie industry because there was something she was meant to do. She'd always thought there was another life waiting for her, a life she was meant to live, and it had nothing to do with red carpets, makeup artists, directors and boom operators.

Or her new husband. How could she tell him the marriage was over before it ever began? They hadn't even taken a honeymoon. Their happy-couple faces still beamed out from magazine covers around the globe.

"You look beautiful, as usual," he said. Then he looked around. Fiona knew he was always looking for paparazzi because he was an attention-whore. She, on the other hand, was exactly the opposite. She hated all the attention.

"So do you," Fiona said. And then she cleared her throat. "Luke, I have something to tell you."

"Oh?" He looked concerned. "Fiona, I know your last movie didn't do as well as all the others, but everybody in this business has a bum movie here and there. Don't worry about it."

Fiona scrunched her eyebrows. It was true her last movie didn't exactly clean up at the box office, but it wasn't that kind of movie. It was an independent movie, a passion project off the beaten path. She loved the story, the character and the script, so she agreed to make it. Just because it didn't make $100 million-plus like all her other movies didn't mean it was a flop.

She cleared her throat again. "This dinner isn't about that, and, anyway, my last movie did fine."

"Of course it did," he said in a condescending, mansplaining tone. "So, what's up?"

"I'm retiring."

"You're what?"

"Retiring. To run a bookstore on the beach and to bond with my family in town." She didn't tell him the truth. She really wanted to retire because she was tired. She only got into acting in the first place because she needed to fill a void in her heart. Now that she'd found her family, that void would be filled. She really wanted a normal life, and running a bookstore on the beach sounded absolutely like heaven to her.

"What family in town? Fiona, are you crazy? You're at the top of your game. And we just got married. It's important to both our publicists that we stay in the public eye. We're Hollywood royalty. It wouldn't do for you to just become a bookstore manager."

Fiona nervously took another sip of her wine, although she noticed his first concern was for her career. His second concern was what this would mean for their marriage. Maybe he didn't love her either, so her guilt would be assuaged.

But Luke wouldn't understand her motivation. He wouldn't understand that her soul was crying out for it. She didn't know why her soul was awakening to this move, and every fiber of her being was telling her this move was right for her. She only knew there was no question about it - she would do this, her career and marriage be damned.

"Don't tell me how many millions of young women would kill to be where I am. I already heard from Michael."

"You know that was exactly what I was going to say. You're an idiot. Just think about all those women waiting tables and trying to catch a break, trying to get a walk-on part, anything at all. You're spitting in their eye. You're exactly where they want to be, and you don't want it. What's wrong with you?"

"Nothing's wrong with me. Nothing at all. In fact, for the first time in my life, I'm certain things will go right for me. I'll have a family, Luke. You don't know what it's like to not have roots. You have your mom and dad, your brothers and sisters. What do I have? I've never had anything like that. And now I will. And, I'm sorry, Luke, but some things in life are worth so much more than starring in the next blockbuster or winning the next Oscar."

Fiona couldn't believe Luke was being so insensitive. Didn't he know how important it was to have a family? No, he probably didn't. He just took for granted that people had families. That's how it was in his world. It wasn't something he thought about. And why should he? He'd never experienced the bone-aching loneliness that came from not knowing where you came from and being raised by strangers.

Camille was really her only family. Camille wasn't just her best friend, but her sister, her confidante, the only person who understood her.

Luke took a deep breath. "And what about us? What about our marriage?" He somehow knew this whole thing would impact their marriage. He was right. If she was going to retire, run a bookstore and find her family, she would start fresh. That would mean she wouldn't want to be tied down to Luke, who was still in the middle of the very world she wanted to leave behind. She couldn't live a quiet life while being married to one of the biggest male movie stars in the world. She wanted nothing more to do with red-carpet events, industry parties and paparazzi. She needed to end her marriage, and Luke seemed to understand this.

Fiona raised her eyebrows. "Luke, I think you know the answer to that question. Don't you?"

"No," he said. "I don't."

Fiona fiddled with the stem of her wine glass. Her eyes didn't meet his because she knew how hurt he was. She was a bad person. Luke didn't deserve this.

"Luke, I think you know the answer. You just don't want to admit it."

Luke leaned back in his chair. "What, that our marriage was a sham? That it was dreamed up by our publicists who wanted the tabloids, Facebook, Tik Tok, and all the rest to gush over our happily-married asses so their own asses would get into theater seats to see us on the big screen?" He shook his head. "I had a feeling you felt that way. I didn't want to believe it, but inside, I knew it. I knew you were only marrying me because Amelia talked you into it."

"Luke, I'm so sorry," Fiona said. "I wasn't fair to you. I should've never accepted your proposal because my heart was never in it."

Luke's eyes got wide. "Wow. You're just laying it on the line, aren't you?"

"I guess I am," Fiona said. "Finally. I'm sorry I couldn't speak my truth until the train was barreling towards the station. You'll say I used you, and maybe I did. But I was desperate for somebody to belong to. Somebody who could look at me and say I was his. I wanted a family so much that I married you because I wanted you to become that."

"And not because you love me?"

"No," Fiona said. "I'm so sorry. Damn, I'm a terrible person."

Luke raised an eyebrow. "Nah, Fiona, you're not a terrible person. You aren't the first woman to marry for security or stability or whatever, not for love. And you won't be the last." Then he shrugged. "Ah, well, this sucks. But I can turn these lemons into lemonade yet. I'll call my publicist. He'll put a bug into the tabloids and influencers' ears so I come out smelling like a bottle of *Bleu de Chanel*." That was his favorite cologne, and Fiona loved its woodsy smell with notes of lemon, ginger, mint and pink peppercorns.

Fiona knew what Luke was saying. She'd look like the bad girl, the user, the manipulator. Oh, well. She worried about her image before she married him but wasn't worried now. So what, the Tik Tok influencers would talk smack about her? So what, the tabloids would run unflattering pictures of her while quoting "sources" that would make her look like a slut who ran out on her 72-hour marriage to shack up with God-knew-who? She bared worse before. She had a family, and that's all that mattered.

A family! God, that sounded amazing to her.

Chapter Seventeen

Jack

Jack Barclay stared out the window, watching the rain come down, which it often did in the wintertime in The Pacific Palisades. Maybe he just noticed it more than he used to. Before the accident, before he was paralyzed from the waist down, he hardly noticed how much it rained. He was too busy going to class at UCLA, playing rugby, hanging with his friends at the bar, and chasing after pretty girls. His life was full and fun before the accident.

After the accident, it was different story. His friends came around for the first few months to cheer him up, even though, at that time, he didn't want to be cheered up. He drove them away with his surly attitude that was so unlike him, because before the accident he was nothing but a sunny guy. What he didn't know was there was a transition period between being an active guy and becoming an invalid. There was a mourning period, a period of adjustment where you go through the stages of grief after losing everything you knew in one fell swoop. One of those stages was anger, and another one was depression, and Jack went through both of those stages intensely.

Depression hit him first. He refused to see anybody who came to the door, telling his mother to send them all away. It was bad enough that he was in a wheelchair for life, but he also was forced to move back in with his mother, which was the ultimate in humiliation. All of his friends were living on their own or in University housing, which was the case with Jack before the accident as well. He was deeply ashamed about having to move back home, even though he knew it was necessary in his situation. So, for the first few months after the accident, he just wouldn't see anybody at all.

A few of his more persistent friends finally came to see him when he was ready. Unfortunately, even though the depression had somewhat lifted by then, it was replaced with rage at his situation. He was bitter and sarcastic and just plain mean to his well-meaning buddies. It was nobody's fault what had happened to him. It was just an unfortunate diving accident. Yet he was mad at the world, and he took it out on anybody fool enough to visit him.

He eventually came out of all of the grieving stages and moved into acceptance, but by then, everybody had fallen away. He was back to being his good-natured self, but nobody was around anymore to enjoy his new attitude.

So now, in the six years since the accident happened, all of the other terrible emotions that he experienced after the accident were just replaced with one terrible emotion - loneliness. He just couldn't figure out how to get out into the world again. Leaving the house seemed overwhelming. His mother was always trying to encourage him to get out and meet people, but he felt too self-conscious about his situation to even try. As far as Jack knew, there weren't a whole lot of people in his situation, being young and confined to a wheelchair.

So, he spent most of his time in his room, watching Netflix or HBO Max practically nonstop. And, just recently, he also did a lot of his artwork. He was a very talented artist, but, ever since the accident, even creating works of art seemed overwhelming for him. But, within the past few weeks, he started painting again. It wasn't as easy as it was before, since he never got out of the house, so he lacked inspiration. He used to paint and sketch people that he would see in his travels, and he also was always inspired by nature. He loved to paint the forest, wildflowers, and the sea. But he hadn't really been out too much since the accident, so he didn't get a chance to be inspired.

He turned away from the window and turned on his television. He needed inspiration for his artwork, any inspiration, so he painted what was on his television screen. He found a Netflix show starring his favorite actress, Fiona Kennedy. He sighed as he looked at her beautiful face. She was so luminous, so radiant.

He stilled the picture and got to work on his canvas. He tried to capture her essence, which wasn't hard for him because something about her made him think he knew her. It was like he could see beneath her skin, into her soul, and capture it. Lately, he painted her in watercolors, but he also sketched her in charcoal and did a few photorealistic portraits resembling a photograph. His work was quite good, so he was always told. Back in the day, before he lost control of his legs and his confidence, he had dreams about being a working artist. But that was before his life was destroyed, and his friends stopped coming to visit. Before he started to feel like a failure.

Just then, his mother was knocking. He knew he worried her. She always meant well, but sometimes he just wanted to be let alone.

"Jack," his mother, Jean, said when he opened the door to let her into his room. "I hear there's a book club starting up. You always liked to read, at least when you were a boy. Maybe that's a good way for you to get out there again."

"Mom, where will the book club be? I haven't been out of the house in many years."

His mother started wringing her hands, a sure sign she felt uncomfortable. "Well, I thought maybe we could host a book club here. I could bake your favorite white chocolate macadamia nut cookies. We could even serve wine. That would be such a good way to meet people. I want you to have friends again."

His mother wanted something positive to happen to him. He loved her for how she cared about him, and he felt sorry for her because she had many sleepless nights of worry. He wanted to take the burden off her, but he felt stuck. He didn't know how to assuage her worry. "I think you want me to meet a girl," he said teasingly. "Most book club members are females, after all."

His mother smiled. "That's true. Most book-club goers are ladies. But you love to read or used to love to read, and I want you to return to that. So, I thought it would be nice to invite some of the customers at the bakery over for a book club."

At the moment, Jean was working for a small bakery on Venice Beach. It was a part-time job because his mother wanted to be home as much as possible to tend to him. She couldn't afford a caretaker for him, and he couldn't afford to hire one, either.

He wanted his mother to have a life again. He wanted

his mother to date and fall in love. And he wanted her to work full-time at the bakery, which she wanted to do and would have done if she didn't have to look after him. But that all seemed like hopeless dreams.

"Mom..." Jack wanted to tell his mother he'd love to host a book club at the house, but that would be a lie. He'd been alone for so long he didn't know if he could socialize. What would he even say to people anymore? Nothing he could say would be interesting to anybody.

Jean waved her hands at her son. "Okay, okay. I'll ask again sometime about gathering people here at the house. You'll have a good time once you get people over here. Just think about it. I must go to work, but I'll see you this afternoon. And hopefully, you'll change your mind about the book club thing, or if you don't want to do that, maybe you can come up with another idea to host people over here."

So this was her game, Jack thought. His mother was finally tired of trying to get him out of the house, so now she'd try to find ways to get people into the house. If Mohammed doesn't go to the mountain, the mountain comes to Mohammed.

"Mom, okay. I get the point. You want me to have something else in my life besides the television. I have something in my life - my art. So, don't you worry about me. I have something to interest me."

She looked worried, which she always did. "

I know you're doing your artwork. But you're sketching things you see on the TV, so you're not getting away from that thing. I just don't know what else to do." And then she started to cry, which broke Jack's heart.

"Mom," he said. "I'll think about the book club thing. Okay?"

She nodded. "I must get to work but I'll be home in a few hours. I love you."

He forced a smile. "I love you too, mom."

After she left, he returned to his TV. He really wanted to make his mother happy. She'd been through so much with him over the years; she was patient and caring. It wasn't fair for her to sit there and watch him waste away, feeling helpless to do anything for him. So, he would have to try.

Sometime soon.

Chapter Eighteen

Cora

Cora had a hard time sleeping the night before. It wasn't that Daisy kept her up. The baby was now sleeping through the night, thank God. The 2 AM feedings were starting to get to her, so she was relieved the baby was now sleeping all the way through. But that didn't mean Cora would get a good night's sleep because there was a lot on her mind.

She wondered what it would be like to meet her sister or if Fiona would even bother visiting them. Her mother got notice from her attorney that Fiona would pay them a visit at some point, but Cora didn't know when that would happen. Would Fiona be this stuck-up movie star who wouldn't want anything to do with her poor relations? Would she see Cora's tiny trailer and turn up her nose? Would she think Greer's profession as a tarot card reader was just too weird to associate with? Cora really didn't care if Fiona liked them or not. She was just worried her mother would get her heart broken if Fiona met them and decided she didn't want to have anything to do with them.

She didn't know if her mother was awake yet. It was only 7 o'clock in the morning, and she had a feeling Greer wouldn't be up and about just yet. Greer was always a bit of a night owl who liked to stay up until all hours. Her mother was a very social person, who made friends all over the trailer park, and there was always somebody or another hanging about her mom's place, sleeping on her sofa or just drinking wine with her mother until two or three in the morning. Cora had yet to learn what those ladies did so late in the evening or early in the morning, depending on how you looked at it. She imagined them all gossiping like old hens, cackling like crows over this or that.

She was about to call her mother when Daisy apparently woke up. Cora could hear her baby cooing in her room, so she knew it was time to nurse her and change her diapers. And, every day she went into her room, she prayed she could look at the beautiful girl and feel the overwhelming love and joy she was supposed to feel. And every day she went into her room to feed and change her, she was disappointed because she still felt nothing.

Nevertheless, she would do her duty, so she entered Daisy's room and picked up her little daughter. She nursed Daisy after she changed her and rocked her softly.

"Little Daisy," Cora said forlornly. "You're going to have an aunt around pretty soon. She's apparently this glamorous movie star. Won't that be great? Oh, you're not impressed by that, are you? No, you're just impressed with… what are you impressed with? What do babies know?"

Cora felt a bit silly talking to Daisy as if the little girl would understand a word she was saying. She just knew it was important to talk to the baby. She'd read a few books before giving birth, and the universal advice to new mothers was that they were to talk to their newborns. She also read a few studies about playing classical music for the baby. Apparently, playing classical music to little babies helped them develop motor skills and speech and language. So, Cora dutifully put on her Beethoven CD while she nursed Daisy.

Daisy made two fists and punched the air, and her little legs kicked a little. It was almost as if she was trying to dance to the music. Cora smiled at her daughter's antics despite herself. Was the sun peeking through the clouds? Was her heart finally starting to crack open just a little to let her daughter in? She closed her eyes and prayed again she'd feel the overwhelming love for her daughter she was supposed to feel.

Just then, she heard her doorbell ring. It wasn't her mom. Her mother would just walk in the door without ringing it. No, there was somebody else at the door. And Cora wondered who it would be. She didn't think it would be any of her friends. It was too early for that.

So, she took Daisy to the front door and opened it.

Standing on the veranda was a very pretty woman with bright red hair who looked much like Cora herself. She almost looked like Fiona Kennedy, the actress, but not quite. This woman was wearing big black stylish glasses and was tiny, freckled, and incredibly pale.

"Can I help you?" Cora asked her, curious.

The woman smiled. "I'm Fiona. I'm your sister."

Chapter Nineteen

Fiona

The next day, after Fiona broke the bad news to Luke about her future plans, she decided she couldn't wait to meet her sister. Even though it was early in the morning, she decided to knock on Cora Morrison's door. She hoped Cora was an early riser. Otherwise, she'd be very disappointed when she knocked on the door and found nobody was awake. Then again, from what she understood, Cora had a newborn baby, so Cora probably wasn't sleeping much anyways.

Her heart was pounding as she drove to Cora's trailer home. This was her sister. This was her flesh and blood. What would Cora be like? Would her sister greet her with open arms or be suspicious? Would Cora think Fiona was some posh movie who wouldn't be worth getting to know? Or would Cora be open-minded about meeting her? She dearly hoped it would be the latter, but she feared rejection just like anybody would in this situation. She was so invested in having a family that her heart would be broken if her family wanted nothing to do with her.

Cora's tiny mobile home was in a beach trailer park in the Pacific Palisades. It was part of a group of manufactured homes and small trailers. Although it was beach living, and the trailer and manufactured homes were on the Will Rogers beach and very close to bike trails and the Santa Monica Pier, it was affordable - the space rent was only around $1,200 a month. The trailers cost less than $100,000 for single-wides and less than $200,000 for double-wides. So, her sister Cora definitely wasn't rich, but Fiona didn't care about that. Cora was her sister, and that was all that mattered.

Fiona knocked on the door, half hoping that maybe Cora wasn't really home or maybe Cora was sleeping in. She hated that she was so timid about doing this, and she tried to get into the head of one of her characters. She'd played some tough characters on screen, namely a series of movies where she portrayed a detective on the hunt for serial killers and other evil characters who fill people's nightmares. That detective, Elle Mason, wasn't afraid of anything. Elle definitely wouldn't be afraid of confronting her own sister. So, Fiona closed her eyes, trying to imagine herself in Elle's shoes and she tried to access Elle's courage.

After what seemed like forever, but was probably only a few minutes, Cora opened the door.

Fiona put her hand to her mouth when she saw her sister. If there was ever any doubt in Fiona's mind that maybe this whole thing was just a big mistake and she didn't belong to this new family, it was erased when she saw her sister's face. It was like looking in a mirror. Same bright red hair, same slightly round face, same pug nose, same crystalline green eyes with just a hint of hazel around the pupil.

Like Fiona, Cora didn't have any eyelashes to speak of, and her eyebrows also were barely visible. The only difference was that Cora's red hair was straight, while Fiona's was naturally curly.

In Cora's arms was a little baby who was probably only around four or five months old. The baby looked just like Cora, with bright red curly hair, big crystalline green eyes with the same hint of hazel around the pupil, and a round face. The baby smiled at Fiona, her beautiful green eyes crinkled at the edges. The baby stared at Fiona for a long time, probably seeing the resemblance between Fiona and her mother Cora, then smiled again and reached for her.

Cora narrowed her eyes as she cradled her baby in the doorway. "Can I help you?"

Fiona felt taken aback. Surely Cora knew she would try to find her family? "I'm Fiona. I'm your sister."

Cora narrowed her eyes again. "You're crazy. You look nothing like Fiona Kennedy, the movie star." Then she raised her right eyebrow. "You look just like me, so I don't believe you are Fiona Kennedy, the movie star. If you are, then call me Gisele Bündchen."

"Okay. I'd rather call you Cora, but if you want, I'll call you Gisele Bündchen. Even though you don't resemble her in any way, shape or form." And then Fiona smiled, hoping that Cora got the joke, but, by the look on Cora's face, Fiona's little joke fell flat.

"Excuse me," Cora said. "I'll be right back."

At that, Cora shut the door in Fiona's face. Fiona looked around and saw it was starting to rain. Fiona sat on the rocking chair, patiently waiting for Cora to reappear. That didn't happen, not for a good 20 minutes. But the next thing Fiona knew, a lady approached the home. She looked like an older version of Fiona, Cora and the baby. She was slightly taller than Fiona but was just as thin. Her features were slightly more angular, and her eyes were blue. But she had a mop of red hair, the same as Fiona, Cora and the baby. She smiled a big smile at Fiona as she grew closer, and her smile lit up the dreary sky. Fiona recognized that smile as being her own, and that smile was one of the reasons why Fiona became such a popular actress. Critics always mentioned it when they reviewed her movies, saying it was a huge part of her winning charisma.

When this new woman smiled, and Fiona recognized it, Fiona knew exactly who this woman was. It was Greer Davidson. Her birth mother. Her heart started to pound as she realized she was coming face-to-face with the woman who gave her life. Again, if there was ever any doubt in Fiona's mind that she was really and truly finding her birth family, it was erased when she saw the smiling woman who was almost to the porch.

"Fiona," the woman said, with her arms outstretched. "Oh, my land. I never thought I'd see the day when I would come to see my first-born."

The woman was now on the porch, and Fiona was enveloped in her arms. Fiona inhaled her apparent mother's scent, Tom Ford's Soleil Brûlant, which had notes of mandarin, bergamot and pink peppercorn, with a hint of black honey. It was a scent Fiona recognized because that was the only perfume she ever wore herself. Was that just a coincidence? Or would she find she had much in common with her sister and mother, like when they studied twins who were raised apart and found they had the same jobs, same hobbies, married similar spouses, and sometimes had the same car? Fiona wondered how much of her make-up was nature and how much was nurture. It would be interesting to find out.

Fiona was surprised to find tears coming to her eyes as the woman, who Fiona now had no doubt was her birth mother, held her on the porch. She felt this was the most natural thing in the world, being held by this woman and inhaling the same perfume Fiona wore religiously. And when her mother finally ended the embrace so that she could look at her, she saw her mother also had tears in her eyes.

Fiona swallowed the lump in her throat and wiped away the tears. "You're my mom," she said. "Oh, my God. You're my mom." It was so profound for Fiona to say those words to this woman, who was a stranger, yet had such a deep connection to Fiona that she could feel it. The connection was palpable, like an entity she could reach for and cherish.

Her mother just nodded, unable to speak because she was crying. And then Cora finally opened the door again and came out on the porch to join the two. "Mom, I'm sorry to keep you waiting on the porch, but I had to put Daisy down."

Greer just nodded, her eyes still fixated on Fiona. "Cora, aren't you going to invite your sister inside? Please don't be rude."

Cora just looked at Fiona with curiosity and vague hostility. "Mom, can you come in for just a second? I need to ask you a few things."

"Now, Cora, this is your sister. You can say whatever you say to me in front of her."

Cora just sighed and pointed at Fiona. "Okay. This does not look like Fiona Kennedy, the actress. She looks just like a college student." And then Cora blinked a few times. "No offense," she said to Fiona. "I'm quite sure you're fine, but I was expecting this glamorous movie star I've seen in a million movies. You're just a tiny thing. The Fiona Kennedy

I've always seen in movies is tall, with porcelain skin, red eyebrows and beautiful long eyelashes. And she has a chest that always looked magnificent on screen."

Fiona was well aware that her breasts were quite small, in keeping with the rest of her frame. "Well, if you think my chest is anything but flat, it's because of a very talented bra that pushes them up when I wear my red carpet evening gowns."

Cora started to laugh. "Are you saying that all those pictures I've seen of you are-"

"Fake, air-brushed, makes me look perfect when I'm obviously anything but? A product of hours in the make-up chair? The end result of a professional hairdresser who spends a ton of time either giving me a Brazilian blowout that makes my hair perfectly straight or putting so much product on my curls that they always look bouncy and perfect? You're on the nose."

Fiona subconsciously put her hand to her hair and felt the frizz. Yes, it probably was startling to see Fiona Kennedy looking like a bespectacled and frizzy drowned rat instead of the glamorous air-brushed movie star everybody was used to seeing. Still, it was odd that Cora was so invested in telling Fiona how different she looked in real life. It was almost like Cora was already trying to put her sister in her place.

"Well, it's just that I never thought looking at Fiona Kennedy in the flesh would be like looking in the mirror. In all your movies, red carpet appearances, and magazine covers, I never thought that movie star Fiona looked anything like me. Yet, I'm looking at you, and there's no doubt you're my sister. I'm just having a hard time imagining you as the Fiona Kennedy I've always admired."

Fiona furrowed her brows. "I'm sorry to disappoint," she

said. "But I am your sister. I think that's obvious, don't you? Your daughter seemed to recognize me as her aunt, considering how big she smiled at me and reached for me when she first met me."

Cora just nodded. She was obviously looking for the beautiful, larger-than-life movie star and was bitterly disappointed that Fiona looked like every other girl on the street. "Yes, I suppose Daisy did seem to take to you immediately."

Greer went over to Cora. "Now, dear, I know you imagined something in your head. Maybe you thought Fiona would show up in a limousine with a trail of servants following her around and peeling her grapes. But look at her. She's obviously just an ordinary girl. And I think that's a good thing. She wouldn't want anything to do with us if she was too posh. Now, I think it's about time you invite us in."

Cora just shook her head rapidly. "No. My place is so tiny and bare, Fiona will turn her nose up at us, her poor relations. Why don't we all go down to the bar? We can have a beer and have some fun."

Fiona put her hand on Cora's shoulder. "Cora," she said. "I think you have the wrong idea about me. I'm not what you think I am. I'm just a girl, standing before another girl, asking for her love," she said, inverting the famous *Nottinghill* line. That was one of her favorite movies. "Not to mention, the cottage I inherited out in the woods apparently is tiny, and I plan on living in it, assuming it's habitable. I'd love to see your home." Fiona had already decided to give up her Malibu mansion in favor of the cottage in the woods. She'd tired of seeing the paparazzi outside her door all the time, and she thought they wouldn't do the same for the cottage. She hoped she wasn't being naive about that. Besides, a cottage in the woods seemed romantic to her because it was rustic, and isolated, which sounded heavenly. Plus, she was tired of cleaning her enormous house. Time to downsize.

"BS," Cora said dismissively, waving her right hand. "I don't believe you. All those big movie stars live in these hundred-room mansions. I've seen it in the magazines. Hundred-foot ceilings, enormous swimming pools, an army of servants, huge screen TVs all over the house. Priceless paintings on the wall. And yachts. These giant yachts where everybody is beautiful and drinking champagne, and nobody has a care in the world. You can't tell me you're not one of them."

Fiona was almost amused by how badly Cora was stereotyping movie stars. The truth was, Fiona had never been on a yacht. She had a nice home on the beach, but it wasn't a giant mansion. She'd been inside those enormous homes Cora was describing but never wanted to own one of them. How could she explain to Cora that just because she was wealthy and famous didn't mean any of it went to her head? She was always aware that she was living a fantasy life and was so anxious to live in reality. And this was reality, having a mother and sister. This was life. She couldn't care less what Cora's home looked like. In fact, she imagined it being cozy because it looked that way from the outside. And, to Fiona, cozy was what she craved.

Greer finally just took the bull by the horns. "Oh, grow up, Cora," she said, pushing her daughter aside. "Fiona, my precious first-born, follow me."

Fiona followed her into the house. Fiona was charmed by what she saw inside. A well-worn sofa in blue suede, with some beautiful colorful pillows, was next to a reclining chair that had seen better days and did not match the sofa, as the reclining chair was bright red. There was a loveseat that also did not match anything, as it was yellow. But it worked as it was all pulled together by a bright throw rug with the same yellow, red and blue woven throughout. The hardwood floors were scuffed. In the middle of the living room was a green rocking chair.

The dining room, which was really a part of the living room, had a small table and chairs that looked as worn as the rest of the furniture. Above the dining room set, if you could call it that, was a funky chandelier that was stained glass with some stained-glass colorful birds surrounding the bowl of the light fixture. It was very whimsical, as was the beautiful throw rug that pulled the living room together, and Fiona loved it. She realized her sister didn't have much money to furnish her little home, but she made the most of her limited funds by ensuring the living room and dining room had a couple of conversation pieces, both of which Fiona found beautiful.

There was also a large-screen television tucked into the corner of the living room, with beanbags in front of it.

Cora was standing to the side, obviously looking ashamed and embarrassed. She looked down at the floor, and it looked like she was about to burst into tears. "My husband works for a fishery," she said. "And having a new baby is expensive, too. There just doesn't seem to be enough money to go around these days, so I have to make do with what I have."

Fiona smiled. She didn't quite know how to approach the situation. She didn't want to come off as condescending or pitying, but, at the same time, she wanted Cora to know she thought her home was perfectly lovely. It was just as cozy as she imagined, and she could imagine having a cup of hot tea as she tried to get to know her new family.

"Cora," Fiona began. "All I could think when I saw your throw rug and beautiful light fixture is that you and I have the same taste. I've always loved whimsical, and you do too. I believe you and I have more in common than you might think."

Fiona didn't say anymore. She didn't want to gush because it would come off as insincere. But she wanted Cora to know that she found her home quite cute.

Cora still looked doubtful that Fiona was being sincere. "Excuse me," she said, leaving the room. "I think I hear Daisy."

To Fiona's surprise, when Cora left the room, as she walked down the hall to her daughter's bedroom, Fiona could hear Cora sobbing. "I don't understand," Fiona said to Greer, who was just standing to the side and shaking her head. "Is Cora okay? I thought getting to know her might be rough, but I didn't expect hostility."

"Child," Greer said. "My Cora has been having difficulty bouncing back after the baby was born. Her husband is on a boat and will be there for the next two months. I believe she's overwhelmed. I try to come over to help as much as possible, and she tries to act like she's in good spirits, but I know there's something wrong. Just don't take her behavior toward you personally. I think she's not at peace with her lot in life."

Fiona tried to suppress a smile. "Boy, we have that in common too. I wasn't very happy with my lot in life either." She knew she sounded whiny when she said that. To the outside world, Fiona's life was charmed, filled with red carpet parties, a handsome and wildly successful husband, adoring fans, and a salary in the millions of dollars a year. And, to people like Cora, she was also drinking champagne on yachts, which she had never done. Yet, even though she thought most people would think she was whining for saying her life was anything but sunny and bright, she saw in Greer's face that her mother understood.

"We all have our cross to bear. Goodness knows nobody has it easy, even people who everybody thinks they do. I've never thought that this person or that person has no problems just because they're rich and famous. I suppose you're no exception."

Fiona nodded. "Yes. My issue is that I've always felt disconnected somehow. Like I'm not a part of this world. It's probably because I've lived in other people's shoes for the past 10 years, becoming other people on the screen. It's been difficult trying to find who I am."

Fiona was so surprised these words came out of her mouth. She didn't know this woman, yet, at the same time, she knew her quite profoundly. She felt she could tell this woman anything.

"You know, some of our greatest actors have struggled with depression and anxiety and even suicidal thoughts. So, you're in good company," Greer said gently.

Fiona never said the word "depression" to her mother when she described how she felt, but Greer could pinpoint exactly what was wrong with her. She never wanted to admit to it, not even to herself, but she struggled with depression for most of her years. It was always present. She had dark moments when she would lock herself in her home and not come out for days. This would always happen when she was between movies because Fiona was a professional who always came to the set when she was needed. But there were so many days when Fiona would be on the set and not feel anything. Like she was numb. Like she was mouthing the words while trying to ignore the empty pit in her stomach. She never felt worthy of all the attention, and she often wanted to tell people that she was just not good at what she did, even though everybody always told her she was amazing.

Fiona smiled and blinked. "Yes, I understand that." Fiona had read many biographies about some of the biggest stars around, both recent and in the Golden Age of Hollywood, and many of them, like Fiona, struggled with depression, low self-esteem, anxiety and other mental illnesses. Cary Grant struggled with depression and abandonment issues for most of his life, as did Marilyn Monroe, and both of them had mothers locked up in mental institutions, as did Charlie Chaplin. Steve McQueen was badly abused by his stepfather, had low self-esteem because of it and ended up in reform school. Audrey Hepburn was scarred from the war years when members of her family were murdered by the Nazis, and she, herself, lived by eating tulip bulbs for a year because there was no food. These were just a few legendary actors who struggled with mental issues, and Fiona knew there were many more.

These actors' stories made her feel she wasn't alone in her feelings, but it wasn't necessarily a balm. When she was really low, nothing could bring her out of it.

Greer just shook her head and enveloped Fiona in her arms. She seemed to know just what Fiona needed. A hug from her own flesh and blood.

Cora came back out with Daisy in her arms. And, as Fiona looked at her sister staring at her baby, there was a twinge of recognition. Cora wasn't feeling the baby. It was obvious by the look on her face.

"Mom," Cora said. "Can you take Daisy?"

Greer took Daisy in her own arms, and Fiona saw the bond she didn't see between Cora and Daisy. Fiona suddenly realized just what was wrong with her sister. She knew Cora, like herself, suffered from depression. But she felt that Cora's depression didn't come from a deep-seated sense that she didn't have a place in the world, as with Fiona. Cora didn't become depressed because, at the age of eight, she helplessly watched her parents die in the front seat of a car. No. Fiona thought Cora's depression probably was postpartum. That was one thing she had some knowledge about because she had to research the role of a new mother who wanted to harm her child because of her severe postpartum depression.

Fiona nodded. She suddenly realized she could help her sister. "Cora," she said. "Are you keeping up with your physicals?"

Cora shook her head. "Who has time for that? Certainly not me. I'm basically a single mom."

Fiona looked at Greer, who helplessly shrugged her shoulders. Fiona felt that Greer and Cora probably had more than a few conversations about how Cora was feeling, and Cora was probably not straight with her mother. That was common. Fiona found through her research that women often had difficulty expressing their feelings to others. They usually felt a sense of desperation and aloneness and shame that they didn't feel for their newborns the feelings they should. They often felt they were the only people who struggled with feeling love and bonding with their babies.

"Well, you have a sister now," Fiona said, trying to be helpful. "I'd be happy to watch little Daisy while you take some time for yourself to see a doctor."

Cora's eyes got wide. "Oh, I see. You think you can just show up out of the blue and tell me what I need. Well, I can tell you what I don't need, and that's to have some posh movie star who doesn't have a care in the world try to say there's something wrong with me."

Fiona suddenly realized she'd overstepped. She didn't know this Cora, even though it was so obvious, literally plain as the nose on her face, the two were sisters. She knew she was so desperate to connect to her family that she wanted to help in any way she could. But Cora obviously wasn't ready for her help.

Greer rolled her eyes. "Cora, you're being incredibly rude to your one and only flesh and blood sister. Now, why don't we go put a kettle of hot water on the stove and choose a good Earl Grey from your tea collection, have some cookies, and we can all get to know each other?"

Cora stared at Greer with hostility. It was as if she resented her mother for telling her what to do. "Mom, I have a headache. That means I don't feel like having a cookie and a cup of Earl Grey tea." Then she turned to Fiona. "Real people in the real world get headaches and feel tired and don't feel like socializing."

Fiona took her cue. "I get it. I came over here unannounced, and that was incredibly rude of me. I was just so anxious to meet my family, and I didn't have anybody's phone numbers because my lawyer didn't give me your phone number or my mother's number, only your addresses, so I couldn't necessarily call either of you to announce I was coming."

Cora furrowed her brows. "You could've Facebooked either of us or emailed us. I know you had our email addresses."

"Yes. I could have. And I should have. I don't know why I didn't, except that it just seemed so impersonal. You know, sending an email saying, 'I'm your kin. How you doing?' I wanted my first contact with both of you to be face-to-face. But that was a mistake, and I apologize. If I would've sent you an email, we could have arranged a time for us to meet that was good for both of us. I didn't do that, so I've obviously come at a bad time."

Cora nodded. "Yes. It's true I'm not having a very good day. I'm sorry."

Fiona got the message. "Okay. Well, let me give you my address and phone number so you guys can get in touch. In the meantime, I'll probably check out the bookstore I've inherited and the cottage. I don't know how long it's going take me to check everything out, but I'll be back home this evening. If either of you wants to see me. And, of course, I'll leave my phone number."

Greer looked like she wanted to strangle her daughter Cora but kept her mouth shut. Then she finally opened it. "Fiona, I'll call you later this evening. Maybe we can get together and visit some more."

"I'll be looking forward to it."

"I'll show you out," Greer said, shooting Cora a look.

Greer walked out with Fiona. "I'm so sorry about Cora. I don't know what got into her. I'll have a talk with her."

"I'm sure it's all very overwhelming for her. Having a new sister. Having that sister show up out of the blue. I shouldn't have done that. I was so anxious to meet my new family that I lost my head. Apologize to her for me, will you?"

Greer waved a hand dismissively. "Child, there's nothing to apologize for. Cora's just had a hard time of it lately, that's all. I'm sure we'll all get along famously. Eventually."

"I hope so," Fiona said. "In the meantime, I'll see what awaits me in the woods and the new bookstore. But I don't suppose maybe Cora is hostile towards me because I inherited the cottage and the bookstore? Really, those things should be yours and Cora's, not mine."

"Oh, don't you worry about that," Greer said. "If Ewan

wanted us to have them, then he would've given them to us in his will. But, he apparently wanted to give the property to you, and that's that."

"But if he didn't will them to me, you would've gotten them, and Cora would also be entitled to something. So, she probably resents me for that reason alone."

"I suppose," Greer said. "But I don't think we would've benefited from inheriting those two things. We would've been forced to sell both pieces of property at auction, and it was obvious that Ewan wanted his cottage and bookstore to remain intact. We don't have the money to renovate the cottage, and we don't have the time or inclination to run the bookstore. So, it's better you get the property. I'm sure you'll do a wonderful job fixing up that cottage and running the bookstore."

"Thanks," Fiona said. "For being so welcoming and for your faith in me."

"You're my first-born," Greer said. "I loved you when I held you in my arms as a tiny baby, and I couldn't quit crying when I gave you up. I regretted that day. Every day of my life, I've regretted giving you up. So, I'm looking forward to getting to know you. And don't you worry about Cora. She'll come around. Just wait."

Greer gave Fiona a big hug, and Fiona closed her eyes and tried to beat back the tears forming. She always had a hard time crying for some reason. Ever since the day she lost her parents, she had a hard time expressing her emotions. She'd bottled up what had happened to her, stuffed it down so far that she could never come to terms with it. Yet, here she was with her birth mother, about to cry the tears she didn't cry for her own parents. Maybe she was turning a corner with her emotions.

Fiona left. Her destination was to find her cottage in the

woods. In her fantasy, she would've taken her mother and her sister along to the cottage. They would've laughed and gabbed like old friends the whole way. And then they would've worked together to decorate the little cottage. And, as far as the bookstore went, Fiona's fantasy was that her mother and her sister would help her run the place. Fiona would've been happy to put the bookstore into the name of her mother and sister and give them all the profits from it. She didn't need the money, to say the least, and all she wanted was for her family to be around her, helping her establish her new life. But Cora and her hostility threw cold water all over those plans.

Well, Fiona thought, Cora obviously disliked her immensely. For whatever reason. But Fiona would have to find the path to ensure she and Cora became true sisters.

It might take her a long time, but she would do it. She was used to doing difficult things well.

She would have to do this difficult thing well, too.

Just a half-hour later, she arrived at her new bookstore. She was excited about getting this place up and running again. Even though the bookstore had not been a going concern for the past few months, it looked like it had been preserved in amber. All the bookshelves still had books on them, and some cozy sofas, chairs, and loveseats surrounded the fireplace in the nook. She loved this bookstore on sight. She loved the smell of the books, the hardwood floors, the high ceilings, the exposed brick, and the loft. Her favorite part was the fireplace and the cute little furniture surrounding it.

Fiona had never run anything, so she'd have to get a business plan together. She had no idea where she would order books or how to get the word out about this place. But, then again, this was a bookstore on Venice Beach. There probably was a market for this place, and since it faced the famous boardwalk, with all the foot traffic, she would have people lined up in no time.

One thing was for sure, this place would have to be deep cleaned. Unfortunately, cobwebs were everywhere, and every single book probably had a layer of dust on them. In fact, just being in the place made Fiona cough, as she was allergic to dust. She felt temporarily overwhelmed when she thought about what would have to happen before the bookstore was ready to open. She would have to get an inventory of new books, she would have to clean this place from top to bottom, she would have to get employees, and she would have to schedule events. And she would apparently have to do all this alone because her family didn't want her around. Well, that wasn't fair. Greer was still very kind to her. But her sister seemed to hate her, so Fiona thought Greer probably would take Cora's side because Cora had been her daughter all along, and Fiona was somebody new.

In other words, the more Fiona thought of it, the more she thought she might be ostracized by her mother and sister. She was disappointed, but then again, she was used to disappointment. Her professional life had always been on point since she fell into acting. Her personal life had always disappointed her, however. It was more than just that she felt disconnected from most people, aside from Camille and, on occasion, Luke. It was that she had never been in love. Before Luke, she had dated many guys, none of whom were men she could truly lose herself in. She imagined that true love was something that was... well, even though she had been in love a million times on screen, it seemed, Fiona was still not sure what true love really was. All she knew was that true love was something she'd never experienced. At least, not yet.

Fiona wandered over to the books, thinking of why she'd landed on such a depressing subject as her inability to fall in love. What was love? Was it witty banter, *a la* Elizabeth Bennet and Mr. Darcy? Was it all-consuming passion and chemistry, as with Maggie Cleary and Father Ralph in *The Thornbirds*? Or was it something else? Perhaps it was wanting more for somebody else than you want for yourself. Somebody comfortable and safe, somebody who's your best friend, who always has your back, somebody who you could have real conversations with. Somebody who won't bore you 30 years down the line.

Fiona didn't know. She thought she'd know love when she found it, but she didn't know if that was the case.

Perhaps Fiona would always be alone in her life.

Although she hoped not.

Chapter Twenty

Cora

"Don't say it," Cora said to her mother when Greer stormed back into the house after saying goodbye to Fiona. Her mother was very upset with her, and Cora didn't blame her. Cora was very angry with herself.

She surprised herself at how mean she was to Fiona. She had no reason to be so hurtful to her sister. And she really didn't know why exactly she treated Fiona so badly. She supposed the reason why she was so mean was because she was jealous of Fiona. Her sister was this wealthy, talented, and immensely famous woman who was loved by people around the world and was married to a hunk of a man who also was loved around the world. And, when Fiona came into her home, she didn't think she imagined that Fiona was sticking her nose up at Cora's bare furniture, her tiny surroundings, and even at her tiny daughter. Fiona coming to see her made her suddenly feel so small and insignificant. She'd never felt that way before and didn't like feeling that way.

"Cora Jean Davidson," Greer said to Cora, using her full name. Greer never called her "Cora Jean Davidson" unless she was really angry with her. And, of course, Cora's current last name was Morrison, but when her mother was really angry, she didn't hesitate to remind Cora that she was Greer's daughter, and she better act accordingly. "I can't believe how rude you were to your sister. What has gotten into you?"

Cora wanted to strike back at her mother. She wanted to cry to her mother that she was drowning, and she didn't need some highfalutin movie actress to come into her life and make her feel even worse about her situation. She wanted to tell her mother about her constant fantasy that she could give Daisy to somebody else to raise. She wanted to divorce her husband, move far away where nobody knew her, and just start a new life. She wanted to be anywhere but where she was.

But her mother would tell her the words of wisdom she always told her when she thought running away from her problems was the answer. And those words were, "Wherever you go, there you are." No matter where Cora went, she couldn't get away from herself. Which made her feel all the more hopeless. But she couldn't tell her mother any of these things.

"Oh, she comes in here so posh and so much better than us," Cora spat. "She hated this house. She thinks I'm beneath her. And what does she have that she feels so uppity? Just because she happens to look great on a big screen? She doesn't know about my life or about anybody's life. She only knows about her wealthy friends. That's all she cares about, I'm sure. And she'll sell that house and that bookstore and be gone as soon as you can say the word boo. Mark my words."

Greer shook her head. "You couldn't be more wrong. Your sister is a very down-to-earth, caring woman. You have this vision in your head that she's some stuck-up Hollywood star, and you're not letting go of it, all evidence to the contrary."

"Mom, you better wake up," Cora said. "Don't you think for one second that a wealthy and famous movie star will want anything to do with us. She'll turn her back on us so fast your head will swim. And your heart will be broken. I've been here all along, and I know that after she stops returning your calls, you'll only be thinking of her, not of me and your granddaughter."

Greer's face softened. "Child, don't ever think I love her more than I love you, or I'll ever love her more than I love you. You're both my children. You're both my heart. And if she decides to turn her back, I'll miss her. I won't lie about that. Now that I've found her, she's a part of me. She's always been a part of me, but now she really is. But that doesn't mean I'll ever love you any less."

Cora felt about 2 inches tall. What was getting into her? She was 26 years old, but she was acting like a teenager. Jealous of her sister, afraid of losing her mother's love, and wanting to escape her life. She wasn't acting her age, and she knew it. But there was no way she'd know how to act her age.

Cora crossed her arms in front of her, feeling very defensive. "So you say," Cora said. She wanted to say that if her mother truly loved her, she'd see her daughter drowning. Her mother never seemed to notice how overwhelmed she was getting. It was so hard being away from Alistair all the time, never being in contact with him, because he couldn't call her from the fishing boat he was on. And she hated herself for feeling so hostile towards her own daughter. But Greer never seemed to notice just how depressed she was. Oh, Greer was wonderful about coming over every day and helping out, watching Daisy while Cora took much-needed naps, and helping with the housework, cooking and grocery shopping. But her mother never asked her how she felt about her situation.

And what really hurt Cora's feelings was that her sister, who just met her, somehow figured out there was a problem. Fiona asked her if she was keeping up with her physicals, which meant Fiona was wondering if Cora had seen her primary care doctor. Cora hadn't because she hadn't gotten around to it, but she was secretly impressed Fiona knew there was something wrong with her. She just wished her mother would notice the same thing.

Greer shook her head. "Child, I don't know what to do with you. You've never been like this. You've never doubted my love or been cruel to a perfect stranger for no reason. You've always been such a happy child."

Cora shrugged. "I'm just having a bad day, that's all. I'm really happy you're here because I need a nap. I appreciate you coming over here and watching Daisy so I can get 40 winks once in a while."

Greer just took Daisy out of Cora's arms. "You just take a nap; hopefully, when you wake up, you'll be in better spirits."

Cora went into her room, shut her door, and lay on the bed. She could hear the sea rolling in when she opened the window. She imagined the entire trailer somehow rolling into the sea. She'd drown, and that would be welcome.

She had those kinds of thoughts all the time.

And there was no way she could think about what to do about it.

Chapter Twenty-One

Hallie

Hallie had arranged for Willow to see Pete and hopefully hypnotize him, and so, on a very sunny Wednesday, Pete and Hallie left the retreat to head down to Venice Beach, which was where Willow had a storefront. She had gone into business with a lady by the name of Greer Davidson, who apparently was the biological mother of Fiona Kennedy. Hallie was very excited. She knew that there was a good possibility that she could meet Fiona Kennedy, and even though she wasn't as crazy about the actress as Ava was, she still really loved Fiona's movies.

But that was not on the agenda for that day. On the agenda was Pete hopefully getting to the bottom of what happened to him when he was 11. And, if that happened, maybe Pete could move on from it and quit eating his feelings.

They got to Willow's shop, and she was waiting for

them. Also in the shop was a woman about Hallie's age with bright red hair, pale skin, and freckles. Since she resembled Fiona Kennedy, and Hallie knew that Fiona Kennedy's mother was working with Willow, Hallie surmised this was Greer.

When the lady smiled at Hallie, all doubt was erased in Hallie's mind. This was definitely Fiona's mother. Their smiles were identical, and both would light up a pitch-dark sky. Something about this Greer made Hallie feel warm and fuzzy inside. She could feel the positivity exuding from the lady.

"Hey," Willow said to Hallie and Pete when they walked in the door. "I want you to meet my new business partner, Greer. Greer, this is Hallie, a friend of mine, and Pete, who is apparently a friend of Hallie's."

Hallie shook Greer's hand, as did Pete. Greer continued to smile that dazzling smile. "It's so good to meet you."

Willow looked at Pete. And then she nodded her head. "Come on back," she said. "And just relax."

Pete looked nervous, but he followed Willow to the back room.

Hallie looked at Greer. "How long will this take?"

"About an hour. So if you want to go to the beach or grab coffee at the café down the street, feel free."

"I think I'll be taking you up on that," Hallie said.

Hallie went out the door and was immediately on the boardwalk. It was a very warm day, unseasonably warm considering it was only January, but there were few people on the beach. It was almost deserted. Some people were out surfing, a sport Hallie really wanted to learn. It looked like such a freeing experience. The surfers almost seemed to fly when they caught a good wave. She also heard that most surfers saw great white sharks when they were out on their boards. The sharks always left them alone, but Hallie wouldn't want to chance that. She had to overcome her fear of sharks, which she picked up when she was 8 years old and saw *Jaws* on the big screen for the first time.

Hallie sat down on the sand and closed her eyes. Why was she still so confused about her life? She never imagined when she was 18 years old, so full of life and dying to go into her future, that she would get to be 55 and still not have a clue. Maybe she would never have a clue. Maybe that was her fate. Not that she was the only one of this age who still knew nothing about life or love, but maybe she was one of the few who got to this age and could honestly say she'd never been in love. What did it even feel like, romantic love? She wished she knew the answer, but she didn't.

Her mind drifted over to Pete. Her heart went out to him. At the same time, she knew he needed to accept himself at any size. He had lost 10 pounds but gained back a couple more, and was frustrated with that. Hallie tried to tell Pete that was how weight loss was - it was never a straight line. It was one step forward, two steps backward, three steps forward, one step backward, etc., etc. And keeping it off wasn't fun. What was fun was eating cinnamon rolls and cotton candy at the county fair, drinking (non-skinny) margaritas while the sun set behind the mountains, and eating pizza, Reese's Peanut Butter Cups, fried chicken and mashed potatoes, cherry cobbler, donuts, and Little Debbie snack cakes whenever the mood struck. All these foods were Hallie's biggest weaknesses. She still missed them every day of her life.

Perhaps Pete didn't want to give up his own junk food list. Maybe he wanted to live a normal life. If that was the case, Hallie needed to help him accept himself and love himself at any size. And she knew he had a lot of work to do to get to that point of self-acceptance and self-love.

This self-love and acceptance was an important part of the retreat because even the people who left the retreat having lost weight probably would gain it back. That seemed to be the case for at least 90% of the people who lost a significant amount of weight, or even just a small amount. Taking your eye off the ball was easy, and your biology works against you at every turn. Your body doesn't want to lose weight once you gain it, so your metabolism goes down, and your hunger hormones go up. Once you lose weight, it's a constant battle against your biology to keep it off. It was a cruel aspect of human biology that Mother Nature apparently wants you to stay the weight you are and does everything in her power to ensure that happens.

An hour passed, and Hallie returned to the storefront to get Pete. He was waiting for her, and he looked shaken. He was very pale, sweating, and shaking. Willow was sitting next to him, her hand on his. When Hallie walked in the door, Willow gave her a look and motioned her to talk to her in private. "Let's step outside," she said to Hallie. "Pete, we'll be right back."

Hallie and Willow went outside the door. "What's going on?" Hallie asked Willow.

"Pete told me I could tell you everything. But here's the gist. He was kidnapped at the age of 11 by some men who were holding him for ransom. They kept him in a closet for weeks while his father desperately tried to get the million dollars to give to them. I guess his father wasn't very liquid, but he owned a lot of property that he could sell to pay off the kidnappers. His father finally got the money together, and the kidnappers released Pete."

As Willow talked about the incident, it had a ring of familiarity for Hallie. That's what was teasing her brain about Pete's situation, come to think of it. She remembered now reading the story in *People* magazine when it happened. The kidnappers didn't get away with it, thank God. They were caught and were now serving a life sentence in Pelican Bay, a Supermax prison in Crescent City. Pete's father got his money back, too.

"Oh my God," Hallie said. Then she took a deep breath. She wondered what to do next. She wasn't a therapist, and she wondered if the retreat was even right for Pete now that he knew the root cause of his overeating. At the same time, she saw Pete had been blossoming at the retreat. She didn't want to take that away from him. She'd let Pete decide whether the retreat was right for him or if he needed to go into long-term therapy about his childhood issue.

Hallie walked back into the store, and Pete was sitting there, still looking shaken but quite a bit calmer.

"Pete," Hallie said. "How are you feeling?"

He shook his head. "I don't know. I finally know the root cause of my depression, anxiety and overeating. But I don't know how to deal with it. It's in the past, but I know it's always affected my life, even if I haven't acknowledged it."

"You have the choice to leave the retreat if you want to seek therapy," Hallie said.

"No. I'm enjoying myself at the retreat. I know I've gained back a few pounds after losing the first 10, but that's okay. I have to give myself a break and stop beating myself up so much. I survived something not many children could survive, and that's not nothing."

Hallie was happy to hear Pete say those words. Because

that was so important for Pete and for anybody, really. He needed to accept himself. And now that he knew the root cause of his issues and realized that he wasn't to blame for his depression and anxiety, he might, with the help of the right therapist, move past it and live a better life.

"You have a good attitude," Hallie said. "And maybe with your next group therapy session, you can tell the group what happened to you and solicit advice about how to move past it. If you are willing. In the meantime, you're in a safe environment at the retreat."

Pete smiled, perhaps the first genuine smile Hallie had seen on Pete's face. "Thank you, Hallie. Thank you for being in my corner."

Pete squeezed her hand, and Hallie felt some butterflies. But she also felt butterflies when she looked at Conrad, and she really felt them when they kissed the other night. She and Conrad had not spoken about the kiss, and Hallie thought he might not remember it.

"Let's go back to the retreat," Hallie said. "If you're ready."

"I'm ready," Pete said. "Maybe for the first time in my life, I'm ready to tackle my issues." And then he looked at Hallie shyly. "And maybe you can be in the picture after the retreat? I mean, I know you and I can't get together until after I leave, but I think there might be something there between us."

Hallie swallowed. She was feeling a burning attraction to Pete, especially now that he would start his recovery process in earnest. But she couldn't act on it. Not until Pete left the retreat.

"Maybe," she said.

She closed her eyes and leaned into Pete. She wanted him to kiss her. She wanted to know if there were fireworks with Pete, as much as the fireworks she'd experienced with Conrad.

He kissed her, and, yes, there were definitely fireworks with him, too. As much as with Conrad.

Hallie was more confused than ever.

Chapter Twenty-Two

Ava

Sarah and Quinn announced to Ava the words Ava never wanted to hear. They were moving into their new home. And they would be moving out the very next day.

The renovation of their Venice Beach home was finally finished.

Ava was so used to having the girls around, and their mothers, and she just knew that her giant home would feel like a tomb once everybody left. She loved hearing Emerson and Julia compose their songs in the piano room. She adored having Sarah and Quinn around to talk to, bounce ideas off of, have a glass of wine with at the end of the day, and have many Netflix evenings. She loved everything about having Quinn, Sarah, Julia, and Emerson around, not to mention the dogs, Kona and Bella. And Mia's dog, Roxy, always came with her when she visited, which was often. Roxy, fortunately, got along beautifully with Kona and

Bella, so the three of them romped and played on the beach all the time.

Her favorite evening time, when she wasn't working nights, was dinner time. She, Sarah, Quinn, and Mia would typically dine out on her back deck and listen to the ocean come in and out. The girls, Emerson and Julia, would often join them and then go down to the beach and play with the dogs. Hallie would often come over and join them. It was an idyllic and wonderful time in Ava's life to have everybody around, and now it would be just her and her six-bedroom house.

There wasn't much for Quinn and Sarah to pack up to go to the new house. They didn't have furniture at Ava's house. They had nothing but their clothes and toiletries. Quinn, the interior decorator, had chosen the new furniture that would go into this place with Sarah's approval. That furniture would be delivered within the next few days.

So, that evening, all of them had one last hurrah. Well, it wouldn't be one last hurrah, exactly. After all, it was the ritual for the four of them - Hallie, Sarah, Quinn and Ava, plus Mia – to have a get-together at least once a week, usually on Ava's deck. And that would still go on. But it wouldn't quite be the same. Now, once the evening wrapped up, Sarah, Quinn and their girls would go to their own home. There would be no running into them in the middle of the night when Ava couldn't sleep, and somebody in the house would inevitably have the same problem. Ava would end up talking and bonding with that person, be it Quinn, Sarah, Emerson, Julia or sometimes Mia, until both of them felt sleepy again. There would no longer be anybody around to have breakfast with.

This would be the first time Ava would be completely alone in a long time. Technically, when she lived on

Nantucket, she lived alone. But she was never alone because she ran a bed-and-breakfast out of her home. So she couldn't be lonely. There was always somebody around, even if they were strangers.

Ava tried not to think about being alone in her big house. But it would feel like the ultimate in empty nests.

That night, they talked and laughed and joked around. There was a full moon, so the waves were even bigger than usual. They were drinking wine from Ava and Sarah's winery and eating pizza from South End, one of Ava's favorite pizza places on Venice Beach.

"Oh, I'm going to miss you guys so much," Ava said.

"Sugar, we'll be literally forty minutes away in traffic. Twenty minutes away without traffic. It's not like we'll be on the moon," Quinn reassured her.

"I know," Ava said. "But it won't be the same."

Sarah just laughed. "Oh, the irony. For twenty years, we didn't speak at all. I might as well have been on the moon during those twenty years, or you might as well have been. Now, I'm moving to Venice Beach, and you're here in Malibu, and we'll be living just a few miles apart. And we're going to miss each other." Sarah had tears in her eyes, which made Ava want to cry, too.

But then, both Ava and Sarah laughed at the silliness of it all. Quinn joined in with the laughter, and Mia smiled.

After the laughter subsided, Ava just looked at her wineglass sadly. "I envy you guys," she said to Sarah and Quinn. "You'll still have a vibrant, busy house full of laughter and music. I'll have my Netflix and books, and that's about it."

"And the beach," Mia said, sweeping her hand in the air. "Man, what I wouldn't give to have a house right on the beach. What my Roxy wouldn't give for that luxury."

"Yes," Ava said wistfully. "But nobody to share the luxury of having a beach house."

Quinn put her arm around Ava. "Well, sugar, there's always Elijah."

Ava smiled. Elijah. Her handsome physician step-brother. "Oh, thanks," Ava said. "That's a creepy thought." It really wasn't a creepy thought for Ava. It was a fantasy, a very welcome one. But Ava knew her friends thought it was creepy, so she wanted them to think she thought that, too.

"Not so creepy," Sarah said. "I've been thinking. It's really okay to date your stepbrother."

Ava looked around and saw everybody nodding their heads in agreement. "Well, it's a moot point," Ava said. "Because I don't think Elijah wants that."

"But if he did?" Quinn asked.

Ava smiled and took a sip of her wine. Then she raised her eyebrows and giggled. Just the thought of Elijah and her dating filled her with warm fuzzies from head to toe.

"Let's change the subject," Ava said. "And if we'll be out here much longer, we should call Hallie."

The sun had long since set, and the air was chilled. Ava had the outdoor heaters going but knew it was getting late, and everybody needed to get to bed.

"I'll have to beg off," Sarah said, stretching. "Long day tomorrow with moving and everything. I have to get all my stuff out of my storage locker and unpack, as does every-body else."

"I'll help, of course," Ava said. Sarah and Ava had hired some wine tenders, Amber Holt and Shane Purdue, and they would work the next day. So, Ava cleared her schedule to help with the big move-in.

Quinn yawned. "Long day," she said. Quinn was busy working on a mansion in Bel Air for a finicky billionaire who hit on her like most men in the world. Quinn always put the guys in their place, and this time was no different. But it was annoying, especially now that she was spoken for by Mia. But the billionaire, Rex Mondale, kept Quinn on the job and was very demanding of her time, working her long hours. Not that Quinn minded. She loved the work, but it tired her.

The ladies, except for Ava, retired, leaving Ava alone on the deck.

Better get used to being alone, Ava thought ruefully. *Better get used to it...*

Chapter Twenty-Three

Jack

Because Jack wanted to show his mother he could get out into the world again, he decided to wander to the Venice Beach boardwalk. So, he called a wheelchair-accessible Uber after Googling how he could ride-share, and took the ride over to Venice Beach. His mother had recently bought him a special beach wheelchair with large, fat tires because his mother wanted him to enjoy the beach again. He would finally get the chance to use it.

It was a beautiful day, the kind of crisp January day Jack craved. It wasn't warm, but at least it wasn't raining. It had poured rain that morning, but now the sun had come out, the birds were singing, and he could hear the ocean rolling.

He realized how much he missed this – just being outdoors, breathing in the fresh air, feeling the sunlight on his shoulders. He couldn't remember the last time he'd been outside the house. It probably had been years. But this was a good thing, him getting out of the house, because he needed inspiration for his art. And that was how he looked at the day – as inspiration for his paintings.

He wheeled onto the boardwalk and was cheered by the people he saw walking, biking, and roller-blading. He was out amongst people again! He was actually seeing people who weren't related to him. There were a couple of girls outside a café, one of whom had a very cute German Shepherd lying at her feet, snoring. A guy and girl were outside this same café, looking at a laptop computer and laughing. As Jack passed by this couple, he could hear snippets of a YouTube video they were both watching. Apparently, this YouTube video was hilarious because they continued to laugh.

He was tempted to go into the café, which he knew sold delicious cookies, scones, hot chocolate, and various sandwiches and salads. They also sold various French sodas, made with different kinds of sodas, generally fruit-flavored ones, mixed with cream and ice. He loved French sodas, and their relatives, Italian sodas, which were French sodas without the cream. But he didn't go into this café because he wanted to continue his journey.

As he wheeled along, he was comforted that not much had changed since he had been away. There were still the same delicatessens, restaurants, and bars. The same clothing boutiques, wine bars, bakeries, health food stores, yoga/pilates studios, dry cleaners, florists, and art galleries. Street performers were singing and playing guitar for money. Just beyond the horizon was the Santa Monica Pier, and Jack could clearly see the Ferris wheel.

And then he came upon the bookstore he used to love to go to when he was younger but hadn't been a going concern for a few months. At least, that's what his mother told him. He peeked in the window, and he saw a woman in there.

She was a lovely woman, redheaded, slight, wearing heavy black glasses and freckled. She looked almost like his favorite actress, Fiona Kennedy, but that was impossible. Nevertheless, he felt excited there was somebody inside that bookstore because it meant the place might open up again.

He remembered being a younger man and taking part in poetry slams. Those slams were so much fun! He really got into them, cheering the poets on, writing his own poetry and reading the poems aloud, and, on occasion, he was a judge of the poets.

The bookstore used to really thrive, with different events every night. Some nights there was live music, with a guitarist in the corner, and sometimes people even got up and danced. On other nights there were readings given by local authors. And, there were quite a few local authors, surprisingly. Not all of them were successful. In fact, most of them weren't successful at all. But it was still exciting to attend a reading because sometimes he discovered new writers that way. And, several nights a week, book clubs would meet there. There were children's story hours. Once a week, there was a paint night, where people gathered around to paint and drink wine, and he loved doing that, of course. He was even asked to lead one of these paint nights because he was considered a local artist, but then he had his accident and was never able to do this.

Now somebody was inside the bookstore, so the place might open, and the fun events would begin again. Jack would love that because that would be the best way to return to the world. He could meet people naturally if the bookstore opened again.

Right at that moment, the redheaded woman looked at him. He realized he was just longingly staring in that window. She smiled at him, and her smile was the kind that could light up a pitch-black evening.

Damn, she sure looked like Fiona Kennedy when she smiled.

The woman came to the door and opened it. "Hello. Would you like to come in? My name is Fiona, and I will be opening this bookstore again soon."

Jack looked closely at the woman's face. How strange. This woman looked so much like Fiona Kennedy and her name was Fiona. "If it's not too much trouble," he said shyly. "I have so many good memories of this place. Name's Jack, by the way."

He wheeled into the store and looked around. It had a musty smell; it had not been occupied for many months, but everything looked intact. He closed his eyes, remembering the good times there for many years. Fiona was just standing next to a bookshelf, shaking her head.

"It will be a monumental task getting this place up and running. Are you a local?"

"Yes," he said.

"You don't know of a good cleaning service, do you? That's what I need more than anything. Someone to come in here and shine up these floors, steam clean these area rugs and all the furniture, and dust off these books and bookshelves."

He took a deep breath. He'd been so detached from the world for so long that he didn't know how to help her. He had no idea who would be good for this job.

"No, I'm so sorry," he said. "I really haven't been out so much lately."

She nodded. "Well, I'll have to use the Google machine to figure it out."

He gazed at her, thinking how much she looked like his

favorite actress. "Has anybody ever told you that you look like Fiona Kennedy?"

She smiled. "I get that a lot." And then she paused. "Well, I might as well tell you. If you're hanging around, and I hope you do, because I need all the friends I can get, you'll find out who I am." She took a deep breath. "I am Fiona Kennedy, the actress."

He cocked his head, thinking he was hallucinating all this, or maybe it was a practical joke being played upon him. "You're crazy," he said with a smile.

Fiona started to laugh. "I'm sorry. I don't mean to laugh, but you just said exactly what my sister said when I met her."

That was weird. Why would her sister say she was crazy when she claimed to be Fiona Kennedy? "I don't understand?"

Fiona smiled and shook her head. "Oh, this is such a long story. But you know what, I feel very comfortable around you for some reason. You seem like an old soul."

And then Fiona told Jack a crazy story about how she was just working in Hollywood, not feeling very connected to anybody but her best friend named Camille, just floundering in her personal life, when she discovered she had a birth mother and birth sister right there in the Los Angeles area. As she spoke, Jack suddenly realized she really was Fiona Kennedy, the actress. It was in her voice and mannerisms, which he had memorized by now.

And, all at once, he felt extremely inadequate and shy. This was Fiona Kennedy. *The* Fiona Kennedy. Why would she want to befriend him?

She finished the story, and Jack didn't say anything at first. "Wow, that's quite a story," he said. "And I really have to go." He didn't feel worthy of even being in her presence.

And that was too bad because he thought she could become a new friend.

Fiona shook her head. "Oh, okay, if you have to go," she said, looking disappointed. Then she walked over to one of the bookshelves, put back some books, and hung her head. "Please don't do this," she said after a long pause. "I've already been rejected by my sister because she thinks I'm too stuck up. I don't want to appear needy, but I really need a new friend, and like I said, I instantly felt you were someone I'd like to get to know."

Jack furrowed his brows. Was this really a world-famous actress who was anxious to become his friend? He'd been out of the social scene for so long, only hanging around his mom, so he was out of practice. He didn't feel confident in himself.

"Okay. I don't have anything to do. So I could hang around and help you do whatever."

Fiona cocked her head. "Would you like a job? Working here?"

"That would be fantastic," Jack said enthusiastically. "My mom has been telling me I need to get out of the house. Nagging me, really. Working here would be the perfect way I could get out of the house and quit being such a nuisance."

"Well, you could help me out right now if you like. Maybe look for some cleaning outfits to help me get this place up to snuff. Of course, I'll pay you. Would $20 an hour be fair?"

Jack had been living off disability for six years, which didn't pay much, so $20 an hour sounded amazing. "That sounds more than fair, actually."

So, for the next few hours, Jack looked up cleaning firms, got some quotes, and invited one to the bookstore on

Monday. While he did that, Fiona busied herself with looking at the book collections and brainstorming with him about arranging the books. "For the fiction books, I think we should have a mystery section, a Y.A. section, a sci-fi section, a romance section, a classics section, and a special World War II fiction section. Since that seems such a popular genre, it should have its own section. Then the non-fiction sections should include cookbooks, travel, memoirs, and a million others."

Jack raised an eyebrow, amused. "A million other sections? Are you going to have the room for that?" he teased.

Fiona smiled and then laughed. "I tend towards hyperbole."

They bantered about like that as if they were old friends. Jack was amazed at how easy their connection seemed and how ironic it was that he was just thinking that if he ever met Fiona Kennedy in person, they'd become good friends. It seemed that was already happening. She was just as the salt of the earth as she seemed, like Prince Harry shopping at T.J. Maxx or buying Ikea lamps, which he apparently did, according to his memoir, *Spare*. He supposed some people didn't become affected by fame and fortune and stayed true to who they were, and Fiona Kennedy happily fell into that category.

Several hours later, Fiona announced she was ready to quit for the day. "I need to go and see my new cottage in the Santa Monica mountains. Would you like to come along?"

"I don't know," Jack said, not knowing if the vehicle she drove could accommodate him and suddenly being too shy to say anything about that. And the very thought that Fiona would somehow pick him up and place him in the vehicle mortified him. And just like that, he thought this entire afternoon was some kind of dream from which he would awake. "I really should get back. My mom will probably worry."

"Text her and tell her you'll be home in a few hours," Fiona said. Then she looked embarrassed as her cheeks flushed. "Oh, I'm sorry, I'm being way too pushy. I'll let you go."

"Actually," Jack said, "I don't want to go to the cottage because I don't know if your vehicle will accommodate me. And I can't ask you to try to pick me up to put me in the car. Unless you have an SUV."

Fiona nodded. "I have a Land Rover."

"Can you help me into the car?"

Fiona nodded. "I'm an actress, which means I've played many roles. And in one of my roles, I was a caretaker for a paralyzed man, so I had to learn how to maneuver him in and out of cars and buildings. So, yeah, I can do it."

Jack remembered that movie. She was quite good in it. If he remembered correctly, her character quarreled with the paralyzed man before they finally became friends and, eventually, lovers.

Jack swallowed his pride and nodded. "Okay. Right. If you don't mind, I'd love to go to the cottage with you."

So, Jack and Fiona went to Fiona's Land Rover, which was parked down the street. Fiona was quite adept in putting Jack into the car, much to his secret delight, and she had no trouble putting the chair into the trunk, either.

"Can you put on your Google map for me?" Fiona asked once they were safely in the car and strapped in. "I really have no idea how to find this place."

"It's in the mountains?"

"Yeah, that's right," Fiona said. "Maybe you could help me find this place."

"I've lived here all my life, so I'm familiar with the mountains." Jack had fond memories of camping in the mountains with his friends back in the day. They'd build a fire and tell ghost stories while they drank beer. By the end of the evening, they were singing every song they knew, their drunken voices ricocheting throughout the woods. People would've shouted at them to be quiet if they were in a populated area.

Jack directed Fiona to the forest in the mountains, and as they entered it, the smell of pines, moss, flowers and rain hit Jack's nose, making him feel nostalgic for his old life. The Land Rover bumped along on the narrow and rocky road while Jack held onto the handle that hung from the roof of the Land Rover, and Fiona, evidently nervous about driving over such rough terrain, concentrated on the road. She was hunched over the steering wheel, her hands tightly gripping the edges.

It started to darken as the blanket of trees formed a roof of sorts, with the light shining through in shimmering ribbons here and there. The sky opened up, and rain poured, making the conditions even more treacherous. Jack felt bad for Fiona and her white knuckles, which still gripped that steering wheel for dear life.

She chuckled. "Not used to these conditions. It's been raining more than I've ever seen in these parts. And I'm not used to driving on backroads like these."

Jack nodded. "Well, it's been raining a lot lately. That's no lie."

Fiona smiled. "I guess you get used to it, huh? You ever think about how people lived 100s of years ago? No running water, no indoor plumbing, no air conditioning or penicillin? I can't imagine living that way, but if that's all they've ever known, I guess they probably didn't think they had it particularly hard."

"That's funny because I often think about these things myself," Jack said. "My friend John and I, in college, used to stay up late in bull sessions. We wondered about reincarnation, and John thought we'd come back again after we die, but we might not come back in the future, but maybe in the past. And I said that would be perfectly awful because no plumbing. I couldn't imagine using an outhouse, let alone cleaning one. He said that if you lived in those times, you probably don't even think about the hardships because that's all you know."

"Yes," Fiona said. "And I wonder what people 200 years from now would think about us. What kind of hardships are we going through that we don't even think about, but that future people would say, 'How could they live like this?'"

"Well, they'll have flying cars, so traffic jams would be one thing they'd wonder about. Other than that, I don't really know. We live in a pretty good period. Not a lot of hardships, really."

Jack closed his eyes, knowing he lived in a state where he knew a different life and had to adjust to a harsh reality. He sometimes wondered how people felt when they were handicapped from birth, and that was all they knew. Did they feel bitter that they never got to experience a normal life, or did they even know the difference?

Fiona sighed. "I sometimes wonder if we'll get to a point where we have flying cars or if we'll blow ourselves up long before that happens." Then she laughed. "Sorry, that got dark in a hurry."

"Dark is good," Jack said. "It makes you appreciate the light."

He knew from where he spoke. He had so many days of darkness, days when he couldn't imagine getting out of bed, and days when he thought about ending it all. He couldn't imagine living like a prisoner in his body, not cliff diving, motorcycle riding, and rugby playing. Those black days made him appreciate days like today so much more - he was hanging with one of the biggest stars in the world, and, more than this, he was actually looking forward to tomorrow. Because tomorrow would be something different than what he'd experienced today. Finally. After so many days that blended together because they were all the depressingly same, today was different, and tomorrow would be ever more so.

So, today seemed so much sunnier than anything he could've ever imagined before. Even though the weather was anything but, as the rain was now coming down in buckets. His previous darkness made this light much brighter than anything he could've imagined.

Fiona looked at him with a smile that lit him up from the inside out. It was the same smile he'd seen hundreds of times on-screen, it seemed. It was broad, blinding almost, and it reached her eyes, which meant it was genuine. That smile was enough to erase all his darkest days, and it was enough to make him glad that he didn't end it all six years ago. If he could close his eyes and remember that smile in his mind's eye, it might make any future dark days brighter.

He realized he sighed out loud when she flashed him that smile and was embarrassed, so he immediately looked away and out the window at the rain. "Here we are," he said, pointing to a thatched-roof stone cottage that appeared out of nowhere. "I guess this will be your new home, right?"

"Right," Fiona said with a nod. "It looks adorable and

cozy. And I hope it has a working fireplace because I'm already freezing, just looking at all this rain."

Fiona opened the door of the Land Rover, went to the trunk to get his chair, then opened his door and carried him into the chair. Then she pushed him up the ramp - the raised porch thankfully had a ramp instead of steps - and opened the wooden door into the cottage.

The cottage had the same musty smell the bookstore did and had the same drafty feel. It wasn't a big place - just a small living area, an even smaller dining area and a kitchen with appliances from the 1950s. The refrigerator was big and white and had a metal handle, while the ancient stove, also white, had paint that was wearing off and showed the metal underneath. Fiona walked into the bedroom, and he followed, and it was much the same. A tiny space, just big enough for a bed and dresser and not much more. However, the place had a large stone fireplace, which was one positive aspect.

Jack's heart sunk as he looked around. This cottage wouldn't do for a big star like Fiona. Not at all. He knew how women like Fiona lived, and they didn't live in tiny hovels like this one. No, Fiona probably wasn't happy in any place that didn't have fifty rooms and a saltwater pool.

Yet, Fiona was looking around the cottage with a look on her face that told him she was pleased. She nodded her head. "It doesn't look like much, but it'll shine like a new penny in the right hands. I just have to find a good interior decorator who can replace these floors, install new appliances and give everything a fresh coat of paint." Then she furrowed her brows. "The only thing is, it's so isolated out here. This place is kind of in the back of beyond."

"It is," Jack said. "Well, you could always sell this place. You live in Malibu, don't you?" Jack knew this because he read about Fiona in a magazine. This magazine showed the fans and readers inside Fiona's magnificent home, which featured a swimming pool, hot tub, 8 bedrooms and beautiful high ceilings.

"No," Fiona said. "My father owned this place. My birth father. I think I should stay right here in this house. I need to feel close to my roots, and, I don't know, I can feel his spirit in this house." She went over to the fireplace and ran her hand along the dusty ledge. "I don't know if you can relate to the feeling that you've never been grounded to anything on this earth, but that's always how I've felt. But here, in this house, I don't know. I finally have a home."

Jack allowed a tiny glimmer of hope to crack the contours of his heart. Just a tiny sliver that maybe this beautiful woman, beloved worldwide, might brighten his life with her presence. He never thought, not for a second, that they could be more than friends, but just being with her was enough. "I can't say I've never felt grounded because I live with my mom, and she's great, although I don't know my dad. He was never a part of my life. But my mom has always been good. She works hard but doesn't make much money, so things have been tight. But there was always a hot meal, and she's always there for me."

Fiona smiled. "You actually don't know how lucky you are," she said. "There really is something to knowing where you came from." Then she frowned and put her hand on the fireplace ledge again. "I'm finding out where I came from, but my sister seems to hate me for some reason. But my mother seems great. Anyhow, I think things will even out sooner or later with my sister. I just have to find out a way to help her."

"What's wrong with your sister?" Jack asked.

"Well, I strongly suspect she has some kind of postpartum depression. At least, the way my mother described her mood since she gave birth makes it sound like she does. She's also really overwhelmed. I'm waiting for my mother to call me before I return to Cora's house because she gave me the bum's rush when I went there before."

"Well, if she's depressed, you must keep on it. Make sure she's okay. If I didn't have my mom after my accident and went into a very dark place, I probably would've offed myself. Depression can do horrible things to your mind, and when you're in it, you think you'll never get out of it. You think it's your lot to live in blackness for the rest of your life, so ending it all would be the right answer. I know how your sister is feeling. I've been there."

Fiona nodded. "I agree I need to be there for her. But she doesn't seem open to my help just yet. I'm sure that'll change, though. At any rate, I think I need to go home. I'm sure you probably need to be getting home, too."

Jack felt disappointed. He wanted to hang around with Fiona as long as possible. But she was right - they'd been hanging out for a while, and Fiona no doubt had places she needed to be.

Fiona headed back, dropping Jack off at his home. When he went into the house, his mom was home, and she looked happy. She clapped her hands when she saw him. "Oh, Jack, you got out of the house. I can't tell you how happy that makes me."

Jack nodded. "Yes, Mom. And I have a job. At the old bookstore that will be reopening soon. I met the new owner, and she'll get things rolling again. So, I'll soon have someplace to be every day."

Jack didn't tell his mom that the person who owned the bookstore was Fiona Kennedy.

He didn't think she'd believe him. Not in a million years.

Chapter Twenty-Four

Cora

On the day she met her sister, Fiona, Cora went to bed feeling incredibly guilty and ashamed. She really should've given her sister more of a chance. She wanted to be happier about meeting Fiona. Nothing made her happy anymore.

Not even when Alistair made a surprise appearance at the house the very next day. He wasn't supposed to be home for several more weeks, months even, so Cora should've been thrilled to see her husband. But she wasn't.

"Hello, beautiful," Alistair said as he bounded through the door. "Surprise! I'm home for a week or two." He kissed her on the cheek and playfully grabbed her rump. "I missed you."

Cora smiled, but, as always, she wasn't feeling her smile. She didn't feel lit up from within like she used to feel when she looked at Alistair's clear blue eyes. "I missed you, too," she lied. Well, it wasn't really a lie, she thought, because she did miss him in a way. She missed his help with Daisy, and he really was a big help with the baby when he was around. He was a modern man who changed diapers, got up to feed Daisy with Cora's pumped milk and read her bedtime stories. Now that Alistair was home, Cora just might get some sleep.

And that was important. Maybe her problem was a lack of sleep. Even though Daisy was now sleeping through the night, Cora wasn't. She found herself tossing and turning all night, and then, during the day, she wanted to crash, but she couldn't because she had to care for Daisy. So, if her mother didn't come over, Cora had to drink gallons of coffee just to stay awake for her daughter.

But Alistair was home, so maybe, just maybe, Cora could find some rest. So, for that reason alone, Cora was happy to see her husband.

But that was the only reason why Cora was happy to see Alistair. And that made her feel even more depressed.

"Where is my beautiful little girl?" he asked.

"She's in her room," Cora said, realizing that she hadn't checked on Daisy yet and feeling ashamed. Daisy probably had a full diaper and needed her breakfast, but Cora just couldn't bring herself to tend to her baby, so she just left her in her crib that morning.

Alistair kissed her on the cheek again and playfully mussed her hair before going to the bedroom to get Daisy. He returned in a few more minutes, Daisy in his arms. "I just changed her," he said. "I assume she's been fed."

Cora didn't know what to say. It was 9 AM, long past time Daisy's breakfast time of 7 AM. She didn't want to admit she was so negligent. Yet, she couldn't lie. Daisy needed her breakfast. "Uh, no, not yet."

Alistair just nodded his head. "Okay, little one, let's look in the fridge to see if your mom put some lovely breast milk in there."

"I haven't pumped," Cora said helplessly. She felt tears coming to her eyes and blinked rapidly, willing them not to come. She didn't want Alistair to see her so exposed. Laundry had piled up, the place was a mess, and little Daisy was starving because of her.

Alistair seemed to sense Cora's distress, for he put his arm around her. Cora loved her husband, loved having him close, but she just couldn't muster up the feeling of love right at that moment, so his arm around her didn't make her feel the way she should. The way she used to feel.

Would she ever return to normal, or was this what she would look forward to? Feeling nothing when her handsome husband lovingly touched her, feeling zero when she looked at her daughter, feeling angry at the sight of her poor sister?

"It's okay, love," Alistair said. "There must be some formula around here somewhere."

"Formula? Formula?" Cora was suddenly angry. "What kind of a mother do you think I am? Don't you know Daisy must only have breast milk at least for her first six months, or else she'll be sick all the time and crazy? She'll be fat and get diabetes and will have all kinds of infections. I know all about that formula. No, thank you."

Alistair raised an eyebrow. "You do know my mom couldn't breastfeed me, right? As far as I know, I don't have diabetes. I weigh 170 pounds even though I'm 6'2". I'm fit as a fiddle, have few allergies, and am healthy as a horse. It's just nice to have formula around so I can feed the little baby as well as you."

"I have no formula around," Cora said, putting her

arms out so Alistair could give her Daisy. "Give me Daisy. I'll get her breakfast."

Alistair smiled devilishly. "Oh, and I'll see your beautiful breasts after all this time at sea." He rubbed his hands together and raised his eyebrows.

Cora just shot him a look as she unbuttoned her shirt, and Daisy latched on. "Oh, please, Alistair, I'm feeding her. These aren't for you right now."

Alistair just laughed. "I know, I'm just joking. Just trying to get a laugh out of my beautiful honey."

Cora wanted to banter with Alistair like they used to. They used to tease each other back and forth, and she used to have quite a sense of humor. She wasn't feeling it, though, and she had difficulty pretending for Alistair. She had enough of pretending when she was around her mother. She just didn't have the energy for it with her husband.

Cora fed Daisy and then handed her back to Alistair. "Here. You can put her back in her crib now."

"Nothing doing," Alistair said as he stared into Daisy's eyes. "She's wide awake, and I haven't seen her or her beautiful mother for all this time at sea. I want to spend some quality time with both my girls."

Alistair sat on the sofa with Daisy in his arms and pulled Cora beside him. He bit Cora's ear playfully as he pulled her close. "Tell me how you've been. I've been thinking about nothing but seeing you this whole time I've been gone. My friends on the boat were tired of hearing me mooning on about you, so they were more than happy we got some time to come home."

Cora suddenly felt a sense of dread that maybe Alistair wanted some nooky. That was the last thing she wanted, but she knew her husband, and that was on his mind.

"Come on," she said. "I'm really tired, and I'm feeling fat." She moved away from him and then self-consciously took a strand of her hair and twirled it around her finger.

Alistair shrugged and tickled little Daisy, who laughed out loud. "Listen to that," he said. "My beautiful little girl just laughed. When did she start doing that?"

"I'm not sure," Cora said.

"Where's the baby book? We need to write something about this. She'll start college before you know it and want to know about the first time she laughed."

Cora shook her head. She still needed to put something in that baby book. Alistair had been gone for the past two months, and before he left, he documented everything little Daisy did. The first time she held her head up, the first time she pushed up with her arms while lying on her stomach, and her first smile - all documented by Alistair. Since then, Daisy met a few other milestones, like laughing aloud, babbling and cooing, and she could roll over on her back. Cora was supposed to write all this down in the baby book, but she didn't.

"Just a second. I'll go and get it."

Cora went into Daisy's room, where she promptly burst into tears. She had been doing that a lot lately. They just came unprompted, and she couldn't stop them. She tried to quietly sob because she didn't want Alistair to feel bad or, God forbid, think her tears were about him.

But Alistair, being the sensitive, poetic soul he was, quietly came into the room and put his strong hand on her shoulder.

"Love, you've been having a hard time of it, haven't you?" he asked her. "I'm so sorry I've been gone for so long. You've had to do without me these past few months, and it's unfair to you."

Cora shook her head. "No, it's not that. Really. My mom has been helping me, so it's okay." The last thing Cora wanted was for Alistair to guiltily quit his job because what would they do if Alistair wasn't working on the fishing boat? He loved the boat, he loved his friends on the boat, and it paid enough that Cora didn't have to work to make ends meet. Cora didn't know what Alistair could do that paid nearly as much as the fishery, so there was no way she would make him think that he somehow needed to be home to help her with the baby.

He gently put Daisy into her crib, sat on the rocking chair, and pulled Cora onto his lap. He stroked her hair and kissed her forehead, and his gentle and loving touch made Cora want to cry even more. He was such a good man, such a wonderful man. Just like Daisy, he deserved somebody better than her. They both deserved somebody better than her, better than what she could give either of them.

Like Virginia Woolf, she could walk into the river, her pockets weighed down with rocks. Alistair would have the chance to find a better woman than her, and Daisy could find herself a better mom. She wasn't cut out for motherhood or being a wife, and there was no way of undoing any of it aside from taking herself out of the equation.

"How can I help you?" he asked. "Would you like me to find somebody to watch little Daisy for a few hours every day, so you can get some proper sleep?"

"No," Cora said. "We can't afford that."

"Well, I ran into your mom before I got here, and I guess you have a wealthy movie star as a sister, so maybe-"

"NO," Cora spat. "Don't even say what you're about to say. I will not ask Fiona, my so-called sister, for a single cent. Don't you dare be an idiot and tell me to go begging from Fiona Kennedy for anything."

"Relax, my beauty. I was just going to suggest that she could look after Daisy a little during the week. I know you're proud and won't take a penny from anybody, but you must accept help when needed."

Fiona was a sore subject with Cora, so she resented her husband even bringing her up.

Then again, if Cora decided to end it all, maybe Alistair could find new love with Fiona. After all, Fiona strongly resembled her physically, and Cora wanted Alistair to be happy. So, she could get the two together, Cora could slip out, and everybody could be happy without her.

Cora shook her head. She must stop thinking these dark thoughts. She must stop thinking that she would end it all because she wanted to live when it came right down to it. She did. But she didn't want to burden her loved ones, and she knew she was.

"I'm fine," she said.

"You're not," he said. "You're unhappy, I can tell. You're not the Cora I fell in love with, and I don't know how to help. I want to help. Please let me help."

"Don't be crazy," Cora said, intentionally brightening her voice to sound like the Cora he used to know. She plastered on the smile she had practiced for her mother, but she knew from Alistair's expression that he wasn't buying it. "Things are good." She kissed him quickly on the forehead and got off his lap. "Come on, let's have some tea and let me hear about your adventures at sea."

"Cora, don't," he said, following her into the kitchen. Cora put some hot water on the stove and got out the assortment of teas.

"Some Earl Grey, Chamomile, or Green Tea? Also, I found this amazing *Downton Abbey* tea at the little tea shop in town. I bought the tea because it has a picture of Lady

Mary, Lady Sybil and Lady Edith, but it's actually quite delicious." *Downton Abbey* was Cora's favorite show and the one thing that could take her mind off of her depression.

"Cora, don't avoid this," he said. "You were crying just now. I want to think you weren't crying because I came home early. You have to be straight with me."

She couldn't possibly be. If she told him all her dark thoughts - about her fantasies about giving Daisy up for adoption and her fantasies about drowning herself in the river - he would surely put her into the nut farm.

"I can't," Cora said. "I can't be straight with you. You wouldn't understand. All I can say is that I'm not crying because you're home."

"But you clearly aren't happy to see me," Alistair said. "Even if you aren't crying about my being here, you aren't exactly jumping up and down about it, either."

"Don't say that," Cora said unconvincingly. "I love you." And that was true. She *did* love him desperately. She had a good man, and she knew it. But that didn't mean she was happy to see him, because he was right - she *wasn't* happy he was home. She just couldn't be happy about anything, including that.

The tea kettle started to whistle, and Cora put a bag into Alistair's cup and her own and poured the hot water over each bag.

Alistair blew on his cup and tasted the tea. His beautiful blue eyes were trained on Cora's face the whole time.

"Do you like it?" Cora asked. "Raspberries, rose petals and hibiscus. Subtle, fruity and sweet."

"It's fine," he said. "But you're not fine, and I can't enjoy this tea while my wife is hurting."

She wished he'd never caught her crying in Daisy's room. There was no putting that horse back in the barn, though, because now he knew something about her despair.

So she changed the subject. She needed to do anything at all to get out of this conversation. "Fiona inherited the bookstore in town from my dad. My mom told me she'll be there today. Why don't we bundle Daisy up and go down there and help out?" As much as Cora didn't want to be around Fiona, she also didn't want to be at home alone with the prying Alistair.

"Okay," Alistair said. "You're shutting me out, but that's okay. You'll come clean when you're ready. In the meantime, it sounds wonderful to go into town with you. Let's go to the café we used to go to for brunch and then to the new bookstore."

"Okay," Cora said with a nod and a fake smile. "That sounds like fun." A trip to the café on the way to Fiona's new bookstore sounded like anything but fun to Cora. Yet, it seemed that she was stuck doing just that.

Alistair looked skeptical that Cora really wanted to do these things, though. It was in his eyes. But he shrugged and put his arm around Cora again. "Sounds like we have a date. Now, let's bundle up this beautiful little girl, get a bite in town, and see your new sister." He cocked his head. "And is it true that your sister is a rich actress?"

"You haven't heard of Fiona Kennedy?" Cora said. "How is that possible?"

Cora was sure the two of them must've seen one of Fiona's movies at some point. They hadn't been living under a rock, after all.

Alistair shrugged. "I don't know who she is. Should I?"

"I think you've been on a boat for too long. Yes, she's a famous actress, one of the most famous in the world, and my sister."

"Oh, my," Alistair said. "I'm impressed. I have a famous sister-in-law then?"

"Looks like it," Cora said. "Well, come on. Let's go to Venice Beach, eat at our café, and go to Fiona's bookstore."

So, Cora bundled Daisy up, put her in her stroller, and headed into town.

Chapter Twenty-Five

Fiona

Fiona woke up the next morning, excited to face the day. She was more excited than she'd been in a long time. As overwhelming as the task seemed - getting her bookstore up and running and finding somebody decent to renovate her little cottage - it was still something Fiona looked forward to.

She thought about calling Jack because she was anxious to see him again, but decided against it. It was a Saturday, and Jack would start working for her the following Monday. Fiona wanted to avoid pressuring him to come in and help her before he was due to start formally working.

Besides, she hoped Greer might drop by, and Fiona wanted to give Greer her full attention. Her birth mother deserved nothing less than Fiona's complete focus.

So, she headed over to her bookstore early that morning, wanting to get a head start on taking inventory and starting the cleaning process. She would hire people to help her clean the bookstore and her home, but she had yet to settle on anybody, so she'd start all on her own.

She got to her bookstore and started taking the books off the shelf, dusting them off, one by one. About an hour into this process, she came across an unusual book. It was a book that wouldn't be for sale, but rather, it was a photo album.

Was this a photo album left by her birth father? It was tucked away in a nook where people wouldn't be looking for a book. Fiona felt excited about seeing a picture of the man who gave her life.

She loved photo albums, anybody's photo albums. She never really cared who owned the album - she just enjoyed seeing people's pictures. She was one of those odd ducks who could watch people's vacation videos with rapt fascination, even though everybody else would be bored. And this album possibly belonged to Ewan Davidson, her apparent birth father, so she was excited to crack it open and see pictures of her birth family.

She sat cross-legged on the floor and opened up the dusty cover. There were pages and pages of pictures of people, none of whom looked familiar. She looked for pictures of Ewan, Greer and Cora, but the book didn't show them. The pictures were just of random couples of all different ages, all of whom looked rapturously in love.

Fiona studied each picture, putting her hand on each photo, then wondered why she was touching each photo. It was as if she was trying to pick up the energy of each couple, trying to ascertain if the people were as in love as they looked or if they were faking it for the camera.

There was no doubt about it. Fiona knew in her gut that these couples were soulmates, whatever that meant. She believed in soulmates, even though she hadn't experienced it yet. Or maybe she had? As Fiona understood the term "soulmate," it was two people who meet and feel as if they'd known one another their entire life. They just meet and start talking about everything under the sun, as if they were best friends from childhood, never having met each other before. When they meet for the first time, it's as if they remember each other from a past life or something.

In a profound way, Fiona and Camille were platonic soulmates. They were best friends from the very beginning. Fiona felt comfortable with Camille from the start, and Camille apparently felt the same. Fiona had never before experienced that kind of connection with another person. They were never more than friends because they were straight, but they got each other on every level. They finished each other's sentences and could almost read each other's thoughts. They were always there for each other, no matter what. They had what Fiona never had with Luke.

Now there was Jack, and Fiona felt something similar with him. She met him and immediately felt she'd known him forever. Just like with Camille, she and Jack started talking immediately, as if they were picking up an earlier conversation and continuing an ongoing comfortable relationship.

Fiona shook her head. She supposed that if soulmates were a thing, perhaps Jack was hers. Whether or not he would turn out like Camille, and she and Jack just became the best of friends, or if it would be a romantic soulmate thing, remained to be seen. But Fiona was sure there was some kind of profound connection between them. She felt it from the start.

And as she looked at each of the couples in the photo album, she knew they felt a profound connection with the person next to them. She didn't know how she knew this. She just did, on a deep level.

She got to the end of the photo album and was disappointed that she never saw a picture of Cora or Greer, so she also probably didn't see a picture of the mysterious Ewan.

What she did see was a small hand-written note.

Time getting short. Must find the one.

And that was it. That was the only thing written on this note.

Fiona had no idea who had written the note or what this photo album was about. It was certainly an unusual photo album. Usually, photo albums featured families - adults, children and babies, usually who resemble one another because they were family members, and, very often, there would be older pictures of ancestors. Most of the photo albums Fiona had seen fit a familiar pattern - pictures dating back to the 1970s or so, babies who age throughout the book to children to adolescents and to adults by the end of it. Older pictures of relatives who lived at the turn of the century, always frowning. Why were they always frowning and never smiling? That was always a mystery to Fiona. People in older generations just seemed so unhappy, at least judging by their photos.

Anyhow, this photo album showed different couples instead of the usual multigenerational documentation of a family over the years. So, Fiona had a feeling this was a special photo album, although she couldn't quite put a finger on what it all meant.

Just then, she heard the little bell jingle, which told her she was getting company. Her heart skipped a beat as she thought maybe it was Jack. But it wasn't.

It was Cora, her baby Daisy and a handsome, strapping

man with gentle blue eyes, dark wavy hair and a huge grin. The man was presumably Alistair, Cora's husband, but wasn't he supposed to still be at sea? But it was obvious this man was deeply in love with her sister. Fiona could see a thread connecting the two, like a gossamer rainbow running from one to the other.

She frowned as she realized something very off about the two, though. They were meant to be. That much was certain. But the energy coming from Cora to the man, presumably Alistair, wasn't the same positive, pure energy going from Alistair to Cora. It was as if something was blocking her energy.

And then Fiona shook her head. What was this sudden burst of insight she was getting about people around her? She'd never been able to sense energy between people, never before had seen the gossamer rainbow thread she was seeing between Alistair and Cora, never before had been able to put her hand over a photograph of two people and feel the love and connection leaping off the page. Yet, she felt in tune with people's energies on a level she'd never experienced.

Well, that wasn't necessarily true. She was a good actress because she could become different people, and she could become these people - actually inhabit her roles in a way few people could - because she could read about her character and feel the energy of the person she was supposed to become. That was always an ability she had.

But becoming a character was different from what she was now experiencing. It was as if something happened in the universe when she opened up that photo album. Something happened to her. Something was brought out of her that maybe was always there, just dormant.

It was as if she could see love as a tangible thing. Something she could touch and feel and keep safe. And, there was something inside her that shifted.

She had a calling, maybe one she never even knew about.

But she needed to figure out exactly what that calling was.

In the meantime, Cora was in the bookstore, looking like she wanted to be anywhere but there. And this handsome smiling man was somebody who Fiona liked instantly, although she could sense a broken heart. His heart was breaking because of something that was beyond his control, and Fiona knew it was up to her to try to do something about it.

"Hello," Cora said, her arms crossed in front of her defensively. "Fiona, this is my husband, Alistair. Alistair, Fiona."

Alistair extended his hand for Fiona to shake, which she did. But a part of her wanted to give him a huge hug. It just looked like he needed it, poor guy.

"Good to meet you," Fiona said. "I guess you're back early."

"Yes and no," Alistair said. "I'm only back for a week or so because our boat captain had a family emergency. Then it's back on the high seas for me."

Fiona looked at Cora, trying to see if Cora was happy about Alistair's unplanned visit. It was obvious she wasn't. She looked at the hardwood floor and twirled her hair around her index finger. Fiona noticed the hand twirling the hair was shaking like a leaf.

"Anyhow," Cora said. "You've now met my sister, so maybe we should get going." Cora took a deep breath and traced her foot on the floor. "We've got things to do."

"No, we don't," Alistair said. "What do we need to do that's so important?"

Cora had no answer for that.

"Cora," Fiona said. "Maybe you can help me out."

"I'm sure I can't," Cora said.

Alistair sighed. "I can help. What do you need, Fiona?"

At that, Fiona went to the photo album and brought it out. "Look at this handwritten note. Do you recognize the handwriting?"

Alistair studied the note. "Looks like Ewan's handwriting. Cora's dad." Then he furrowed his brows. "But I don't know. It sounds pretty cryptic."

Cora's curiosity finally got the better of her. "Give me that," she said, snatching the paper out of Alistair's hand. She looked at the paper. "That's my dad's writing, for sure. But I don't know why he wrote that time was getting short. He wasn't dying at any point. And what does that mean, 'he must find the one?' What one? This makes no sense."

"That's what I thought," Fiona said. "But do you recognize anybody in this photo album?"

Even though she tried to hide her interest, Cora apparently still had a real curiosity about the photo album and the note. She looked through the photo album, studying all the pictures. "Here," she finally said, returning the album to Fiona. "I don't recognize anybody in this photo album."

Alistair took the album next. "Yes," he said, looking at one of the pictures. "This is John and his wife, Sheila. They live in our mobile home park." He looked at a few more, recognizing them, as well, as people who lived in the mobile home park. "Sure," he said after he saw each of the photos. "I recognize quite a few people in this book."

"How do you recognize people I don't?" Cora asked.

Fiona knew without Alistair even answering that question. It was obvious that Alistair was, in general, much more in tune with his surroundings than Cora. He looked at people when he went out. He seemed the observant type.

On the other hand, Cora was very much inside her own head and probably had a hard time exploring the outside world. Fiona wondered if Cora had always been like that, or maybe that was something new.

"Dear, I don't know," Alistair said. "I meet people when I go out. It's a tight-knit beach community. Everyone knows everyone."

"Alistair's much friendlier than I am," Cora said. "He can go to the butcher shop and come out of it 10 minutes later with three new friends."

She said that like it was a bad thing.

Fiona shook her head. "Oh, what was I thinking? You guys have dropped into the bookstore, and, you know, there's a cappuccino machine I brought in. I just bought it this morning. I thought it would be great to offer cappuccino and scones, donuts and things to people who come into the store. I can make both of you a cappuccino. I don't yet have any baked goods, but a little kitchen is attached to the bookstore, so I think I can make some goodies for people."

Fiona had discovered the little kitchen just that morning. For some reason, she never noticed it before because the door to the kitchen was covered up by one of the bookshelves.

"Sure," Alistair said. "We'd love to stay for a cappuccino."

Cora looked like she wanted to leave but reluctantly sat with Alistair in front of the fireplace. "One cup of cappuccino," she said. "And then we go home."

Fiona clapped her hands and entered the kitchen to bring out the espresso. She ground the beans and put them through the French Press before steaming them with milk. She'd learned how to make the perfect espresso and cappuccino when she worked for the Italian restaurant waiting tables. Just thinking about that job made her think again about Camille, and she smiled. She wished her best friend was there with her. But she was working a double shift at the restaurant that day.

Fiona proudly poured the cappuccino into two glass mugs and brought them to Alistair and Cora. "Here," she said, sitting down next to them. "I hope you love it."

Alistair raised his glass with a smile. "A toast," he said. "To Cora's new sister."

Cora and Fiona raised their glasses, and the three took tentative sips of the still-steaming liquid. "Delicious," Alistair said. "You make a mean cup of cappuccino. I will tell you this."

"Thanks," Fiona said. "It all starts with quality beans. Thankfully, a cute little shop on the boardwalk sells really good beans. I got this machine there, too."

"The Better Bean," Cora said with a nod. "I love that place. They have really good teas there, too. That's where I picked up my *Downton Abbey* tea."

Fiona smiled. "You love *Downton Abbey*?" That could be a jumping-off place for Fiona to get to know her sister, a way to break the ice. After all, Fiona loved that show, too.

"Of course," Cora said. "They're all posh and all, but, for some reason, I feel like I could be friends with all of them. Especially Edith."

"Oh, you loved Edith? I was more of a Sybil person, but Edith has her appeal. And I'm one of the few who really loved Mary. I think she was misunderstood," Fiona said.

"What about Bates and Anna?" Alistair chimed in.

"That guy went through hell, and so did his wife. But they were stronger for it."

"And Mrs. Hughes," Fiona said. "She was stern in her way, but what a heart. An iron fist in a velvet glove. And everybody would love to have such an understanding boss. Unlike Carson, who was just plain judgmental and mean most of the time."

"But he was a Cheerful Charlie," Cora said. "You forget that he sang and danced onstage, so he wasn't all bad. And he did have a big heart sometimes. He just covered it up with his gruff demeanor."

Fiona laughed. "True, true. But he was so ashamed about the Cheerful Charlie thing that he bribed that other Charlie to keep quiet."

Cora genuinely smiled, which made Fiona think that maybe the thaw had begun. This conversation made Cora happy, so Fiona wanted to keep the ball rolling.

Cora sighed. "Not many things in this life make me happy, but *Downton Abbey* is one of those things. And it's not because I'd like to live in a palace, but because I love the characters. The writers for that show are absolute geniuses, you know."

Fiona put her hand on Cora's forearm. "Oh, I agree. I aspire to be a writer, and that show is a good one to study to see why it's so compelling."

Cora just nodded and looked at Daisy.

"You'd like to be a writer?" Alistair said, obviously trying to keep the friendly conversation going. "What type of a writer?"

"Oh, I'd love to write screenplays." Fiona had seen her share of screenplays over the years, more than her share, really, and she knew what made a good story. She'd learned early on what to look for in the screenplays sent to her, and she had enough clout in Hollywood that she could turn down the bad ones. And thank God for that because there were more than a few box-office bombs she'd turned down because the screenplay wasn't up to snuff. If she would've been associated with some of the weaker movies she'd turned down, her career probably would've been well and truly over.

Which it was at that moment, but on her terms. She'd walked away from Hollywood, retired. She wasn't run out of town in a cloud of stink bombs like some others were, and she was grateful for that.

Of course, her agent, Michael, didn't know she'd retired. After all, she promised him to keep an open mind about returning to Hollywood. She'd have to break the news that she was never coming back. She knew that now. She'd found what she had been desperately looking for all her life with her new family and this bookstore - happiness and roots. She couldn't put her finger on why she felt so happy here. She only knew she did.

Cora just rolled her eyes. "Oh, I suppose you could give Julian Fellowes a run for his money, do you?" Cora asked, referring to the man who wrote almost all *Downton Abbey* episodes.

"No, no," Fiona said. "I couldn't be that brilliant. Not many people could be. But I'd like to explore some kind of screenwriting sometime in my life. It's on my bucket list."

"My bucket list includes just getting through until tomorrow," Cora said. "Nice to know you have something broader in mind."

At that, Alistair shot Cora a concerned look. Fiona knew that look. Alistair knew Cora was drowning. That much was obvious. It was also obvious he had zero idea what to do about it.

Fiona sucked in her breath. "Cora, you know, I have this little bookstore and all, but I plan on hiring help. I already have hired a guy named Jack Barclay, but I plan on hiring more. I guess I'm trying to say that the bookstore won't be an all-consuming thing for me, and I could watch little Daisy once in a while. So, maybe you can leave the house, visit the ocean, go to the cafés, just enjoy the fresh air. It might do you some good."

"Jack Barclay?" Cora said, ignoring the rest of what Fiona said to her. "The guy in the chair who lives in my mobile home park?" She shook her head. "What a sad thing that happened to him. I didn't know he'd even left his house, let alone get a job."

Fiona cocked her head. "What happened to him?"

"Oh, he and some other guys got drunk one night and went cliff diving. They dared each other to dive off a stupid cliff into the ocean. He landed wrong and broke his spine. To tell you the truth, he was lucky he didn't drown."

"Oh, my," Fiona said. "That sounds terrible."

"Well, it happens when you combine too many beers with a dark cliff and a raging sea below," Cora said. "It's too bad that happened, but he's lucky he didn't get the Darwin Award."

"Darwin Award?" Fiona had heard the term before but couldn't quite place it.

"Yeah, you know, The Darwin Award. When people die doing dumb things, they're proving Darwin was right - only the fittest survive, including the mentally fittest. It's related to The Death Pool, where people bet on what public figure will die soon. As I said, the guy is lucky he's still alive after that."

"He is," Fiona agreed. And she was thinking how happy he didn't die. Because truth be told, he was the first person since Camille to make her feel alive, and that was not nothing.

The three drank their cappuccinos for a few more minutes in silence. Fiona felt it was an awkward silence, and she wanted to keep talking because it was obvious Cora wanted to leave, and Fiona didn't want her to. She knew that if she kept trying to keep the conversation going, this wouldn't happen.

As for Alistair, it seemed he was so focused on Cora's mood that he didn't have many words to say, either. That was the problem with Fiona because she was also focused on Cora and anxious not to say the wrong thing. She felt like she was walking on eggshells around her own sister.

"So, Cora, what do you think about what I said earlier about my looking after Daisy a few hours a week?" Fiona finally asked after a few minutes of silence.

Alistair looked at Cora hopefully, but Cora just shrugged. "Thanks, but if it's all the same to you, I can look after her just fine. I've been doing it for four months now, long before you appeared on the scene out of nowhere."

Alistair looked annoyed. "Cora, I've only been gone for two months, and before I left, I did my share of caregiving. So, you haven't been alone the whole time Daisy's been alive."

Cora nodded and put her hand on Alistair's knee, which struck Fiona as patronizing. *There, there, you just think you do your share,* the move, and Cora's expression, said.

"Of course," Cora said to Alistair. "Okay, Fiona, your cappuccino was delicious, but we must go." She stood up and gestured to Alistair with a look. "Daisy needs her nap."

Alistair looked reluctant, but he shrugged and finished off the rest of the cappuccino. "Fiona, it's been good to meet you," he said, extending his hand again.

With Daisy in her arms, Cora was already at the threshold of the bookstore, looking at Alistair with impatience.

Alistair leaned down and spoke in a low voice as Cora looked out the window. "I'm sorry about this," he said. "I wanted to invite you to tea at our place, but I don't think Cora's in a fine enough mood for all that."

Fiona just nodded her head. She understood. And she really wanted to help her sister. She just didn't know how.

And it was obvious that Alistair didn't know how either.

Chapter Twenty-Six

Greer

Greer was anxious to get to know her new daughter. But she didn't want to tell Fiona the real story about why she put her up for adoption. Fiona would never understand the desperation that Greer was feeling at that time.

Cora was already wondering about all of it. Greer had no idea what to tell Cora either. How can you explain giving away a loved child born into a loving marriage? But she was desperately afraid that Cora and Fiona would find out the truth, and they would shun her for it. So, a part of her was apprehensive that Fiona was back in her life. But a bigger part of her, the dominant part, couldn't be happier about the situation. Even if she was really sad about the turns Fiona's life had taken.

She never imagined it would end so tragically when she bundled off her tiny infant and handed her to the beautiful half-Asian woman and her strapping Irish-born husband. Not that what happened was anybody's fault, of course. It was just one of those things, an auto accident. Still, Greer felt incredibly guilty, as if she and her actions way back when started the entire thing in motion.

So, she felt that Fiona being back in her life was, in a very real way, purging her own guilt. At least, it gave her a chance to try to make up for the tragic life she had given her daughter indirectly when she put her up for adoption all those years ago.

Just then, her best friend Bridget Graham was knocking on her door. Bridget often popped by just out of the clear blue sky to say hello or to fill Greer in on the latest gossip around the trailer park. Greer confessed to her about Fiona, not telling her that Fiona was this posh movie star and hoping that Fiona, who didn't look like she did in the movies or magazines, could get away with being anonymous around her friends. Of course, Greer didn't really believe that. It was just a matter of time before somebody opened their gob about Fiona, and then everybody would be agog about the star in their midst.

But, for now, she instinctively knew she had to protect her daughter from all the attention she would get when the truth got out. She knew Fiona really wanted to live a quiet life. She just got that sense about her. So, Greer would give her that. That was the least she could do for Fiona.

"Hello, Greer," Bridget said cheerfully. Bridget, like herself, was in her early 50s and, like herself and the other ladies in her informal group, was on her own, having been married with children, but now, through either death or having a no-good husband who left them in the lurch, was alone. Not that Bridget and Greer's other lady friends, including Erin Brown, Maeve Buchanan and Siobhan Walsh, were against remarrying. They only needed a man if they could find their soulmate, which seemed impossible.

Yet, Greer knew she and all her lady friends were still looking for that elusive soulmate.

In other words, they all were too old for the nonsense that a rubbish marriage can bring, so they all were trying the find the elusive non-rubbish relationship and, thus far, couldn't. But they were always ever-hopeful because nobody wants to die alone, do they?

"Bridget," Greer said, giving her friend a hug. "Good to see you."

As usual, Bridget was bearing gifts. She always brought something over to Greer because her adult daughter Nora, who lived with her, loved to bake. It was very relaxing for Nora to bake cookies and so forth, so Greer was always trying to fend off the latest offering. If she ate everything that Bridget gave her, she would be big as a house.

In this case, Bridget had half of a cake in her hands.

"Thank you," Greer said. "What a lovely cake."

"Chocolate Guinness," Bridget said. "Made with sour cream, a cup of Guinness Stout and all the usual. I had a slice last night, and it's quite delicious."

"I'm sure it is," Greer said, her mouth watering. She knew she would do what she usually did with the tasty treats Bridget always brought over. She'd have a slice with Bridget, and then, after Bridget left, Greer would throw the rest of it into the trash. It was a matter of self-preservation not to overindulge. But Bridget always meant well and tried to get rid of Nora's baked goods, so she pawned them off on Greer and the others. Really, Nora was the original sin, so to speak, because she liked to bake when she was under stress. And judging by the number of sweets Bridget was always trying to pawn off, Nora had been particularly unhappy lately.

Greer went into the kitchen to get some plates and

brought them out, along with a cup of coffee for Bridget. And then she went to open the window, so she could hear the sounds of the roiling sea while she enjoyed her rich and delicious slice of cake.

The second she bit into the cake, she knew she found Nirvana. And she also knew this cake would go into the trash for sure. Otherwise, she'd start eating it and never stop.

"So this is what heaven tastes like," Greer said as she savored the treat, which was sweet and rich, with just a hint of bitterness that tempered the sugar and brought texture and character to the cake. Greer always loved competing flavors, such as chocolate with a dash of chili powder, ice cream made with caramelized garlic, and, apparently, chocolate cake made with beer. She thought whoever decided that salt went well with caramel and chocolate was a genius who deserved the Nobel Prize. So, this cake was right up her alley.

"Right," Bridget said. "Nora is trying out for an amateur reality baking show. She's been trying to create an original cake recipe to help her stand out, so she's starting with this."

"A reality baking show? Which one?"

"It's called *Is it Cake?* Contestants bake all kinds of cakes that look just like something else. Like a cake that looks like a hamburger or a shoe. So, Nora has been working on that, too, making her cakes look identical to different things. She'll be sending her audition tape to the producers next week."

Greer nodded. She'd caught a few baking shows and knew all about it. *The Great British Bake Off* was the grand dame of the baking reality shows, but Greer had also heard of *Is it Cake?* It was hosted by Mikey Day, who was on *Saturday Night Live.* She was impressed Nora was trying to get on that show.

"Well, she's on the right track with this cake," Greer said.

"Yes," Bridget agreed. "She is. She dreams big, but she'll have to start somewhere else to get on a show. Something smaller."

Then again, Nora tended to not do anything small. She was currently working for a bakery, making everything from cookies and fairy cakes to elaborate wedding cakes. Nora was very talented with her wedding cake-making skills; she was creative, had a keen eye for detail and beauty, and had excellent baking skills.

Of course, Nora was always looking for a man to sweep her off her feet, so she could have her own wedding. But somehow, it never had happened for the 23-year-old lady. Greer knew it would happen for Nora one day, but Nora was very choosy, having seen her mother's terrible relationship with her dad, not to mention all of her mother's friends' relationships with their various no-good guys.

Greer finished off her slice of cake, dabbed her mouth with her napkin, and then used her fingers to pick up the crumbs. Oh, when she got to heaven, this cake would be there. Greer knew in her heart that heaven was like that – you get to have all the foods you love without worrying about gaining weight or becoming unhealthy because of them.

She also knew she'd be reunited with her loved ones, such as Ewan, who she loved dearly. She was therefore looking forward to the next life, even though she wasn't in a hurry to get there, which was part of why she couldn't eat cakes like this all the time.

That was one thing she had that many of her friends

never did – she had a good relationship with her husband. What happened to him was tragic, but Greer was lucky she could experience great love, and she knew it. But she was ready for another great love if one happened to come along.

Greer polished off her tea and then stood up. "Well, thanks very much for bringing this delicious cake by. I was going to Venice Beach to see my daughter."

"Your new daughter or the daughter I know?" Bridget asked.

"My new one. Would you like to come along?"

"Sure. I'd be keen to do something like that. I'm excited to see what will happen with that new bookstore. We've needed the bookstore around here, let me tell you. My granddaughter has been asking when she can go to story hour again, and I haven't been able to answer that question. Now I can."

Bridget had one other child besides Nora: her son Connor. He was married to a lady named Kiera and was a cop in Malibu. He had one 10-year-old child, Maura, who remembered the story hours at the old bookstore quite well.

The two ladies left the trailer to visit Venice Beach and Fiona's bookstore. Greer was looking forward to seeing Fiona again and really looked forward to introducing her lady friends to her beautiful daughter.

They got to the beach area, parked, and headed to the boardwalk. As they walked along, Bridget looked over at Greer. "So, just so I don't get on the wrong foot, how much does Fiona know about exactly why she was born?"

Greer shook her head. "I haven't quite figured out how to tell her. So, as far as she knows, I simply gave her up for adoption because I wasn't ready for a child at the time. "

Bridget just nodded. "Well, I suppose it doesn't really matter. What she doesn't know won't hurt her, I suppose."

Greer noted that Bridget said "I suppose" twice in one sentence, which meant she didn't mean what she was saying. Greer had long since decoded the subtext of her best friend's speech, so there was no disguising just how Bridget felt about Greer's subterfuge.

"Yes, I agree with that," Greer said, pretending she didn't understand what Bridget was getting at. They were now at the bookstore, and, to Greer's surprise, her other daughter, Cora, was coming out the door with Alistair and Daisy in tow.

She knew Alistair was back because she'd run into him earlier that morning when she was out for a walk, and she was so happy. She absolutely loved her daughter's husband. She found a fine guy that was for sure. Alistair adored Cora, and with his laid-back and sunny personality, he could balance out Cora's sometimes prickly demeanor. And Cora had been pricklier than usual these past few months, so Greer felt sorry for him. Still, he chose his lot and knew what he was getting into when he married Cora.

Alistair's eyes lit up when he saw Greer. "Greer, how ya doing!" he exclaimed when he gave her a hug.

"Oh, it's good to see you, twice in one day, no less," Greer said, hugging him back. "And I forgot to ask you earlier, but how long will you be around this time?"

"A week or two," Alistair said. "My ship's captain had a family emergency. We'll be going back soon, though."

Alistair gave Bridget a hug as well. "Bridget, good to see you. How's Nora coming along with her baking? I should drop into the bakery to see her."

Bridget told Alistair about Nora wanting to get on a baking reality show, and Alistair grinned.

"If anybody can get on one of those shows, it would be Nora. You tell her good luck from me."

"I will," Bridget said. Then she looked at Cora, who was standing back with Daisy in her arms. "Cora, let me see that beautiful girl," she said, putting her arms out.

Cora reluctantly handed Daisy over to Bridget. "She'll catch her death being out here for too long," Cora said. "And I need to put her down for her nap."

Bridget scrunched her nose but cooed at little Daisy, who smiled broadly. "There, there, little Daisy," Bridget said. "Such a beautiful little baby."

Greer looked over at Cora. "You weren't mean to your sister just now, were you?"

Cora shrugged. "No. I wasn't mean at all. I just don't know what to say to her, though. I don't know how to talk to somebody like her."

"What do you mean, somebody like her?" Greer asked.

"Rich and famous," Cora said. "What do I have in common with her?"

"She's your blood," Greer said. "That's what you have in common with her. And she's your only blood at that."

Cora said nothing but looked at Bridget, who was busily baby-talking little Daisy. "Well, it's Daisy's nap time, so we need to be getting on." Cora held out her arms, and Bridget gave Daisy back to her.

Alistair hugged Bridget and Greer, and the trio walked down the boardwalk while Greer and Bridget entered the bookstore.

Fiona was in the store, looking tinier than ever in her jeans, oversized sweater and Wellies. She was still not wearing a lick of makeup and was still beautiful, with her wild red hair sticking up in all directions, clear green eyes, thick black fashionable glasses and a smile that lit up the room. It was obvious that Fiona was happy, which also made Greer happy. That was all she wanted for her children - for them to be happy.

Greer sighed as she realized Cora had that same smile, but it had been so long since she'd seen it that she'd almost forgotten what it looked like. How would she get Cora to smile like that again?

"Greer," Fiona said excitedly as she came over and hugged her. "I was hoping you'd show up. I wanted to show you this photo album and note that my real father apparently wrote. I was hoping you could make heads or tails of it."

She ran over to get a book out and beckoned Greer and Bridget to the spot in front of the fireplace. "By the way, I'd like you to meet one of my best friends, Bridget Graham. Bridget, this is my daughter Fiona."

Fiona shook Bridget's hand with a huge smile on her face. "Good to meet you, Bridget," she said.

"Likewise," Bridget said with a nod of her head. Greer looked at Bridget's face to see if she recognized Fiona, but she didn't. But, then again, maybe she had an inkling of who Fiona was because she narrowed her eyes and put her hand to her chin as if thinking about it. But then she shrugged her shoulders and sat down.

Greer wondered if the ruse would last. It might, because who would ever think that a huge actress would just start running a small bookstore on the beach? And there was true magic in makeup, hair-styling and air-brushing. Plus, she wore glasses in real life, which she never did in her pictures. Greer realized she was holding her breath while Bridget studied Fiona and then felt a sense of relief when Bridget apparently decided that Fiona wasn't familiar to her after all.

Fiona excitedly gave Greer the photo album. "Tell me

about this album," she said. "It's such a mystery, and I love mysteries."

Greer looked through the album, seeing that it consisted of pictures of different couples. However, Greer couldn't figure out what these couples had in common, and she didn't understand why they were all featured in this collection of pictures.

"I know all these people, but I don't know why Ewan put them all into an album like this," Greer said. Then she looked at the cryptic note and shook her head. "And I don't know what this note was about, either."

Fiona looked disappointed. "Oh. I was hoping maybe you could give me some insight."

Greer still stared at the note. It was Ewan's handwriting, that was for sure. But she couldn't make heads or tails about what he was trying to say. What was all this about finding the one? And his time being short? His time wasn't short, not until he got behind the wheel of that boat and got himself killed.

She handed the note back to Fiona. "I'm sorry, my dear, but I fear I don't have an answer for you about any of this."

Fiona nodded. "What was my father like?" she asked.

"Oh, he was a lovely man, just lovely. And thank God he was because he gave my Cora a good example of what a man should be. Caring, thoughtful, funny, and with no temper to speak of. Nipped at the bottle once in a great while, but not too bad." Greer shook her head. "Too bad for him and the rest of us that he was nipping at the bottle when he drove that boat into that other boat. I guess it was lucky that nobody from the other boat was hurt."

Greer smiled when she thought of her Ewan. She was ready to move on and find somebody just as good, but she was sad to think it might never happen again for her. Maybe it was just as well. She was happy living in her little mobile-home community with her good friends and two beautiful daughters.

"Don't forget to tell Fiona about Ewan's second sight," Bridget said, nudging Greer. "Maybe that has something to do with this mysterious note."

Greer dismissively waved her hand. "That was nonsense. Oh, Ewan got lucky once in a while and could see things in the future, but a broken clock is right twice a day, isn't it?" Greer didn't really believe what she was saying, though. She didn't want to admit, even to herself, that Ewan might've known that the end was near for him just because he saw it happening before it did.

Because if he knew he was about to die, why didn't he tell her? Why didn't he prepare her for what was to happen? And why didn't he try to prevent it more than he did? Didn't he love her enough to ensure he didn't do silly and tragic things like drive his boat three sheets to the wind? All those questions bothered her greatly and kept her awake at night.

Bridget shook her head. "Oh, Greer, you know the things he knew were more than just lucky guesses. And he was very good at matching people up, you know. He always seemed to know who would go with who and who would be divorced by the time the year was out in any given year."

And that was the truth, Greer thought. She'd seen him look at two people and instantly knew they were supposed to be together, no matter how much they seemed to have nothing in common. And he'd see two people who seem perfectly matched, tons in common and madly in love - the ooey-gooey type of couples that make everybody sick because they would hang all over each other like two cheap suits - and Ewan would sadly shake his head and mutter to Greer that they would never make it. And, inevitably, they would quietly divorce several months later. No doubt about it, Ewan seemed to have a nose for these things.

But Greer never thought twice about all this. She never thought Ewan had anything special regarding matters of the heart. It wasn't like he was a born matchmaker or anything like that. He just seemed to have a good handle on people and…

Greer just shook her head. And what? Was there such a thing as somebody who could see who fit together and would go the distance? If so, where were these mysterious people? Certainly not in their mobile-park community. If there were such people, all her friends and their daughters wouldn't still be looking for their perfect match. They'd all be happy, and that was the truth.

Fiona was listening to Bridget with some interest. "Are you saying my father was a matchmaker?" She put her hand on her chin and looked like she was considering everything.

Bridget nodded her head. "Yes, I believe he was. What do you know about matchmakers?"

Fiona shrugged. "Nothing, really. I was in a *Fiddler on the Roof* production at one of my middle schools when I was 13 years old. Other than that, I only know about matchmakers who charge out the nose and don't know what they're doing."

Greer had spoken to somebody who used one of those services. Maybe it was called Heart-to-Heart or something of the sort. This person who Greer talked to was a lawyer who was interested in such things as going to galleries and plays, the symphony and other cultural pursuits. She had zero interest in NASCAR racing or any other sports. She was an animal lover who had a heart for all living creatures.

She was matched up with a guy whose only interests were NASCAR and hunting. She asked for her money back.

Bridget started to laugh. "Oh, child, you know what you're saying when you say many dating agencies don't know what they're doing. Because they don't. Anyhow, matchmaking is more than finding two people who love rugby and watching Netflix and getting them together. A true match is between two people's hearts and souls, and it's difficult to match them up. But a real matchmaker has a way of doing just that – matching up hearts and souls."

"Is that what Ewan did? Find two people whose hearts and souls matched and get them together?" Fiona asked.

"He did," Bridget said. "If he matched up two people, they stuck for the long haul. Oh, his couples would get into fights, as people do, and maybe one might take off for parts unknown for a day or two, but they always got back together."

Greer started to get her back up about this conversation. She never thought Ewan had any special abilities to match people up. Oh, he introduced people from time to time, and almost 100% of the time, these people ended up getting married and having children and becoming happy. But if Ewan was some magical matchmaker, she would've known it, wouldn't she? What was Bridget talking about?

"Bridget, you're talking about stuff and nonsense," Greer said. "What's all this talk about my Ewan being some kind of a matchmaking wizard?"

"Now, don't you have cross words for me, Greer. I'm only telling the facts. I'm not saying Ewan was a magical anything. He wasn't a witch, you know. But he had an instinct about people, and that's no lie."

Greer took a deep breath and moved to change the subject. If there was one thing she hated, it was somebody demonstrating that she didn't know her husband as well as she always thought she did. She wanted to be the one who could tell anybody everything about Ewan, not somebody else.

"Anyhow, Fiona, when do you plan to open this bookstore?" Greer asked.

"Hopefully in a few weeks," Fiona said. "We won't have the latest titles right away. I'll have to order them. I'll open up as soon as this place is properly cleaned, and I can get better inventory."

Greer clapped her hands with delight. "Oh, Fiona, I just can't wait for this bookstore to open again. It was such a delightful addition to the beach when it was open. Such a wonderful place for people to meet and so many happy and fun events. I hope you get the poetry slams going again. Those were so much fun. Everybody has been waiting for this place to open again, so I know you'll have no problem filling the store up with happy and shiny people."

Fiona nodded, but she seemed apprehensive. Greer knew why, even without Fiona saying a word. It was strange. Fiona was new to her. Greer didn't know her at all before the day before. But Fiona was from her blood. She came from her body, so Greer felt she had the same almost psychic connection she used to have with Cora. So she knew Fiona was apprehensive because she didn't want much attention.

"I hope you're right," Fiona said. "At any rate, I think I'd like to get the book club going. Once I can get some of the newer books ordered and on the shelves, I can gather some ladies around to read a book monthly and discuss it. Maybe *City of Girls* by Elizabeth Gilbert, *The Midnight Library* by Matt Haig, *Lilac Girls* by Martha Hall Kelly and *The Seven Husbands of Evelyn Hugo* by Taylor Jenkins

Reid. Those are some of the better books I've read lately. And maybe some good memoirs, like Prince Harry and Matthew Perry."

"Sounds like a fun list," Greer said. "I've read a few of those myself."

"I think so, too," Fiona said. "And go with some classics, too. Probably some Jane Austen would be a good thing to start with."

"Can't go wrong with Jane Austen," Greer said. "Everybody loves *Pride and Prejudice*, but I'm partial to *Mansfield Park*. But, as I said, you can't go wrong."

Fiona smiled. "And maybe I could even recommend some books to Cora. Does she like to read?"

"She used to," Greer said. "But I don't know what she likes to do these days." Greer had to admit that she was no longer psychically connected to Cora. She always had been able to help Cora because she knew just what her daughter needed. But, ever since the birth of Daisy, it seemed she was very much out of sync with her daughter. She didn't know what had changed, and, perhaps even more distressing for her, she had no idea how to fix it.

"What did she like to read before? Novels? Self-help? Memoirs? Non-fiction?" Fiona asked.

"She used to read novels a lot. She was very much into romance-type books. And historical fiction. But, as I said, she's not been doing a lot of reading lately.

Fiona handed Greer a book. "Here," she said, handing her a copy of Brooke Shields' memoir called *Down Came the Rain*. "Does she like Brooke Shields by any chance?"

Greer took the book and cocked her head. "I don't know if she particularly likes her or not."

"Well, maybe she'll enjoy reading this book," Fiona said. "It's very well-written and a quick read. It goes into what some women go through after childbirth when they just can't kick the baby blues."

Greer peered through the book, doing what she usually did when she picked up a new book – reading passages here and there, seeing if anything interested her. At the same time, she wondered if Cora would enjoy this book. Cora seemed to have such an attitude about Fiona being a rich and famous movie star, so she might have the same attitude about Brooke Shields. Still, the memoir seemed quite well-written, so maybe Cora would read it while Daisy napped.

"You know, Cora is weird about anybody implying she has something wrong with her brain," Greer said. "I had a feeling that maybe she just had the baby blues too, but it's lasted this long, and it seems to be much worse than what I went through when I gave birth to you girls."

Greer knew she'd given birth three times, not just two, but she didn't always like to think about that. She hated to think about those days when her little Caitlin was sick. It was so painful that she didn't like to think about it. It also made her feel guilty for reasons she'd not acknowledged to her deepest soul.

Still, she bounced back pretty quickly all three times she gave birth. She was always thrilled with her babies - right from the start, she fell in love with them. Cora was different with Daisy, and Greer didn't know quite why. There were times when she thought Cora didn't really love her daughter. It was just the way Cora looked at Daisy, almost as if she was repulsed by her.

This book might help.

And she realized maybe she needed a book too. That was one thing she didn't do after her tragedies of losing Caitlin and Ewan many years later. She didn't do any kind of self-introspection, didn't try to seek help from a local therapist, and didn't even keep a journal about her feelings.

"Well, it's probably not her fault," Fiona said. "I don't think anybody really knows why some women suffer from postpartum depression and other ones don't. It has some to do with hormones, but another risk factor is a stressful event during pregnancy."

Greer nodded her head. "Ewan died when she was eight months along," she said. "But Cora seemed to bounce back pretty well after losing her dad."

Fiona looked like a lightbulb had just come on. "See, that's probably why she's having difficulty bouncing back after having Daisy. She probably hasn't dealt with the grief of losing her father at such a pivotal time. Add in the usual hormonal changes after giving birth, and it's probably not that much out of the realm of possibility that she would have a bad funk at this time."

Greer felt mixed emotions about Fiona's "diagnosis" of what was wrong with Cora. On the one hand, it certainly seemed rational, even probable, that Cora was most likely suffering grief on top of the physiological changes she was going through with the birth of Daisy. On the other hand, why couldn't she figure that out for herself? What was wrong with her? Was she letting Cora drown in her grief and sorrow and not even thinking postpartum depression was the problem?

Bridget, who always had a good head and connection with Greer, put her arm around her protectively. "Greer, I know you couldn't figure out what might be going on with Cora yourself. And you're fighting with yourself, I know. But you also suffered the loss of Ewan not 6 months ago, so you've had difficulty seeing your way out of it. That's why you had a hard time helping Cora. Now don't you pay that any mind that you couldn't see it. What's important is Fiona sees it, and we need to do something about it."

Greer looked at Bridget, who always knew what to say. She took a deep breath. "Do you have a book for me?" she asked Fiona. "I thought I was okay with my Ewan dying, but I think Bridget's right. Maybe I haven't exactly been right with it either. Maybe I've had difficulty trying to help Cora because I need to help myself first."

That was a first for her, in a way. She had a hard time asking for help. Cora was the same.

"Here," Fiona said, handing Greer a book. "*The Year of Magical Thinking.* It's written in very spare, searing prose and gets to the heart of the matter without emotion. But I think what Joan Didion went through after the sudden death of her husband is universal."

Greer took the book and did the same thing as with the Brooke Shields memoir - she scanned it, looking through various passages at different parts of the book, seeing if the words might strike a chord with her. She saw just a few passages and knew this book was for her.

"How are you so good at this?" Greer asked Fiona. "Recommending books to people?"

Fiona smiled. "It's just that I know the power of books. It makes you realize that what you're going through is universal and experienced by everybody at one point or another. And it helps to know that another person has gone through what you've gone through, has been where you are right now, and came out the other side. And I guess I have a bit of a gift for reading people. Also, I'm an actress. Empathy for others and stepping into another person's shoes is vital to what I did in my previous life. Any actress worth her salt has to have one thing – the ability to look through someone else's eyes."

Greer knew Fiona and this little bookstore could trans-form the beach area. She had never thought of it, but everybody really needed this place. They needed a place to go when they were having problems because Fiona was right – reading was really important because it connected you to the larger whole. It was like tapping into the universe's wisdom in a way, reading. And her daughter seemed to have a gift for knowing just what books people might need. That made this little bookstore much more valuable than an impersonal big-box store like Barnes and Noble. Maybe Fiona was meant to inherit this bookstore.

Bridget was smiling. "Fiona, can I tell you how lucky you're here? It's very auspicious you landing here, inheriting this bookstore that'll help people from all over. I didn't think about it, but you're performing a good service for us here. It's not just that people will come in here to find the latest bestseller, although I know that'll happen when you get everything up and running, and your inventory is up to the mark. But you're right. People need stories. There's a reason why we've always had stories. I didn't consider how much this area needs this place until now."

Fiona smiled. "I'm really happy to be here. I just can't tell you how happy I am. It's almost as if I was living my life just waiting. I had success in my former life, but not happi-ness. I never felt like my life had quite begun. And now I'm here, and I feel like this is the beginning. It's strange, and I don't think I thought about it until now that I'm explaining everything."

Bridget nodded. "So, you now own this bookstore. What did you do before?"

Fiona took a deep breath. "I was an actress. And a waitress."

Bridget smiled. "Did you do community theater? We

have a great community theater called the Pacific Resident Theater. You can go over there and see if they need some help. It's a lot of fun doing that, you know. We love our little community theater plays."

So, Bridget really didn't know. Greer looked at Fiona, wondering how she would handle questions about what she did before owning the bookstore. Greer would follow her lead. If Fiona came clean about who she was, then Greer would too. But if Fiona played it down, that was how she'd handle it.

Fiona visibly swallowed. "Actually, no. I was in Hollywood. I know I don't look like Fiona Kennedy, at least how people know Fiona Kennedy. I don't like to wear makeup, and as you can see, my hair is not straight. It's wild and crazy and curly and frizzy in the rain and humidity. And I wear glasses. My eyesight is terrible, and I'm afraid of Lasik Surgery. But I'm Fiona Kennedy."

Bridget's eyes widened, and she put her hand to her mouth. "Oh, my land. You looked familiar, but I never imagined you were the famous actress Fiona Kennedy. I mean, I thought you looked like Fiona Kennedy, but I thought my eyes were deceiving me." Then she turned to Greer. "Greer, why didn't you tell me your daughter was *The* Fiona Kennedy?"

Greer shrugged her shoulders. "I got the impression my daughter didn't want the attention. So I wanted to respect her privacy. It wasn't for me to announce to everybody who she was."

Greer knew Fiona was calculating that it would only be a matter of time before word got around about who she was. And if that were the case, Bridget would wonder why Greer lied to her. Well, not really lie, but it certainly would be keeping important information from her best friend.

Fiona smiled. "I've thought about this angle since I decided to retire and run this bookstore. All I want is to live a quiet, normal life. But I just don't know if it's possible." Then she shrugged. "What are you going to do? But I'd appreciate it if you didn't spread the word about me. Not just yet. Give me at least a few days of blessed, blessed anonymity."

"Of course," Bridget said. "Consider my lips zipped. But I'm so happy to meet you." She clapped her hands together. "Greer, your daughter is simply wonderful. Just wonderful."

Greer nodded proudly. "She is at that."

Fiona blushed. "Thank you, I think you're pretty amazing too." Then she cocked her head. "If you keep my secret, you'll be even more amazing."

"Oh, Bridget can be kept at her word. Don't worry. Now, what can we do to help you?" Greer asked.

"Well, I don't want to put you guys out. Really, I've got this."

Greer shook her head. "Stuff and nonsense. Bridget, why don't you go to that bookshelf against the wall and start dusting off books? I'll do the same for this bookshelf over here."

Fiona tried to protest, but Greer put her hand on Fiona's mouth to silence her. "Child, you have to let us do this. It's a Saturday afternoon, it's raining, and I know Bridget has nothing better to do. And neither do I. So, consider us your help for the day."

So, the three women worked together for the rest of the day to dust off books. At some point, Greer sent Bridget over to get a steam cleaner. She rented one from the local hardware store. She returned with the steam cleaner, and Fiona spent several hours steam-cleaning everything in the store. She steam-cleaned the drapes, the rugs, and the furniture.

By midnight, the three ladies were finished deep cleaning the store. "I was going to hire a professional service to come and do this for me, but I guess I don't need to now. You ladies were really a lifesaver for me."

Greer put her arms around her daughter. "Then I'm just repaying the favor because I think you'll be my lifesaver. You don't realize how much you will mean to this community. How much you'll mean to me."

Chapter Twenty-Seven

Fiona

The next day, Fiona went into town because she would buy Bridget and her mother a "thank you" present. Neither woman would take a penny from her for all their hard work at the bookstore. So, Fiona decided it would be good for her to buy some saltwater pearls for the two ladies. At the local jewelry store, she noticed some beautiful strands, black pearls and mother-of-pearl.

And, on a whim, she texted Jack to see if he wanted to come along. He eagerly texted back that he was free and would love to accompany her to the boardwalk. So, Fiona walked over to his place and knocked on the door.

She was greeted by Jack's mother, Jean. Jean was so excited to see Fiona that she gave her a spontaneous hug as Fiona walked in the door. "Oh, you're here to take Jack into town with you, are you? Well, come on in, come on in. Jack is ready to go."

At that, Jack wheeled into the living room. He looked at

his mother. "Okay, Mom, Fiona isn't the second coming. She's just a new friend who happens to be a pretty lady. That's all." And then he rolled his eyes. "Mom apparently has us married off already," he said with a grin.

Jack rolled his eyes and shook his head but was very happy to see Fiona. And Fiona felt her heart quicken a little as she looked at Jack. With his dark hair, green eyes, and long dark eyelashes, he looked like a Hollywood movie star himself. And he was so shy, with a sweet smile and huge dimples, so Fiona felt comfortable around him. She was so used to narcissists and cocky people who thought the sun rose and set with them. Fiona appreciated Jack's sweetness.

Fiona and Jack went down the ramp and onto the sidewalk. "I'm so excited you came with me," Fiona said to Jack. "I really need to buy some saltwater pearls for my mother and her friend Bridget because they spent 12 hours yesterday helping me clean that bookstore from stem to stern. So, I guess I don't need that cleaning firm after all. And I think I'll open up the bookstore in a week or maybe two."

Jack looked at Fiona. "Fiona, I could've joined that cleaning party yesterday," he said. "You should've called me. I would've been there in a flash."

Fiona laughed. "Oh, I'm quite sure. But I didn't want to be too pushy about the whole thing." Fiona didn't want to tell him she was anxious to call him yesterday because she wanted to see him again. She didn't care if he'd help her clean the bookstore. She just wanted his company. That was all. Just his company.

"Be pushy all you want with me," Jack said. "Believe me, any excuse to get out of the house."

They got to the jewelry store, which was also a crystal store. Behind the counter was a young woman who appeared to be in her early 20s. And coming in the door behind them was a guy. The woman behind the counter smiled at the guy right after she greeted Fiona and Jack.

"Malcolm, hello!" she said to him. She was a pretty young woman, blonde with a smattering of freckles across her cheeks. The man was just as blonde as the woman, fair with blue eyes and a slight frame.

Fiona looked at the two of them and saw the same bright tendril of light between them that she saw with Alistair and her sister Cora. She had no idea why she saw this, but she was fascinated.

The woman came over to Fiona and Jack. "I'm so sorry. Malcolm here comes over every Sunday to help me with my books. I was distracted, so I'm sorry. My name is Skyler. But what can I do for you?"

Fiona blinked. She, too, was distracted, but for a different reason. Why was she suddenly seeing this bright light between people? What did it mean? Was she sick? Did she have some kind of brain tumor or something of the sort? She didn't know. She knew that, generally, hallucinations didn't mean anything good.

Fiona leaned over the counter and pointed to a strand of saltwater pearls and a strand of black pearls. "I'd like one of each," she said. "I was wondering, I know I just met you, and it's none of my business, but is this Malcolm guy single?"

Fiona had no idea why she was so forward with this woman she literally just met. Something told her she should ask that question, though.

"Malcolm? The guy you just saw? Why, I have no idea if he's single or not. We've never actually talked about that."

"You haven't?" Fiona asked. "Why don't you find out?"

Skyler giggled. "Oh, it's none of my business. He just

comes over and does my books. He's saved my life on more than one occasion, not literally, of course, but the IRS audited me one year, and he kept my books clean as a whistle. He had all the documentation and everything right at the ready. I suppose it doesn't matter if he has a wife at home as long as he does a good job with my books, does it?"

Skyler got the strands of pearls and put them into a bag for Fiona. "That'll be $5,000," she said, and Fiona gave her a credit card to run.

Just then, Malcolm returned from the back room, and Fiona saw the same bright light between them. She suddenly knew she would have to find out what that bright light was about. She hoped it was some kind of gift she was given, something her father had left to her besides the bookstore and the cabin in the woods. She hoped it was that and not some deadly disease.

Before Malcolm left out the front door, Skye's books in his hands, Fiona turned to him. "Hello, my name is Fiona."

Malcolm looked at her and smiled. "Hello."

She knew what she had to do. She had to match this Malcolm up with Skyler. But she was an interloper, just another customer. And she was apparently unrecognizable to people now that she'd gone *au naturel*, so it wasn't like she could use her fame to make this match.

Skyler was looking at Fiona curiously. Fiona didn't know if Skyler was trying to place her face or if she was wondering what she was up to. Fiona hoped and prayed it was the latter and not the former.

Fiona cleared her throat. What would she say to this guy? That he was made for Skyler, and he better open his eyes? That, if he happened to have a girlfriend or wife, that person was wrong for him because Skyler was his soulmate? That she knew what it was like to be with somebody who wasn't a soulmate and that he shouldn't settle like she did?

She had just met both of these people. They both would think she was crazy if she tried to match them up.

Malcolm scrunched his eyebrows. "You know, you look so much like that actress. The one who left her guy high and dry after staying married to him for a hot minute."

Fiona put her hands on her cheeks, and Jack looked at her curiously. Oh God, Jack! She was so smitten with the guy that she didn't even think to tell him about her quickie marriage. She was still technically in the marriage because there was no annulment and no divorce.

Jack shrugged. But he looked hurt. Fiona knew by the look on his face that he was probably thinking he didn't have a chance with her anyways, so why should he care if she was married? Fiona wanted to tell him that, for whatever reason, she felt more connected to him than she ever felt to Luke. Her connection to Jack felt so real, and it was what was missing between her and Luke.

Fiona shook her head. She wouldn't confirm or deny that she was, in fact, "the actress who left her guy high and dry after staying married to him for a hot minute." But she would have to address the situation with Jack. Maybe it would be presumptuous because she had no idea if he was interested in her romantically, but if he was, she wanted him to know she was available. Maybe she was not technically available because she still had to have the marriage annulled or, at the very least, terminated in divorce court, but she was emotionally available to him.

"I get that a lot," Fiona said. "Anyhow, can we talk outside?"

"Sure. That's where I'm heading."

So, Fiona and Malcolm walked right outside the jewelry store.

"Okay," Malcolm said to Fiona. "I'm listening. Although I must tell you, this whole thing is bizarre, my talking to a lady who's a perfect stranger. But go ahead. I like weird things."

Fiona nodded. She would have to put it all on the line. There would be no beating around the bush. "Okay, listen. I think I have a gift. I just acquired it, but maybe it's been latent somewhere, wanting to get out. But I can see when people are meant to be together. And you're meant to be with Skyler."

There. She went ahead and told him. He would say she was crazy, but she didn't care. She suddenly realized this might be her calling. Well, that and matching people up with the right books, which was also a form of match-making if you thought about it. Maybe not everybody was meant for another person. Maybe some people just wanted to be alone. But that didn't mean they had to be alone because a good book could always be a good companion.

So that was it. She would be in the business of matching people up with people and books. She wondered if her father had the same gifts. Somehow, she knew her mother wouldn't be the person she could ask about that because her mother didn't seem to know her father had these gifts. For whatever reason. But Bridget seemed to know. So maybe Fiona would talk to Bridget about her father and what he did for people in their mobile home community.

To her relief, Malcolm did not get on his cell phone to call the loony bin on her. Rather, he smiled. "You really think so? I've been keen on her, but I never thought she'd look at me like that. Why do you think I'm meant for her?"

"I have a gift. My father left it to me."

He smiled again, went back into the jewelry store, and returned five minutes later. "We have a date tonight. Thank you so much. I didn't get your name?"

"Fiona."

"Fiona. Like that actress who ditched her husband after 72 hours of marriage?" He raised his eyebrows and got a good look at her. "Okay. You're going to pretend you're not her, and that's okay. You've done me a very good favor, so I thank you. I never would've gotten the courage to ask her on a date if you didn't say something, so thank you."

Fiona smiled. She wouldn't confirm or deny when people "accused" her of being the flighty idiot who left her handsome husband in the lurch after less than a week. She would have to make them wonder.

Except for Jack. Jack knew the truth about her identity but didn't know the truth about her marriage. She would have to talk to him about that.

She hoped and prayed he cared whether or not she was married. Because if he didn't, it meant he wasn't into her like she was into him.

And that would break her heart.

Chapter Twenty-Eight

Jack

So, the woman of my dreams is married. It figured. Jack knew he didn't have a chance with her. What was he thinking? She was this wealthy, famous, stunningly beautiful woman with a heart of pure platinum. And he was a man without functioning legs, who lived with his mother, didn't have a job, and seemingly didn't have a future. What could he possibly offer her?

But he had to admit, after spending time with her at the bookstore and at her cottage, he went home and thought about her all night. Her silky white skin, her placid and clear green eyes, her copper hair, and her glorious smile that lit up the world. And her kindness. She was as kind as he had hoped she would be. She was everything he imagined she would be, but there was no way he could ever get close to her except to treat her as a friend and nothing more. He had to think of her as just like his rugby friends back in the before times. He could talk to her, and she seemed to understand him, but it was inevitable that she would break his heart.

And, with the news that she was apparently married, maybe his heart was already broken. Why didn't he know that about her? He thought he knew everything about the beautiful and glorious Fiona Kennedy. But he didn't know that about her.

He was embarrassed as he thought about the painting he made of her. He made this painting of her last night after spending all that time with her, and he could memorize her face. The crook of her neck, her little upturned nose, her butterfly lips, her freckles, her décolletage, her beautiful hair. Everything about her was burned in his brain, so he could paint her just by accessing the picture of her in his mind. She didn't have to pose for him. She was right there with him when he closed his eyes.

She put her hand on his shoulder, and he felt the electric tingles from her touch. This electricity shot through him and lit him up from underneath the skin. Damn! He was so feeling her, but she was not to be. She was an unattainable golden girl, this world-famous popular actress who would never be interested in an average guy like himself.

"Jack, let's go. I got pearls for my mom and her friend Bridget, and, as a bonus round, I made my first match. That's cool, huh?"

"Yes. Very cool."

Jack and Fiona left the jewelry store. Behind them, Malcolm and Skyler were looking into each other's eyes dreamily. And that was so weird because, before Fiona got involved, they seemed to be just business partners. Malcolm did her books, and Skyler didn't even know if he was single. Yet, as he looked at the two of them, they were clearly in love.

"Jack," Fiona said. "I'm sorry I didn't tell you about my marriage."

Jack just shrugged. "It's not my business. You and I are just friends. So, I don't know why you would tell me about being married. I don't know why you'd think I needed to know about it."

Fiona sighed. "You're right. You and I are just friends. So, I guess it's really not your business. But I still wanted to tell you that I'm no longer married to the guy. Sorry - I guess I technically am still married because we haven't legally had it dissolved. Anyhow, we aren't together anymore because he was not The One. That's really it, you know. There are just soulmates in the world. But I don't think there is just one soulmate for every person. That would be too crazy. Could you imagine? You have to find your soulmate somewhere in the world? If there was just one, your soulmate could be in India, and you could be in Australia and never would meet. But I think everybody has multiple soulmates running around, hopefully close enough that everybody could find their other half. And Luke just wasn't my other half. And I think I finally have figured that out."

"What do you mean? How come you just figured that out?"

"Well, I just was so confused about the whole thing. I was marrying him, knowing it was wrong from the beginning. But there was nothing I could put my finger on why he was so wrong for me. We're both actors, so we understand each other. He's an amazing cook, very talented with the piano and acting. All the critics say he will be looked upon as a legend one day, like Daniel Day-Lewis, Al Pacino, or Leonardo DiCaprio. He's phenomenal in every way and was very good to me. So I could never figure out why he wasn't right. But now I do. I've discovered there really are soulmates."

She was smiling. She looked like a woman who just discovered the secrets of the universe.

Jack shook his head. Why was he getting the feeling that this woman, this Fiona, was his other half? How could he possibly think that? No, that was wishful thinking. Fiona's soulmate was somewhere nearby, but it couldn't be him. As much as he wished it would be.

"So, what are you going to do? With Luke?"

She shrugged. "Well, I will have to make it official that we're not married anymore. Not that he cares. When I told him I was retiring to run the bookstore and live a quiet life, he was more concerned about my leaving the movie industry behind than leaving him behind. And he was already focusing on how to spin it in the legacy and social media. So, I don't think he's heartbroken."

She pushed him along, and they ended up, somehow, at the animal shelter. He looked at her. He was an animal lover, and it broke his heart to see the animals behind bars. And he wanted a dog so badly, but there wasn't enough money. Dogs cost a lot of money, between food and trips to the vet. Besides, he couldn't care for an animal, and his mother wasn't always around to help him.

"I hope you don't mind, but I want to get a dog. I never had time for a pet while working in the movie industry. I was on the set for 17-hour days, so it just wasn't fair for me to get a dog. But I have the best set-up here now. I live in the woods, so there's lots of room for a dog to roam, and I could take him or her to the bookstore with me every day. He or she could be like the mascot of the place. Will you help me find one?"

Jack grinned. Oh, Fiona was going to get a mutt? And,

better yet, she would bring the mutt into the bookstore with her? Which meant he would get to play with the pup? He was very excited about that.

"Of course. After all, I'll be working for you at the bookstore. So, I'll get to be around this little pupper myself. So I'd love to have a hand in finding her or him."

They went into the shelter and spoke with the lady who let them go back and look at the dogs. They were big dogs and little dogs, barking dogs and quiet ones who just looked at them. All of them begging to be taken home.

Jack and Fiona settled on a beautiful mid-sized fawn-colored mutt with a black face, curly tail, and a small set of crooked teeth. The dog had a cone of shame because she had two cherry eyes that were surgically altered recently. She looked at both Fiona and Jack warily. She looked exactly like a tiny English Mastiff, and her little card said she was a pug/shepherd mix. However that worked.

Fiona and Jack went to get the adoption lady, who allowed them into the little room where the dog was. The dog hung her head, and her tail was between her legs, but she approached them carefully and sniffed them both. Then Fiona lay down on the floor, and the dog approached her and licked her face.

Jack was charmed by Fiona Kennedy, this world-famous actress, lying on a shelter floor and letting this mutt give her kisses on her face. Somehow, that little action meant more to him than he could acknowledge because it meant she was more down-to-earth than he had ever imagined.

"My goodness," the adoption lady, whose name was apparently Sheila because that's what her nameplate said. "That little puppy is so shy, she won't go to anybody. Yet, she's coming to you like you're giving her filet mignon."

And that was the truth.

Fiona just giggled. "This is the one. I was drawn to this shelter right now because I felt a dog was meant for me, just waiting to be found. And I found her. This is the one. I'll call her Lucy."

Fiona wasn't lying on the floor anymore, but she was on her knees, and Lucy was no longer shy but was covering Fiona's face with kisses. No longer was Lucy hanging her head. And her tail was no longer between her legs, for it was now curled around her back. Lucy's entire little body was shaking with joy.

"This is my pupperoni," Fiona said. "Give me the paperwork, Sheila, so I can take her to her forever home."

Sheila smiled. "Oh, good. I was afraid this one would have difficulty being placed because she's been so shy around everybody that everybody has passed her right by. But it looks like the two of you are made for each other."

Fiona smiled. "Yes, I think we are."

Chapter Twenty-Nine

Fiona

Fiona was so happy about Lucy that she felt ready to burst. It was weird - after she left the jewelry store, she felt a pup calling out to her. She knew her dog soulmate was waiting for her, and as she took little Lucy out to the car, leash and dog food in hand, she knew she was right. Lucy was hers, and she always was meant to be hers.

Just like Jack. Fiona's heart broke when Jack acted so nonchalantly about her marriage. And it broke further when Jack said she was just a friend, so it wasn't his business. She was feeling, more and more, that maybe Jack was her person. That elusive person she was looking for desperately in Los Angeles and could never find. So, she settled for Luke. Now here was the one she was supposed to be with, and she wasn't free. Not really.

She hadn't spoken to Luke since she decided to leave Hollywood and run the bookstore. She needed to be away from him because he represented Hollywood to her and the life she was ready to leave behind. If she still hung out with him, she would still be in that world, going to industry parties and red-carpet events, still being harassed by the paparazzi whenever they went out together. She would still have to talk about everybody in Hollywood to Luke. That was his life, and it wasn't hers anymore. And she didn't want it to be ever again. Plus, she needed to explore her feelings for Jack without Luke bothering her. And Luke hadn't called, so maybe that was all the answer she needed. He was a part of her past; hopefully, Jack would be a part of her future.

She dropped off Jack at his home and then went to her own home. For the moment, she lived in a beautiful and spacious home on a cliff overlooking the Pacific Ocean. Her home was behind a gate, and when she approached her house, she saw hundreds of paparazzi and reporters clustered outside her gate. She looked at the remote camera on her phone and saw many more inside the gate. She didn't know how they got inside her gate, but they did.

She groaned. Luke must have put the word out about their impending divorce. She knew she'd have to face it eventually, but didn't want to.

She sighed. She remembered that her mother worked at a psychic storefront on Venice Beach, so, not knowing what to do, Fiona went to her mother's storefront to ask for advice. She didn't want to face the paparazzi and the reporters. She was so happy. She had so many great days since she decided to retire. And now, it seemed her happy little bubble was about to burst.

But not if she had anything to say about it.

She drove down to Venice Beach with Lucy in tow. Lucy was completely excited, bouncing off the walls to be going to her forever home. The only problem was, her forever home, Fiona's home, was overrun.

It was after four o'clock, so she could take Lucy on the boardwalk. So, she parked, harnessed Lucy, and walked rapidly towards the boardwalk. Even though it was now dusk, she wore sunglasses, so she didn't attract attention amongst the rollerbladers, bikers, joggers and dog-walkers on the famed Venice Beach.

She got to Greer's psychic storefront and walked in. There was a beautiful younger woman, about her age, with dark hair, green eyes and lots of tattoos. She was visibly pregnant, and she looked at Fiona with curiosity. "You're here to see Greer," she said. "You're Fiona."

"I am." She gestured to Lucy. "Is it okay if I bring her in?"

The woman just smiled. "Of course. She looks like a happy mutt." Then she went to the front desk, reached down, and brought out a couple of dog treats. "Here's a treat. It's just beef liver, so I assume your pupper can eat it."

Fiona smiled and took the treat. "Thanks." She gave Lucy the treat, and Lucy eagerly wolfed it down.

The woman nodded her head. "You need a place to stay, don't you?"

Fiona cocked her head. Actually, that's what she really needed. A place to stay. She could go to a hotel, no problem, but she didn't trust that option. She thought it would be only a matter of time before somebody at the hotel tipped off the press, and they would hound her there, too.

"Actually, yes. I didn't realize it before I came in the door, but I need a place to stay. How did you know?"

The young woman just smiled. "I didn't use my psychic powers, I promise you. I knew you were Fiona when I saw you because it's obvious."

239

Fiona subconsciously put her hand to her hair. "It is?" She felt disappointed that she thought she was unrecognizable without makeup, airbrush, hairstyling, and with glasses. But maybe she was wrong about that.

"Of course. It's not like you're Clark Kent, and somehow everybody, even Lois Lane, who's in love with the dude, doesn't know you're Superman. Although, I'll admit, if I didn't know that my business partner had a long-lost daughter named Fiona Kennedy, I probably wouldn't have known who you were."

Fiona knew this young lady was just saying that to make her feel better. "Okay. I guess my disguise isn't as good as I thought. But how did you know I needed a place to stay?"

"Now that I can chalk up to intuition. You just have the look of somebody who's haunted and hunted."

Haunted and hunted. That actually was not far wrong. She was haunted by her past, what happened to her parents when she was in the car, and all the foster families that came afterward. And, in a way, she was haunted by her past in Hollywood. That was why those paparazzi were coming to her home, after all. And she felt hunted by them as well. They wouldn't let her have a private life, no matter what.

She nodded. "Is Greer here?" she asked. "And I didn't get your name."

"Willow Killeen," the young woman said, extending her hand. "I'm Greer's business partner."

"Willow. Good to meet you."

Just then, an extremely handsome man came through the door. In his hands were two large coffees from Starbucks and a few things in a bag.

Fiona looked at the two of them and saw that same bright tendril between them. These two were made for each other, soulmates. Fortunately, both Willow and this new man seemed to feel the same way about one another. Neither of their energies was blocking the other. Fiona smiled. This would be fun, being able to see the thread between two soulmates.

"My lifesaver," Willow said, taking one of the coffees from this man. "If I have to work until 10 o'clock tonight, which I do, I need to mainline this stuff."

While Willow eagerly drank her coffee, the man looked at Fiona. "I'm Jackson," he said.

"Fiona," Fiona said, shaking his hand.

Jackson raised his eyebrow. "Wait, I know you."

Fiona groaned inwardly. What did she expect?

"You do?"

"Yeah. You're good friends with Camille Hudson. We met at a party years ago.

"Yes, Camille is definitely my best friend." Fiona thought she could stay with Camille until her cottage was renovated, but that wouldn't work. The paparazzi already knew Camille's house, and they also knew Fiona and Camille were best friends, so it would only be a matter of time before Fiona would be tracked to Camille's house. There was probably at least one scout stalking Camille's house as it was, right at that moment. The second Fiona moved in with Camille, the locusts would descend. She wouldn't put Camille through that.

Jackson nodded and smiled as he looked at her closely. "Wait. You're Fiona Kennedy," he said. "I'm an actor, too. I have the part of F. Scott Fitzgerald in a biopic coming out this spring."

Fiona knew about that project. She was approached for the role of Zelda but was too busy with other movies to take the offer. Too bad. If she had accepted the offer, she could've worked with this Jackson, who seemed cool. He just gave off good vibes and positive energy, and Fiona needed all the positive energy and good vibes she could get.

"Oh, right," Fiona said. "I've heard a lot about that. People are really buzzing about that movie and your performance in it. Congratulations. It sounds like you'll soon be on your way."

Jackson nodded. "Can I say you have the dream career? I'd be a happy man if I could have even 1/10 of your popularity."

Fiona didn't want to hear that. Not that Jackson knew all of what happened in the past few days – her decision to retire, to divorce, and her wish to live a normal life. But she felt guilty hearing that she had the career other people coveted. She knew it was true, but she didn't enjoy hearing it.

"Well, I appreciate that. But I've decided to retire. I inherited a bookstore on Venice Beach I'm going to run. I've decided it's time for a quiet life."

Willow rolled her eyes. "Don't say it, Jackson. I know you want to, but don't."

"What? What did you think I was going to say?" Jackson asked Willow playfully. Then he looked at Fiona. "You might think it's cool to be in love with a psychic, but I'm here to tell you, it's not all it's cracked up to be."

Fiona just laughed. "I might find that out. I won't be in love with a psychic, but my birth mother is one."

"Your birth mother?" Jackson asked. "I'm sorry, I always thought -"

"That I'm an orphan? I thought that too until just a few days ago. But I'm not. I have a birth family in town. They live in the Pacific Palisades. A mother and sister. And my mother is Greer."

"Greer? Willow's business partner?"

"Yep. One and the same."

Jackson laughed. "Oh, my God. You're Greer's daughter. That's crazy. Talk about six degrees of separation."

Willow apparently just finished her coffee and bagel. She came over to Jackson and Fiona. "Anyhow, Greer has a client with her right now. She's doing an hour-long reading. But I already know where you can stay."

Fiona felt excited. She didn't know when she came into the shop that she needed a place to stay until her cottage in the woods was ready for her to move into. But it made sense that it could solve her problem regarding the paparazzi camping out at her house.

"You do?"

"Yeah," Willow said. "Well, I shouldn't talk out of turn. Jax, can you call your mom and ask her if Fiona Kennedy can stay with her?" Willow turned to Fiona. "Jackson's mom Ava just got rid of her long-term houseguests, whose house was being renovated. She's feeling kinda sad and lonely, and she's a huge fan of yours. We're talking huge. She could probably recite every line to every one of your movies."

Fiona just laughed. "Well, I won't hold her taste in movie actresses against her. But it would be great if she would say yes. Just until my new cottage is renovated, which won't be long. Well, it might be long, seeing as I haven't had the chance to find an interior decorator for the project."

Willow laughed. "I have somebody for that, too. Quinn Barlowe. Ava's best friend. I'm sure Quinn could pencil you in."

Jackson chimed in. "And you know what? My sister Samantha baked the cake for your-" And then he put his hand to his mouth. "Oh shit, sorry for bringing up a sore subject."

"You know about the divorce?"

"Yeah," Jackson said. "I'm in the business. People talk. I've heard it on the set." He looked stricken.

Fiona put her hand on Jackson's shoulder. "Don't worry even a second about bringing up a sore subject. It was a mistake, my marriage, but not a painful one. Just a stupid one."

"Okay," Jackson said. "My sister Samantha baked the cake for your wedding. She's amazing, my sister. So talented."

"She is," Fiona agreed. "That cake was delicious and beautiful. Traditional, yet gorgeous. She does fantastic work."

Willow nudged Jackson. "Get a move on. Call your mom."

"Right, right," Jackson said. "What do I tell her?"

"That I can't stay at my house because it's overrun with paparazzi. The ending of my marriage is already coming back to bite me," Fiona said.

Jackson stepped outside the door with his phone in his hand.

"What was Jackson going to say?" Fiona asked. "When you told him not to say what he was thinking."

"Oh, that he couldn't imagine anybody walking away from acting. It's in his blood. He's been acting since kindergarten when he got the lead in the school play. He's taken every acting lesson he could afford and every Masterclass there is. He waited tables for six years before breaking in. He finally got a major part after getting a lot of walk-ons and extra parts. He's put his blood, sweat and tears into his career. So, no offense, I'd imagine he's dumbfounded that you have the fame and fortune he wants, and you're retiring to run a bookstore."

Fiona raised her eyebrows. "Acting was never in my

blood. I only did it because it sounded fun, and I didn't know what to do with my life."

"Ah," Willow said. "Don't tell Jackson that. He'll think you're nuts for not having acting in your blood. He thinks everyone in Hollywood has it in their blood. But go on. This is fascinating."

Fiona nodded, somehow compelled to tell this stranger her life story. "When I started acting, I thought it was good for me to constantly become other people. But that's only because I never liked the person I was. I never felt grounded. It's hard growing up with nobody permanent in your life. I don't know. I think I've been hiding behind my roles all this time. And now that I have a family and a purpose, I don't need acting anymore. It's time for me to live my life as a normal person."

Jackson came back into the store. "Well, I talked to Mom," he said. "And she screamed so loudly into the phone when I asked her to put you up, Fiona, that I think I'm deaf in one ear."

"So, that's a yes?"

"That's a hell yes," Jackson said. "She thought I was pranking her, though." Jackson shook his head. "She'll be bouncing off the walls, fair warning."

"And you told her I have a dog?"

"Yeah. She loved that, too. She had two dogs living with her, and now she has none. She misses the puppy love."

Fiona suddenly felt lighter than air. This would work out! At least, it would for a time. She didn't know how to open the bookstore with nobody alerting the press.

Well, she didn't have to think about that just yet. The bookstore wouldn't be ready to open for another couple of weeks, at least. That would give her time to hire Quinn Barlowe, maybe have her speed up the renovation and just do some cosmetic things - buff the floor, replace the light fixtures and appliances, and give the place a new coat of paint - and she could move out of Ava's before the paparazzi got wind of her whereabouts. She wanted to avoid putting Ava through the publicity meat grinder, and maybe she didn't have to for another few weeks.

In the meantime, she could get some blessed time to decompress. Just relax. Go to the bookstore daily, do everything she could to get the inventory up to the mark, brainstorm with Jack about opening week events, and do some crash learning on running a business. She knew nothing about taking inventory, billing contractors and suppliers, and overhead. But she would learn in a hurry. Because this would be her life.

Of that, she was determined.

Chapter Thirty

Ava

Ava just got off the phone with her son and was absolutely floored. Fiona Kennedy was coming to stay with her! She couldn't believe it. It didn't seem real. But Jackson had assured her he wasn't playing some kind of elaborate prank. Besides, it wasn't April 1, which was generally the only day Jackson played pranks.

Fiona was on her way over right at that moment. How did the house look? Ava nervously walked into each room, making sure there weren't dust bunnies around and no bits of food on the kitchen floor. She was a meticulous house-keeper, which was one reason her bed-and-breakfast on Nantucket did as well as it did. Still, this was Fiona Kennedy. The house needed to be spotless.

Using her Bluetooth, she called Quinn and hurriedly checked every room for cleanliness. "Hey," she said as she rushed into one bedroom and looked under the bed. "Guess what?"

"What?" Quinn asked.

"I'm about to have a houseguest. And you won't believe who the houseguest is."

"Elijah," Quinn said immediately.

"Guess again," Ava said. "Although that's a good guess."

"Prince Harry," Quinn said.

Ava started to laugh. "You're getting warmer."

"Prince Harry is getting warmer? My, my, it must be a big deal if your guest is anywhere close to being Prince Harry."

"Let me just give you a hint. It's somebody whose movies I love and adore and can't get enough of."

"Chris Hemsworth."

Ava laughed again. "Another good guess, and you're getting even warmer. And, might I add, I wish that guess was right. But it's almost as good."

"Wait," Quinn said. "Is it Fiona Kennedy?"

"How did you guess?"

"Elementary, my dear Watson," Quinn said. "You said my guess about Chris Hemsworth was getting even warmer. You mentioned the other day that Fiona Kennedy was the daughter of Willow's business partner. So, you thought you might meet her one day, anyhow. And Fiona and Chris were in a movie together. So, there you have it."

That was right. Chris Hemsworth and Fiona were in a rom-com. They singled-handedly brought the genre back into popularity. Who knew Chris Hemsworth had such comic timing? He was the perfect leading man, playing against type as a nerdy, klutzy scientist who falls in love with a bad girl on the run from the law. It was a modern re-telling of the classic comedy *Bringing Up Baby*. The two actors had chemistry galore. The movie made buckets of money and brought the genre back from the dead.

"Well, you guessed. What do you think about that?"

"I think you got a much better houseguest than us. How did you manage that?"

"Jackson just said she's retiring from acting and left her husband. She apparently went to her house and saw it was overrun by the paparazzi and reporters and needed a place to hide out. She went to visit her mother at Willow's storefront. Jackson was there and offered my house for her and her pooch to stay."

"Wait. Fiona is leaving the movie business? And she left her husband? She just married him."

Ava suddenly felt bad for gossiping about her soon-to-be houseguest. "I don't know about all that. I'm just hearing it from Jackson."

Just then, Ava heard the doorbell ring. All at once, her heart started racing. "Quinn, I'll have to talk to you later."

At that, Ava hung up the phone and went to the door.

On the other side of the door, there was Fiona Kennedy and a beautiful little pup. She didn't seem to have an overnight bag.

"Hello," she said. "My name is Fiona, and I know your son called to ask if you mind putting me up for a few days. I don't have a change of clothes or anything, but I called my best friend Camille, and she's going to come up here with a change of clothes, toiletries, and everything. She has an overnight bag for me at her house for just this kind of occasion."

Ava opened her mouth, but nothing came out. She was so shocked that this was actually happening to her. She felt she was dreaming, and she pinched her forearm. Yep, she felt the pinch. She wasn't dreaming.

Ava finally opened the door wider and swept her hand

in a motion that told Fiona to come on in. Fiona smiled broadly, lighting the night sky, and entered Ava's home.

"Thanks," Fiona said. "You're a doll for doing this for me."

Ava nodded. What was wrong with her voice?

She finally croaked something out. "I'm happy to help. I mean..." She didn't want to sound like a stupid fan girl. How to sound like a mature, 55-year-old woman who was a high-powered Harvard-educated lawyer, ran her own bed-and-breakfast and was now part owner of a successful winery in the Santa Monica Mountains? And not like a 13-year-old girl squeeing?

"I'm just happy to help," she finally said. "Um, let me show you to your new bedroom." Ava would put Fiona up in Sarah's old room, which faced the beach and opened to the large deck that abutted the beach. Fiona could just open the French doors in the morning and hear the ocean rolling in.

Fiona followed Ava to Sarah's bedroom. "Oh, this room is so cool," Fiona said, looking at the clean white walls, the soft blue bedspread, the exposed overhead beams, and the nautical pictures above the bed. "May I open the doors?"

Ava nodded, still unable to speak.

Fiona went over to the French Doors and opened them. Then she stepped out onto the deck. The wind was whipping up, and the ocean was fierce. It seemed to be high tide. Other than the lulling sounds of the ocean rolling in and out, no other sounds came from the beach.

Ava wanted to call somebody who could break the ice with Fiona. Somebody who was talkative, not intimidated by stardom, and bubbly. Somebody like her daughter, Samantha.

What was Samantha up to that night? She hadn't talked

to her beautiful and talented daughter for at least a week. Ava knew it would be lame to get her daughter involved in this situation without telling Fiona, but Ava didn't have the voice to make Fiona feel comfortable. Samantha certainly would be a wonderful hostess.

"Just a second," Ava croaked out. "I'll be right back."

Then Ava shut the door behind her and called her daughter. It was 9 o'clock at night, but she knew Samantha was a night owl. And she also knew Samantha would be very excited about meeting her idol again. After all, Samantha had already met Fiona once before, because she made Fiona's wedding cake and was invited to Fiona's wedding reception. So that was even better. Samantha already knew Fiona, so the ice would already be broken.

"Hey, Mom," Samantha said when Ava called her. "What's up?"

"I know it's kind of late, but do you mind coming over and maybe spending the night?"

"I guess, but where's the fire?" Samantha asked.

Ava looked around to make sure Fiona wasn't listening to her conversation. "Fiona Kennedy is here," Ava said. "And I don't know. I seem to act like an idiot around her. I need somebody to come over and break the ice."

Samantha laughed. "Mom, she's a cool person. I met her. She gave me a hug when we first met. She's just like everybody else. Really. You can talk to her. Just pretend she's your daughter."

Ava suddenly realized that she *was* acting like a total idiot. And she could do this. Samantha was right. Fiona was just another young and very talented lady like her daughter Samantha. Samantha had different talents from Fiona, but Samantha was phenomenally talented just the same. "You don't want to come over then?" Ava asked.

"I would, Mom, but I have to open the bakery tomorrow morning at 5 o'clock."

Samantha lived in Melrose, and the bakery where she worked making wedding cakes was within walking distance of her apartment. It was only about 30 miles away, but in traffic, it often took over an hour to get to Ava's home in Malibu. That would mean Samantha would drive about an hour to Ava's and an hour or more to get to her bakery in the morning from Ava's home. That would be inconvenient, to say the least.

"You're right," Ava said. "I need to put my big-girl panties on, check in on Fiona, and try to make her feel at home."

"Right," Samantha said. "Like you always did with your guests at your bed-and-breakfast on Nantucket. You had plenty of rich and famous people come to stay with you at your B&B. I remember."

"Well, wealthy people, anyhow. I don't know about famous ones."

"Andrew Jameson stayed with you for months," Samantha reminded her. "Remember?"

That was true. Popular singer-songwriter Andrew Jameson had the same worldwide fame that Fiona had, and he stayed with Ava for months while hiding out from his record producer, who was breathing down his neck for a new album. Andrew became very close to Ava's niece, Jessica Bloch, who also stayed with Ava and worked for her doing odd jobs around the inn. They were now engaged.

"Right," Ava said, taking a deep breath. "Well, fortune favors the brave."

At that, she hung up with Samantha, went to the kitchen to get a bottled water, and approached the bedroom where Fiona was staying. "Um, as you can see, there's an attached bathroom, and I put some new towels in there. And here's a bottled water for you."

Fiona was sitting on the edge of the bed. She smiled and patted the bed next to her. Ava walked tentatively over to the bed and sat down next to Fiona.

"Thanks for the water," she said. "Camille will be here in five minutes with my overnight bag." She hung her head. "Oh, Ava, I'm so sorry to be barging in like this. I can't tell you how much it means that you just put me up, no questions asked. I hope the paparazzi don't find me here."

"Well, of course," Ava said. "It's my pleasure, really."

Fiona sipped her water and looked out the French Doors towards the deck. "I'm just sitting here, decompressing. It's been my first chance to breathe and contemplate what I'm doing with my life." Then she looked at Ava. "Do you think the press and pap will ever leave me alone?"

"I do," Ava said. "Things might be bad right now because the divorce and retiring is a new story. But they'll move on like they always do."

"You mean I'll soon be yesterday's news?"

"Yes," Ava said. "If that's what you want."

"That's what I want. God, that's what I want," Fiona said wistfully. "I don't know. Seeing all those paps and reporters in front of my house rattled me. They even got inside the gate somehow. I don't know how they did that. I thought my home was like Fort Knox. Guess I was wrong."

"You can have them arrested for trespassing," Ava said. "The ones who aren't on a public street."

Fiona shook her head. "Nah. That's a surefire way to keep this whole story going. I'll just let it go and hope they don't break into my home." She paused and then continued to look out the door. "Then again, if they break into my home, they won't get anything valuable to me. My Oscar is in a safety deposit box, and everything else in my home is just stuff. Stuff is easily replaceable. You know?"

"I never thought about that, but you're right."

"Yeah," Fiona said. "I mean, I have the top of the line of everything. Expensive TV, I have an awesome virtual reality helmet and tons of games to go with it, surround sound, precious jewelry, designer clothes and shoes. Even my cookware cost me over $4,000 for all the pots and pans." She smiled. "I love to cook. So does Luke, my ex." She took a deep breath. "But none of those things are valuable to me. I value only family, which I've never had until recently. I'm just realizing that the old cliché is true - the only things worth it in this world are free. Everything else is replaceable."

Just then, the doorbell rang.

"That's probably Camille," Fiona said. "Do you mind if I go down and let her in?"

"Of course not," Ava said.

The two ladies went downstairs, and Fiona opened the door. A tall brunette with olive skin and big brown eyes embraced Fiona, who was now crying. Camille had a large bag in her hand and set it down on the floor.

"Shhhh," Camille said to Fiona. "What's all this?"

"I don't know," Fiona said. "I didn't know I'd start crying the second I saw you, but here I am, blubbering like an idiot."

Camille looked at Ava, Fiona still sobbing in her arms. "I'm Camille," she said. "And you're an absolute champ for taking Fiona in."

"No, really, it's my pleasure," Ava said. "And if you two want to step out on the deck and talk, that would be fine. I'll light up the heaters. I even have a bottle of wine you guys can have."

"Is it from your winery?" Camille asked.

"It is," Ava said. "How did you know about my winery?"

"I'm friends with Samantha," she said. "She told me all about it. It sounds awesome."

Ava just nodded. "Well, let me get the wine out, and I'll show you ladies out to the deck."

"Would you like to join?" Fiona asked.

"I'd love to, but it's been a long day, and I must get up early to open the winery. We have an event coming up this weekend that I have to prepare for." Truth be told, Ava really wanted to take Fiona up on her offer, but it seemed the poor girl was in distress and probably wanted to talk to her best friend in private.

Ava showed Fiona and Camille to the deck and brought a bottle of Pinot Noir and one Chardonnay. "I'm sorry. I didn't ask if you wanted red or white, so I brought them both."

"You're a doll," Fiona said. "I'm in the mood for white."

Ava uncorked her Chardonnay, poured a glass for Fiona and one for Camille, and then slipped back into the house.

She heard Fiona and Camille talking quietly and smiled.

Then pinched herself again.

It all just seemed surreal.

Chapter Thirty-One

Fiona

Fiona was surprised at how much she sobbed in Camille's arms the second she saw her best friend, but she wasn't all that surprised. It had been one hell of a week for her. In just seven days, she got married, found out she had a family, left her marriage, decided to retire, inherited a bookstore and a new home, and possibly found a new love. Was it any wonder she was getting whiplash?

She didn't realize how overwhelmed she was by all the sudden changes until she went to her home and saw all those people surrounding it. Her tears were part exhaustion and part anger. She was angry that the paparazzi couldn't seem to let her alone. She knew that all the press attention came with the territory, but it certainly didn't make things any better.

She suddenly realized just how exhausted she was. It was like all those years of 17-hour days on the set, relentless publicity, and all the BS that came with being in Hollywood finally caught up to her. Hollywood was a place where dreams go to die, and usually, that was because so many people came out to Hollywood dying to make their mark and not succeeding. But for her, her dreams of having a normal life seemed like they would die if she couldn't escape all the attention and press.

It all came to a head.

Now, she sat on the deck with her ride-or-die and felt the fatigue in her bones.

She sipped her wine, and Camille sat right next to her. Camille took her hand and gripped it. "I'm sorry I haven't been around the past few days to help you. I've been working a ton. The restaurant has been short-staffed. But what's going on?"

Fiona just shook her head. "I don't know. The past week or so has just been a tectonic shift in what's happening with me. The ground is just shifting beneath my feet. I mean, I'm really happy. I've made my decisions, and they will be very good and healthy for me in the long run. But there will be a reckoning, and it'll be rough for a while." Fiona gripped Camille's hand. "And thank God you're here for me."

"Always," Camille said. "Always. Remember that. After all, I'm the only one who can say I knew you when…"

"Yes, that's true. You're the only person who has been with me from the beginning. You don't know how important that is to me, that you know me and love the person I am. You don't want a thing from me, and you never have. That's important."

Camille leaned over and put her head on the pillow behind her. "So, tell me about everything."

"There's not much to tell. I love my mother. She seems great. I love my sister, too, but she seems to hate me. I'm hoping that changes. I think it will, but she needs some help with postpartum depression. I don't know how to help her get that help, but I will try." Then Fiona paused. "And I've got this new ability. I don't understand it, but I'm going with it."

"Ability? Do tell."

So Fiona told her about seeing the bright lights between people who are meant to be. "And I swear, even though I can't see the light between other people and me, if I could, I think I could see it between myself and this new guy I've met named Jack. I never thought soulmates were things, but now I think they are."

"Jack? Who is he, and what's he like?"

Fiona felt all warm and fuzzy as she thought about her new friend. "He's just this guy I met, and when I saw him, something happened. Something lit up inside. Then we started talking, and it was like he was an old friend. Like I'd known him all my life. I've never before experienced such an instantaneous connection with another person. Except maybe you, but, no offense, you're not my type."

"So, you think you might be a matchmaker? Do you think you can match me up with somebody?" Camille asked.

"I hope so. I really do. And if my calling is to be a matchmaker, it'll make me so much happier than what I was doing before. Because making people happy by matching them up with his or her soulmate is such an important thing. I'm also excited about matching people up with books. I have a knack for knowing what books to recommend to people. At any rate, I'll be helping people find their joy, and I can't think of anything better in the world."

"I'm so happy for you," Camille said. "But never think that your career as an actress didn't make people happy. Because it did. People could go see your movies and lose themselves, forget for a couple of hours any problems they had. But I know the feeling of directly making people happy will be so rewarding for you."

Fiona knew Camille was right. And she also knew there was somebody out there for her best friend. When Camille found that person, that one person who was meant for her, Fiona would see the bright tendril of light she'd been seeing with everybody else who was meant for each other. She personally couldn't wait for that to happen. Camille deserved somebody special. Everybody deserved somebody special.

She couldn't wait to stand up for Camille's own wedding. And she knew she would and knew she could tell Camille if she dated somebody wrong for her. And better still, she'd be able to tell Camille when she found The One.

The two of them sat up and talked until the wee morning hours, when the orange light started to come up over the water. Malibu was unusual in that the sun rose over the water instead of setting over the water because many of the beaches in Malibu faced the East. Fiona had a very nice camera, a professional one used by photographers everywhere, and she loved to shoot sunrises over the water. She saw the brilliant vermillion light coming up over the water and realized they'd been talking through the night. And she immediately worried about Camille.

"I hope you don't have to work today," Fiona said.

"I don't. I have a couple of days off to just chill. So, I'll be there with bells on for anything you need me to do."

The two of them entered the house, where Ava was in the kitchen. "I hope you ladies like orange juice and eggs in the morning," she said. "I made a cheese strata if you're interested."

Fiona rarely ate a lot of breakfast. But she knew Ava

made a great effort to make this special breakfast, so she smiled. "I love cheese strata," she said. "Let's have at it."

Ava set out three plates and put three glasses of orange juice on the table. Ava brought out plates with a small amount of cheese strata and fresh strawberries. "I'm so sorry. I don't know if there are any allergies or food intolerances. So don't feel obligated if you can't eat strawberries, cheese, bread, or whatever. I'm probably trying too hard."

"No allergies or food intolerances, at least with strawberries and cheese," Fiona said. "Unfortunately, I can't eat almonds. I did a food intolerance test, and almonds, cinnamon, clear vinegar and pumpkin seeds are all on my red list. Go figure. I love all those things, but when I eat them, I have a lot of issues."

Fiona took a bite of the strata, and it was absolutely delicious. It was rich, cheesy, light, and fluffy. The orange juice was freshly squeezed, probably from Ava's orange tree in her front yard.

Fiona resolved to do all she could to repay Ava's hospitality. It would start with getting her a pearl necklace, like she got for her mother and her mother's friend, Bridget. But she wondered if she could find Ava a match. Suddenly, that's what she was eager to do. Help everyone find their other half.

And she was also eager to get to know her host. She hoped she and Ava could talk like Camille and she did last night. She was genuinely interested in Ava's life. She seemed like such a nice lady, but she felt Ava was lonely. She could feel the loneliness as she ate a second helping of cheese strata and sipped her orange juice.

She hoped to ease Ava's loneliness. After all, Ava opened her house for her when she didn't have to. Fiona considered that a salt-of-the-earth move and thought Ava was probably also salt-of-the-earth. And she raised a great daughter in Samantha and an equally great son in Jackson. Ava said she had another daughter who lived in Boston, and she missed her terribly. She had one grandchild, who belonged to the daughter across the country, and one on the way with Jackson and Willow.

But Fiona felt Ava was floundering. She needed a special person in her life. That much was clear.

And Fiona was determined to help her find that person.

Chapter Thirty-Two

Cora

Greer had given Cora a book that Fiona had given to Greer to give to her. And, at first, she was upset about the gift. Who was Fiona, getting into her business? Where did she get off?

But, of course, Alistair, being Alistair, was the voice of reason about the book. He saw it on the bookshelf and he picked it up and read the synopsis on the back. "Hmmm," he said as he read the back of the book. "This sounds very interesting."

"What's interesting about it? Some rich wealthy famous woman had a baby and got all sad afterwards. I'm quite sure I have nothing in common with that woman."

Cora was being difficult, she knew that. But she was triggered by this book. Here was a famous actress boo-hooing about her problems. What could Brooke Shields know about Cora Morrison and Cora's trailer with Cora's lack of funds and distinct lack of fame? Brooke Shields probably had a doctor at her beck and call who could tend to her every problem.

"Well, Cora, my love, I think you might learn something from this Brooke Shields," Alistair said. "Why don't you have an open mind? For me at least? I want my beautiful Cora back."

Cora sighed. She would do anything for Alistair, and it was obvious that he wanted her to read this book. "Okay, for you," Cora said.

"But I'd like to be a part of it," Alistair said. "Maybe you and I can read it together before we go to bed every night. I'd like to know something, too, about what this actress went through."

Cora rolled her eyes but said "okay. Starting tonight, we'll read it together."

So, that night, they decided to retire to bed an hour earlier than usual. Cora made dinner as usual, and put Daisy down at 8, and then Cora and Alistair went into the bedroom and Cora opened up the book and started reading it aloud to Alistair.

At first, there was nothing in the book that was relevant to her. It was about the actress' problems getting pregnant, which wasn't Cora's problem at all. So, Cora told Alistair she'd skip through and Alistair agreed.

It was after Brooke Shields had the baby that Cora started to see the similarities. There, the actress talked in unsparing prose about how she felt about her baby. She was disconnected from the baby and couldn't feel anything for her infant. She was suicidal and fantasized about jumping out the window. It was only when Shields told herself that jumping from a fourth story window wouldn't kill her, but would only injure her severely, that she decided not to jump. In other words, if she would've been high up enough to kill herself, she might've gone that route.

The actress talked about not wanting to deal with her daughter and dreading the moment her husband brought her daughter Rowan to her. About feeling nothing for her daughter. About constantly crying and saying she couldn't be a mother. About not wanting to burden people with her problems. She talked about feeling like a failure when her doctor suggested medication. Nobody she knew had to take meds after birth, so she wouldn't, either. She associated prescription drugs with the movie *One Flew Over the Cuckoo's Nest*, and equated antidepressants with drinking and smoking.

It was when the actress talked about her fantasies about leaving her doctor's office and never coming back, and thinking she should leave because her daughter would be better off, that Cora started to understand. Cora realized that this book spoke to her profoundly. She never thought she'd have anything in common with a famous actress and model, but, lo and behold, she did.

And Cora started sobbing as she continued to read the book aloud to Alistair. She felt she'd never stop.

"There, there," Alistair said gently as Cora sobbed in his arms. "You see? You aren't alone, not at all." And Alistair started reading to Cora. "Okay," he said, after he read a passage. "It looks like this happens a lot to women, but nobody likes to talk about it. One woman wanted to put her baby in a microwave. Other woman couldn't be left alone with their baby and others cried all the time, never spoke for months and couldn't leave their houses."

Cora just nodded. "And what happens? How do I get past this?"

"Well," Alistair said as he skimmed through the book

some more. "It looks like Paxil might be a place to start. I also read that hormone therapy helps women a lot. And time. It looks like Brooke Shields came through her depression and started to really love her daughter. That can happen for you, too. But you need help, my love."

Cora sighed and put her head on Alistair's lap.

"Yes," she finally admitted. As difficult was it was for her to admit to emotional issues, because she thought that having a mental problem was akin to failure, she had to admit defeat. "I think I need help."

Chapter Thirty-Three

Greer

Greer was so nervous. She knew the time had come to tell Fiona and Cora the dark secret about exactly why she had Fiona and gave her up. And it would be a very painful confession. Yet, she felt she had to admit to it.

But she didn't know how Fiona would take it.

What she knew was that Fiona was a lovely, sunny, positive, upbeat person. And she loved her daughter dearly. She loved her when she gave her away all those years ago, and she loved her now. She loved Cora just as much, but Cora, for the moment at least, was not a sunny, positive person. But she hoped that would change.

Cora read the book Fiona gave her. And she told Greer that the book profoundly spoke to her. She recognized herself on every single one of those pages of the Brooke Shields book about how the popular actress suffered from severe postpartum depression and had a hard time connecting with her baby for a long time. Cora realized her feelings of inadequacy, not connecting with her baby, and suicidal thoughts weren't her fault. Something was wrong with her hormones, and she knew she needed help.

Greer actually saw a ray of hope for Cora. Maybe what she needed was some antidepressants and hormonal therapy that could help her get out of her funk. And Greer knew she owed Fiona a note of thanks. Fiona somehow saw what Greer could not – that her youngest daughter wasn't just suffering from the baby blues but from postpartum depression.

She'd invited Fiona and Cora to join her for a little cookout on the beach. She wanted to talk to both of them at the same time, so she could tell them the secret of why she put Fiona up for adoption all those years ago. And why Fiona was born. She knew Cora was curious about this. Cora always assumed that it was just a matter of Greer getting accidentally pregnant and not being able to afford the baby. This wasn't true. In fact, it was the exact opposite.

Greer went over to Cora's trailer. Alistair was watching the baby while Cora went to the beach with Greer. She so loved Alistair. There weren't many men as good as him. Cora was so lucky to have him. Greer needed to impress this upon her because her biggest fear was that Cora's current attitude would push him away.

Cora had a red wagon filled with scraps of wood to burn, drinks, and food. She was dressed in shorts and a jacket because it was still around 60° on the beach, so it was slightly chilly. On her head was a blue bucket hat that was cute on her and made her look like a teenager.

"Okay, Mom, I'm ready to go. But it's mysterious about why you want to do this."

"I need to talk to you girls, that's all. And I wanted to

talk to you before Fiona joined us. I need to know what I can do to help you recover from your depression."

They walked down to the beach, Cora's red wagon of stuff trailing behind them. "I have an appointment with my doctor," Cora said. "Alistair and I read the book together. We read it aloud to each other. I have hope that maybe with some hormone therapy and some antidepressants, I can start feeling better. I've been doing a lot of research online about this. I even found a support group in Pasadena."

"Do you need me to go to your support group with you?" Greer asked.

"No, that's okay. But I've been thinking about asking Fiona to go with me."

Greer looked at Cora with astonishment. "Fiona? Really? Does this mean you're willing to let her be a sister?"

"She *is* my sister. And she knew when she met me what was wrong. She gave me the perfect book to help me understand that my dark thoughts and mood are because my body is betraying me. It's not a moral failing like I thought it was." Cora approached a fire ring and sat down, putting an umbrella up to keep out the sun. "And if it weren't for Fiona, I wouldn't be getting help."

Greer gave Cora a spontaneous hug. "I don't believe it. I think it's some kind of miracle. You're willing to open your heart to your sister. I can't tell you how happy that makes me."

Cora just stared at the ocean. "Don't be too excited just yet. It's going to be a long road for me to feel better. But I think I will feel better, just like Brooke Shields felt better after she took Paxil for her depression."

"Was there anything else in that book that spoke to you?" Greer asked.

"God, yes. Everything in that book spoke to me. She

fantasized about committing suicide and couldn't connect with her baby at all. She cried all the time and thought she was just a bad mother. She couldn't talk to anybody about how she was feeling, and she was envious of all the mothers who easily connected with their babies. Just everything she's gone through, I'm going through."

Greer swallowed hard. She didn't know her daughter had contemplated suicide. How could she miss the signs? "You thought about suicide?"

"I did. Every day. I'm still thinking about it, but I have some hope now that things will get better. I didn't have hope for that before. I don't know. I somehow thought I was the only one going through this. But now I know I'm not. That's all thanks to Fiona."

Greer gave her daughter a hug. She knew that's what Cora needed from her most of all. From her, at least. From Fiona, it seemed she was ready to let her sister help her. That meant the world to Greer.

Cora looked over at Greer. "What are you going to tell Fiona today? You said you had some news for her."

"I'll wait until she gets here." Greer wasn't sure if she should confess her shame. What would it bring to Fiona? The truth was that Fiona was conceived for only one reason - to save her first daughter, Caitlyn. Caitlyn had childhood leukemia, an aggressive form of it, and the only hope for her was a bone marrow transplant. No matter how hard she tried, Greer couldn't find a match for Caitlyn, so she had another baby, hoping the new baby's bone marrow would be a match for little Caitlyn.

Greer probably wouldn't have had any other children if it weren't for Caitlyn's disease. She could only afford Caitlyn because of the money her precious Ewan made as a clerk for a local Best Buy. There wasn't money for a second baby, but they made it work with Fiona. But Caitlyn died before Fiona was old enough to donate her bone marrow.

And Greer, in her grief, simply couldn't care for Fiona. Ewan worked full-time at Best Buy, making just above minimum wage with no benefits, so there wasn't money to get Greer help for her grief. Greer was drowning, just like Cora was, but Greer looked at Fiona's beautiful little face and saw nothing but shattered dreams and broken hearts.

It wasn't Fiona's fault at all, of course. She was just an innocent baby. But Greer couldn't care for her. Greer didn't want to live. So, she and Ewan made the heartbreaking decision to give Fiona up for adoption. The time wasn't right for them to have Fiona, and neither could give her what she needed and deserved.

Just a year later, however, Greer had come out of the grieving for her daughter Caitlyn, and Ewan had been promoted to assistant manager at the store. There was more money to have a baby, and Greer was emotionally ready to care for an infant. So they had Cora. That was the best decision Greer had ever made, but she regretted giving Fiona away every day of her life. Every moment of every day.

All at once, however, Greer knew she shouldn't tell Fiona about the circumstances of her birth. What would that accomplish? What good would it do to tell Fiona that the only reason she was ever born was because there was a very sick child, and Greer was absolutely desperate to save her? Would that make Fiona feel like an afterthought, like she shouldn't have been born in the first place?

Greer had been wrestling with whether to tell Fiona, going back and forth, back and forth. She finally decided to do it, and now she had second thoughts.

Cora got a fire going in the fire ring and got some hot

dogs from a small cooler in the red wagon. "I'll make yours black as charcoal," she said, "just like you like them."

She turned around and saw Fiona coming down the beach. Seeing her beautiful daughter's smile, Greer knew Fiona wouldn't benefit from knowing the truth. She would have to come up with another story about the purpose of the meeting.

Fiona hugged Greer when she arrived at the campsite on the beach. "Mom," she said. "I'm so happy to see you."

Greer noticed Fiona called her "Mom," and her heart soared.

"I'm so happy, too," she said.

Cora looked warily at Fiona before putting down her hot dog stick and walking over to her sister.

And then Cora did what Greer did not see coming. She gave her sister a hug!

Fiona hugged her back, of course. Greer saw the look on Fiona's face, and it was obvious that Fiona was extremely surprised but very pleased. There were tears in Fiona's eyes, and she wiped them away.

Cora sat on one of the low beach chairs, set up another chair next to her, and patted it, gesturing to Fiona to sit down. Fiona did so, the look on her face still very surprised and pleased.

"Fiona," Cora said. "I wanted to apologize to you for the way I've acted. I've been severely depressed for many months. At least since Daisy was born. Probably before that. My depression probably goes back to finding out my father was killed. And you cared enough to ask me about seeing a doctor and giving me a book you thought might help me."

"Did it help you?" Fiona asked.

Cora nodded. "It did. I'm still severely depressed, but I no longer feel so alone. And I now know what's wrong with me. I have hope for the first time in a long time that maybe I'll start feeling better again. And it's because of you."

Fiona smiled. "I only did what anybody would do when her sister is drowning. I threw you a lifeline. But you picked it up and ran with it. I was afraid you wouldn't. I was afraid you thought I was just meddling."

"You're my sister. And I would do the same for you," Cora said.

Fiona put her arm around Cora, and Cora handed Fiona a hot dog on a stick. "You probably don't love hot dogs, but we're cooking out on the beach. It's the easiest thing to eat out here."

"You got some mustard and buns?" Fiona asked. "If so, I'm there. Oh, and I have a plastic bottle of wine in my beach bag. Don't tell the guys who cruise around the beach in their ATVs."

Fiona brought out the wine, produced plastic glasses, and poured some out for Cora, Greer, and herself.

Cora giggled. "If we get busted, you can act all snotty and say, 'don't you know who I am?'"

Fiona smiled and giggled, too. "Oh, I haven't had the chance to break that one out yet. I've always wanted to, but I know I'd get a reputation as difficult and entitled if I did. But it would be fun."

"Such a bad girl," Cora said with a laugh. "Guess you really are a bitchy and entitled movie star."

"That's me, bitchy and entitled," Fiona said. "Hey, do you boogie board? Maybe we could rent some boards and get on out there."

"Get on out there? It's colder than a witch's tit in that water, sis," Cora said. "You boogie board, I'll sit up here and sip this delicious wine."

"Yes, it's delicious," Fiona said. "My new friend Ava has

a winery in the Santa Monica Mountains. She really has some delicious labels. I've tried several, and this Pinot Noir is my favorite. You should meet Ava. You'd love her."

Greer quietly stood back and watched her two daughters bond. Finally, Cora was opening her heart to Fiona, and Fiona couldn't have been more thrilled. Greer could tell that by the look on Fiona's face.

As Fiona and Cora got up to play frisbee and playfully chased each other around the beach, Greer knew they would be okay. Her two daughters were true sisters; nothing could've made Greer happier.

Except seeing Cora conquer her depression for real.

And Greer knew that would happen sooner rather than later.

With Fiona's help.

Chapter Thirty-Four

Fiona

Fiona was so happy that her sister finally opened up and let her in. The day after the beach meeting, Fiona invited Cora to go shopping with her and Cora accepted. "As long as you go with me to the doctor," Cora said. That was their agreement. Fiona eagerly told Cora that she'd go to the doctor with her and maybe even go to her support group. Fiona knew that in a support group, the members of the group aren't allowed to talk about what happens in the group, so there was little chance that somebody in the group would go to the tabloids about Fiona's presence.

The sisters met on the boardwalk. Cora was still depressed, she told Fiona, because she hadn't yet seen a doctor to get antidepressants. But she was already feeling better because she finally saw a light at the end of the tunnel.

"And, for the first time in a long time, I no longer think

that light at the end of the tunnel is an oncoming train," Cora said.

It was a Saturday afternoon, and the boardwalk was filled with people. The beach was, too, although it wasn't as busy as it would be during the summer months. Fiona brought Lucy along, although she really wasn't supposed to, at least not until after 4 PM, which was when dogs were allowed on the beach. But other people brought their dogs to the boardwalk, if not the beach, so Fiona chanced it.

"Oh, what a beautiful pooch," Cora said when she met Lucy. She bent down to pet Lucy, and Lucy eagerly gave her kisses on her face.

"She is, isn't she?" Fiona said. "I love this dog so much. It's really my first dog. Can you imagine? As much as I've always loved animals, I've never had the time for one until now."

Cora stood up. "So, where are we headed?"

"Well, I want to go to this jewelry store," Fiona said. She was hoping to see Skyler there and ask her about Malcolm. She also wanted to buy Ava a diamond pendant. She was going to buy Ava a pearl necklace, like she bought for her mother and Bridget, but decided Ava would look better in a diamond necklace. "And then the bookstore."

Jack was working that day. Fiona and Jack had been working hard to get the bookstore open, and Jack was putting the final touches on the inventory that needed to be ordered. Jack was proving to be quite an asset.

"Sounds good," Cora said.

"Anyplace you'd like to go?" Fiona asked.

"No. Just along for the ride."

So, they went to the jewelry store and Skyler was working. She recognized Fiona from before and her face lit up.

"Hello," she said to her. "I was hoping you'd stop by again sometime."

"May I bring my dog in?" Fiona asked.

"Of course," Skyler said. "She looks well-behaved."

"She is."

"So, how can I help you?"

Fiona smiled. "I wanted to buy that diamond pendant there. A wonderful lady is letting me stay with her and I wanted to give her a special gift."

Skyler got the diamond pendant out and put it into a jewelry box and rang it up. "That will be $5,500," she said, and Fiona gave her a credit card to run. Then Skyler leaned down and showed Fiona her ring finger. "Malcolm and I are engaged, and it's because you somehow put a bug in his ear about asking me out. I've been in love with him for years. But how did you know?"

"I don't know," Fiona said. "Something told me that you two would hit it off."

"Hit it off is an understatement," Skyler said. "We went out on one date and he basically moved in the next day. It's been a whirlwind, but I've never been happier."

Fiona lit up inside. She matched up those two perfectly. And of course she would. She knew they were meant to be, so she also knew that when they finally acknowledged as much to one another, they would be married in no time. She was right.

Fiona chatted with Skyler some more while Cora wondered around the store, looking at different crystal necklaces and jewelry. Fiona found out that Skyler's wedding would be in a month, and it would be a completely casual beach wedding. "And I'd love if you could make it," Skyler said.

"I'll be there."

Fiona and Cora left, and headed down to the bookstore. "You'll get to meet Jack," Fiona said. Just saying his name gave her butterflies.

"Jack," Cora said. "I know of him. He lives in my trailer park. He's an artist, you know. I don't think I told you that about him."

"An artist?" Fiona said. "I didn't know that. He's never talked about that."

"He's quite good. Or at least he used to be, before he became a total recluse. It's good that you're getting him out of the house. He needed to. He drove his mother up a tree."

They arrived at the bookstore, and Jack was working on the computer. His handsome face lit up when he saw Fiona and Cora. "Things are ready," he said. "I have the inventory completely covered, and the books will be in tomorrow. I put a rush on it. I lined up a couple of teachers who are happy to do children's story hour this Wednesday and Friday, and I've scheduled a poetry slam. I'm part of a Facebook group dedicated to poetry slams and I've found five people who want to show up next Saturday night. I've also put the slam on the Meetup app and I have some people interested from there, too."

That was the great thing about Jack. He really knew how to take initiative.

It was then that Fiona noticed the new artwork on the walls. And was completely floored. There were two new pictures on the wall, painted by professional artists and they were exquisite. One was of the roiling sea, with two people standing on the water's edge, holding hands. The other was a multi-colored rendition of a wooded area and a house that looked a lot like Fiona's cottage.

"Jack," Fiona said. "These paintings are gorgeous."

Cora cleared her throat and Fiona, startled, realized

how rude she'd been. "Oh, I'm so sorry. Jack, this is my sister, Cora. Maybe you know her from your community."

"Hi, Cora," Jack said. "I've seen you around."

"Hi, Jack," Cora said. "Those paintings that Fiona's looking at are yours, aren't they?"

"Guilty as charged," he said. "Fiona, don't feel obligated to keep the paintings on the wall. I just put them there as placeholders. My mother helped me put them on the wall early this morning."

Fiona shook her head. "No, please. These are beautiful paintings and a professional artist would charge thousands for them. So, I need to pay you for them, and there's more wall space around. Let's go around the bookstore and find other places to hang your achingly lovely paintings."

Fiona felt tears coming to her eyes. Those paintings spoke to her on a profound level, and she didn't exactly know why. All she knew was that they drew her in, and she couldn't quit staring at them. The more she stared at them, the more she noticed little details about them. The way the woods painting used vibrant color, and how the ocean painting seemed to come alive. How the two people on the beach looked at each other with such love in their eyes.

Jack came over. "That's me," he said, pointing to the man on the beach who was staring at a woman with red hair. Both of their backs were turned, but if that weren't the case, Fiona would've thought that the two people in the painting were her and Jack. Except the man on the beach was standing. "That's how I imagine myself. Healthy and whole."

"Oh, Jack," Fiona said. "You're perfect the way you are."

Jack blushed. "Well, no, I'm not, but thank you."

"But you are," Fiona protested. "You're beautiful inside

and out and you have a rare gift. Why didn't you tell me about your artistic ability?"

"I'm not good," Jack said. "Others are much better than me."

"But you are amazing," Fiona said, going over to the ocean painting and touching it. "Truly." Then she remembered something. Ava had her friends over the night before. One of the friends, Hallie, had a daughter who owned an art gallery on gallery row, and Hallie's housemate, Conrad, was one of the featured artists in the gallery. Maybe Jack could display his art there, too?

Suddenly, Fiona was excited. "Jack, I have an idea. Do you have other paintings at home?"

"Oh, yes," he said. "Well, not at home, but I have a storage locker full of them. Why?"

"I have a much better place for your paintings than a dingy storage locker."

"What did you have in mind?"

Fiona told Jack about Hallie's daughter Morgan and her gallery. "They're looking for two more artists to join their co-op," she said. "You'd be perfect for them."

"I don't know," Jack said. "I've never been a working artist. I've always just dabbled."

"But you want the world to know about your talent, don't you?" Fiona asked.

"Well, it would be great if I could sell a few," he said. "It would make me feel like less of a failure."

Fiona was excited, but she knew she was ignoring Cora. She brought Cora along, now she was acting like her sister wasn't even there. "Cora," Fiona said. "Let's go shopping some more on the boardwalk together, just you and me. But I first have to make a quick phone call."

"Oh, it's okay," Cora said. "Go ahead and make your

phone call. I'm going to take a look around if you don't mind."

Fiona eagerly called Ava, who gave Fiona Hallie's phone number. And then Fiona called Hallie, who agreed to tell Morgan about Jack. "Does he have a website?" Hallie asked.

"Do you have a website?" Fiona asked Jack.

"No," he said. "As I said, I've only dabbled."

"No," Fiona told Hallie. "But I'll go to Jack's storage locker and take pictures of his paintings so you can get a feel for his style."

"That'll be great," Hallie said. "I'll be watching for that."

"Thanks," Fiona said. "You're a doll."

Jack looked anxious. "What did Hallie say?"

"She said she'd tell her daughter about you, after I take pictures of your paintings for Morgan. I know Morgan would love to have you in her co-op."

Jack nodded. "Well, I won't get my hopes up. But we can go to my storage locker tomorrow if you like."

"I'd like that," Fiona said. "The sooner, the better."

Fiona and Cora begged off to finish their girls' day. Cora didn't want anything on their shopping spree, but Fiona would note the things that Cora seemed to love in the shops and buy her a few things as a surprise. She had a feeling that Cora's reluctance to shop was mainly because of Cora's lack of funds. Fiona didn't want to insult her sister, but she wanted her to have a few things she loved. So, it would be a delicate balance between giving Cora things and not giving her so much that Cora felt belittled.

The girls' day was a success for Fiona. The two sisters had lunch at an outdoor café, with Lucy sleeping at their feet. They talked about everything under the sun while nursing a bottle of wine and eating sandwiches, all while people-watching. Both of them loved to watch all the crowds on the beach and boardwalk.

Then they went over to the Santa Monica pier and a portrait artist on the pier drew them together. It was a lovely portrait, not a caricature, and Fiona was astounded how much she and Cora looked alike in the picture. They went over to a crowd of people who were surrounding a magician, and, after the magician's show, Fiona slipped the guy $20. Cora and Fiona rode the ferris wheel and roller coaster together, squealing as the roller coaster went down the hills at top speed.

Along the way, during their shopping trip, Fiona noted Cora admiring different clothes, shoes, jewelry and antiques. Fiona made a mental list of all the things she'd gift her sister later.

After the trip was over, Fiona headed to Ava's, feeling warm and happy. She had a lot of fun with her sister, and she knew that things would only get better between them. Especially once Cora started treatment for her depression. Fiona would be there for her all the way.

Best of all, so far, Fiona hadn't been recognized. She'd walked around in a bucket hat, no makeup, and her trendy black glasses and nobody paid her any mind.

She prayed that would continue to be the case.

Chapter Thirty-Five

Fiona

Two Weeks Later

Fiona had arranged a time with Morgan to evaluate Jack's paintings a few weeks ago, and Morgan loved them. She formally invited Jack to be a part of her co-op and Jack eagerly accepted.

The gallery was to have their first showing of Jack's paintings that night.

Things were definitely a whirlwind. Fiona asked Luke for a divorce, and he agreed. Since they weren't married that long, there was no property division necessary. The tabloids, social media, Tik Tok and the Internet ate up the story. For several days, it seemed sFiona couldn't turn on her computer without seeing stories about their quickie marriage and even quicker divorce. But the news cycle did its thing, and, less than a week later, Fiona barely saw anything on the Internet, social media and Tik Tok about their marriage dissolution.

The paparazzi never found Fiona at Ava's house and her cottage in the woods was already ready for her to move into. Which didn't surprise her, as the work on the house was just cosmetic, and Quinn hired a crew that worked around the clock to get the cottage ready for her. Fiona squealed with delight when she saw how cozy her cottage was now with a makeover. New hardwood floors, new appliances in the kitchen and bathroom, and a new coat of paint was all that was necessary to make the place shine like a new penny.

This was her place, and it was her father's. And it truly felt like home. She loved living in the middle of nature, and loved opening her windows at night to hear the crickets chirping, the frogs croaking and the occasional hoot of an owl. Lucy also really loved the cottage, and she loved running around the property even more. She was having a ball. Every evening, Fiona would throw Lucy's rubber chicken, and Lucy would run after the chicken and drop it at Fiona's feet, again and again.

The only thing was, Fiona still hadn't told Jack how she felt about him. She didn't want to ruin things. They were working so well together at the bookstore. They'd already had several story times for children, and had hosted two poetry slams. Fiona was working to put together a book club, and she'd already gotten 10 sign-ups to read *The Seven Husbands of Evelyn Hugo*, a book close to Fiona's heart as the book centered on a world-famous actress with a secret love.

Much like Fiona herself. Jack was her secret love, even if he didn't know it. Camille told Fiona to put herself out there, but Fiona hesitated.

"I'm as afraid of rejection as anybody else," Fiona said.

"And, in this case, if he rejects me, I still have to see him every day. I can think of nothing worse."

Camille rolled her eyes. "Fiona, don't be silly. I've seen the way he looks at you, and, trust me, I don't see rejection in his eyes."

"Even so," Fiona said. "It's too risky."

"Well, you're free to pursue it," Camille said. "You're divorced now."

Fiona resolved to maybe, tentatively, tell Jack that night how she felt. She was going to Jack's art show, after arranging dog-sitting duties with the lovely Ava. Ava was good about that. She was home most evenings, because she worked at her winery during the day, so she was available for dog-sitting duties and loved doing it. Fiona paid her, even though Ava insisted she wanted nothing, but Fiona won that fight and Ava agreed to $20 an hour for watching her pup Lucy when it was needed and Ava was free.

Fortunately for Fiona, she didn't have to ask Ava too many times to watch her pup. Fiona took Lucy everywhere she went, including to her bookstore every day. Lucy was the unofficial mascot for the place and proved to be a great draw, too. Everybody who came in the shop marveled at how beautiful Lucy was, and how well-behaved.

Most people recognized Fiona, even though Fiona was still trying to disguise herself behind her glasses, her hair in its natural state of wild curls, and no makeup. Some even asked for autographs, which Fiona was happy to oblige. Many, many people asked her when she'd have a new movie out, and were disappointed when Fiona told them she wouldn't make anymore. But everybody, by and large, let her be Fiona Kennedy, bookstore owner, instead of Fiona Kennedy, A-List actress. And Fiona was forever grateful for this.

Fiona picked up Jack and the two of them headed to the art gallery. "Are you nervous?" Fiona asked him.

Jack comically put his fingers to his mouth and pretended to chew his fingernails. "No, what makes you think that?" he asked with a laugh.

"I wonder," Fiona said, laughing. "Don't be nervous. Morgan loves your work. Everybody will love your work."

"Do you love my work?" Jack asked nervously.

"I love-" Fiona paused. "You."

Her hand flew to her mouth. Did she really just say that to Jack? Oh, God. She had to cover immediately. "I mean-"

Jack took her hand when they got to a stoplight. "I love you, too."

Fiona closed her eyes, relief and joy flooding through her.

It was a long stoplight. Jack leaned over and kissed her, and everything she didn't feel with Luke, she felt with Jack. Like the sky was opening up and birds were singing. Like her body was lighting up, every synapse firing at once. Like she was completely, totally, head-over-heels in love for the first time ever.

Jack was hers and she was Jack's.

And nothing could've been more perfect.

They got to the gallery, but not before making out in the car in the underground parking lot. Fiona couldn't believe how deeply she felt for this man who was kissing her passionately. It was like she had been underwater, unable to breathe, and she'd finally come up for air, breathing it all in her lungs. She breathed Jack in. His scent of woodsy, spicy cologne and pure man. The faint hint of cherry in his taste. She couldn't get enough of his lips, his incredibly hard pecs and arms, his thick dark hair.

This was her soulmate. Of that, she was certain. He was her future, her past, her present, her soul, her heart. She could see forever in his eyes, and that thought made her want to cry with joy.

She would marry this man. And their marriage would last one helluva lot longer than 10 days, or however long her marriage to Luke had lasted. Their marriage would last a lifetime. Of that, she was certain. There was nothing wrong with her, like she thought when she was marrying Luke. She worried that she couldn't love, because she felt nothing for Luke. But with Jack, she loved with such an open heart that she knew he was The One.

Jack was hers. Luke never was and never could be.

It was really as simple as that.

They went into the gallery, and a party was in full-swing. Many people were surrounding Jack's paintings and admiring them.

"You see," Fiona said to Jack. "I told you you'd be a hit."

Jack blushed. "I might as well confess. These aren't all the paintings I have."

"Oh?" Fiona said.

"No. I have portraits and paintings of you at home. I've been in love with you since the moment we met. I never thought you'd feel the same."

Fiona laughed. "Oh, my God. Me too. I loved you from first sight, too. I never believed in that before, love at first sight, but I met you and I just knew."

Just then, Hallie came in with a very handsome man with a grey ponytail, wearing a newsboy cap. He was dapper in his cap, an ascot over a dress shirt, paired with faded blue jeans and scuffed hush puppy shoes. A perfect blend of formal and informal.

But Fiona was interested in one other thing.

There was a bright light between Hallie and this man.

Fiona wondered if Hallie and this man knew they were meant for one another.

She went over to Hallie. "Hallie, introduce me to your friend."

"This is Conrad," Hallie said, gesturing to the man. "Conrad, this is my new friend, Fiona."

"Fiona Kennedy," Conrad said. "I love your work."

"I love yours, too," Fiona said. "If you're the Conrad with the art in the other room." She loved Conrad's British accent, and she knew Hallie did, too.

"Guilty as charged," he said. They all went to Conrad's wing of the gallery. "Oh, bullocks. One of my paintings is upside down. I'll have to have a talk with the chap who arranged my art. Excuse me."

Conrad went over to the painting and then gestured to Morgan to help him put the painting right-side-up. Fiona then took the opportunity to talk to Hallie about Conrad.

"So, Conrad," Fiona said. "He's your housemate, right?"

"Right," Hallie said.

Fiona took a deep breath. "He's in love with you. And you're in love with him."

Hallie's face flushed bright red. "How did you-"

"It's obvious. I can see it." She didn't tell Hallie that she saw the soulmate light between them. She didn't know Hallie well enough to bust that out. The woman might think she was crazy.

"I am in love with him," Hallie confessed. "I was struggling, though, because I have feelings for a man named Pete, too. Who also has feelings for me."

"I don't know Pete," Fiona said. "But I now know Conrad, and, I don't want to be pushy, but you have to tell him how you feel."

"What if he turns me down?"

"He won't. You guys are meant for each other. Trust me on this. I wouldn't steer you wrong."

Fiona watched Hallie go over to Conrad and put her hand on his back. Conrad put his arm around her and Hallie whispered something in his ear.

"Doll, I thought you'd never admit that you loved me," Fiona heard Conrad say to Hallie. "And I feel the same about you."

Fiona smiled.

Another match made in heaven.

Boy, matchmaking would be fun.

Chapter Thirty-Six

Hallie

So, the secret was finally out. She finally told Conrad how she felt about him, because Fiona urged her to. And she was amazed that Conrad told her that he felt the same way about her as she did about him.

"You love me?" Hallie asked him when they got home from the art show. She whispered to him at the art show that she loved him, and he said it back. But now that they were home, they could really be alone and talk about their feelings for each other.

"Oh, yes," Conrad said. "I've only been in love with you for oh, about a year now."

"A year?" Hallie was astounded. "But we've only known each other about a year."

"Bingo," Conrad said. "But I didn't want to ruin things between us. I thought I'd tell you how I felt and you would go screaming into the night. I'd have to move out, and it would be a whole thing. Houses aren't cheap around here, you know. For that matter, even rentals aren't cheap. I didn't want to be kicked out of the house, so I kept my mouth shut. But yes, I am truly, madly, deeply in love with you, and I have been since the start."

Hallie felt her heart soar. "So that's the real reason why you decided to move out here with me?"

"Yes. You told me you would be moving out here and I was gutted. Absolutely gutted. I couldn't imagine my life without you. So, I invited myself out here, just because I wanted to be near you. And now it's all out in the open, and we can be together. For real."

The two of them kissed, with Hallie feeling the kiss to her marrow.

That night, they shared a bed, for the first time.

And it was as glorious as she imagined it would be.

Chapter Thirty-Seven

Hallie

Hallie and Conrad spent the entire weekend in bed together. Nothing mattered to Hallie except for Conrad, and Conrad felt the same about Hallie. There was a year of pent-up sexual energy between them, and they expressed it to each other many times over the course of the weekend. Hallie had never felt more sexy, attractive, and alive.

One thing was for sure. They were no longer house-mates. They were lovers, through and through.

She told Ava and everybody, and they all were so thrilled for her. "Finally," Ava said. "We all knew it would happen sooner or later," Ava said and everybody agreed.

Fiona was over at Ava's too. She'd joined the group for their Wednesday night ritual of wine and food. She was now one of their close-knit friends, and, just like with Mia, she fit right in.

Hallie never would've imagined that the most popular

star in the world would be their close friend, but that's what happened.

"How did you know we were in love?" Hallie asked her new friend Fiona.

"I just knew," Fiona said. "I have a gift for seeing soulmates. And I saw Conrad was yours."

Then Fiona told everybody about seeing a light between people who were meant to be. "Don't ask me how I developed this gift. I think I inherited it from my father. He was a natural matchmaker."

Quinn and Mia giggled and looked at Fiona. "Is there a light between us?"

"Definitely," Fiona said without hesitation. "You guys are definitely meant to be."

Hallie looked at Ava. "Maybe Fiona can see you and Elijah together and see the same thing."

"Stop," Ava said. "You're embarrassing me."

"Elijah is her stepbrother," Sarah said. "Long story."

"Well," Fiona said. "As long as there's no blood relation, where's the problem?"

Everybody laughed. "That's what I keep telling her," Sarah said. "She needs to go for it."

Hallie saw Pete the next day at the retreat. She dreaded seeing him, because she knew he had a crush on her. They hadn't spoken to one another about the kiss they shared, because they both knew a relationship between them would be inappropriate and could get Hallie fired.

She had a crush on him, too, but now she was firmly in love with Conrad, and she had to let Pete down.

"Uh, can we talk," Hallie asked him when she saw him.

"Sure," he said. "Let's go into the therapy room with the waterfall. I love that room. I've been meditating in there."

The two of them went in there. It was almost breakfast time, after which everybody would go on their nature hike. Hallie dreaded telling Pete about Conrad, but she knew there was something between her and Pete so she had to be honest.

"Um," Hallie said. "About that kiss a few weeks ago..."

Pete looked embarrassed. "Yes. I wanted to talk to you about that." He took a deep breath. "Hallie, I like you. You're a beautiful woman, and so caring. You helped me more than you know. And I don't know how to tell you this, but..." Another deep breath. "Selma and I have been hanging out a lot, and we've fallen in love. We're going to be together after we leave the retreat."

He looked so ashamed and sad, and Hallie felt like bursting. She thought *she* would be letting *him* down. It was the other way around and Hallie couldn't be happier.

"Oh, that's wonderful!" Hallie said. "Really. Selma is such a nice person and you guys will be happy together. Truly."

Pete beamed. "Yes, I think so. We seem very well-matched. And she doesn't care that I'm chubby. She thinks there's just more to love."

Pete lost the initial ten pounds but had since gained it back. But he'd told Hallie he was at peace with his extra weight. "I want to be healthy," he told her a few weeks prior. "But I can be healthy at any weight. I really want to live my life without starving myself to look like Joe Six-Pack on the beach." Hallie thought his attitude was healthy and was happy he was at peace with himself at any weight.

That was what it was all about, really. Living your life without starving yourself into an ideal. That was true for men as well as women, Hallie realized, and being happy with extra weight made for a happy life indeed.

Hallie went out with Pete to join the group. It was then that she noticed just how attentive Selma was with Pete. She'd never noticed it before, but the two looked like they were in love.

She got an idea. She took a picture of the two of them and intended to show Fiona the picture. Might Fiona see the soulmate light in photographs?

Later, when she showed Fiona the picture, Fiona confirmed it.

"Yep, they're definitely meant to be," she said, looking at Pete and Selma together. "A good match."

Hallie smiled when Fiona said that.

She was in love, and so was Pete.

All was right in the world.

Hallie never thought she could be so happy.

vinci-books.com/beachfront-crush

A forbidden crush. A family secret. One unforgettable summer in the Hamptons.

When Elijah invites Ava to the Hamptons to spend a month with his ailing mother and two half-sisters, Rachel and Deborah, Ava eagerly accepts. There, she finds out more about her birth father and his family, which excites Ava, who is desperate to know about her heritage. As Ava grows closer to Elijah, she grapples with the societal expectations surrounding their relationship.

Turn the page for a free preview…

The Beachfront Crush: Chapter One

Ava

Ava was sitting with Sarah, Quinn and Mia on her deck, listening to the waves coming in and out and watching the sun set behind the hills. Julia and Emerson were playing with Bella and Kona, throwing a plastic bone in the water again and again. The dogs eagerly retrieved them from the water and dropped the toys at the girls' feet.

Hallie wasn't with them, because she was having dinner with Conrad. Hallie and her roommate Conrad ending up becoming much more than roommates after all. Hallie was happier than Ava had ever seen her, perfectly content to bask in love with Conrad while thriving at the wellness retreat. She was born to be a counselor, she'd told Ava, and seemed to be born to be Conrad's love interest. Ava was secretly envious of her friend. She found Conrad to be fascinating and complex, a talented artist with a melodious British accent. And Conrad was really crazy about Hallie. That was plain for everyone to see whenever they were around.

Ava and her ladies were enjoying a glass of wine, the smell of salt and brine in the air. It was an incredibly relaxing experience, just sitting in the silence with her sister, best friend and her best friend's significant other, Mia. Mia was fitting in with the fabric of the friends incredibly well, as everybody knew she would. Mia spent much of her time helping the girls craft songs, with Emerson creating the melodies and Julia creating the lyrics. That project was coming along extremely well, and Emerson and Julia were ready to begin their own YouTube channel. Mia was helping them with that, as well, as Mia had her own YouTube channel. Mia sang and played guitar on her channel, but that wasn't her focus. Her focus was on songwriting and had written songs for many big acts over the years.

Ava was also a bit nervous, because she had to confess something to everybody. She was nursing a serious attraction to Elijah, who was technically her step-brother. Elijah's mother was married to Ava's father, but Elijah had a different birth father. As for Ava, she never even knew that James Bloch, the man who Elijah called "father", was her birth father until recently.

Complicating matters was that Elijah, who was a trauma doctor at Cedars-Sinai, was going East and had invited Ava to come along. He was going to take a sabbatical for the next few months from his job because he wanted to visit his mother in Bridgehampton. She owned a beach house out there, and, because it was January and the off-season, it probably would be quiet around that town. Esther, Elijah's mother, was recently diagnosed with cancer and didn't know how much longer she had left. So, she'd summoned her children to the beach house, because that was where Deborah and Rachel, Elijah's sisters, felt a great sense of comfort.

Deborah was a photographer in New York, and, at the moment, was freelancing. So, she could take the time off to spend with Esther. Rachel was a chef in Bridgehampton, so was already local and had a home of her own in the town, but agreed to stay in the beach house for the month that Elijah and Deborah would also be there. It was understood that this homecoming wouldn't be exactly a happy event. More like bittersweet.

Ava was apparently invited because Elijah wanted her to get to know Deborah and Rachel, Ava's half-sisters. Ava had no relation to Esther, but Elijah still was eager for Ava to get to know her. "My mother is the coolest person around," Elijah said. "And she's 93, so she's seen a lot. You can ask her about Truman Capote." Esther ran with and knew Truman Capote's "Swans," elegant and wealthy women who ran with Truman Capote back in the day. Elijah assured Ava that his mother had many colorful stories to tell about her life.

So, Ava looked forward to staying at the beach house in Bridgehampton. But, at the same time, she was incredibly nervous about the prospect. She'd gotten to know her step-brother and was starting to experience the stomach-churning butterflies she'd only experienced once before - with Daniel, the love of her life, who was tragically killed in a car accident when Ava was pregnant.

And, for some reason, she dreaded telling her friends and family about her feelings. Yet, she felt she needed to talk about it. She knew they thought it would've been strange for Ava and Elijah to date. She'd broached the topic before and they told her as much. But maybe if she told them she was falling for Elijah - and that was how Ava was feeling about him, like she was falling for him - maybe they wouldn't give her such a hard time.

The girls came up to the deck, laughing hysterically about something or another. "Mom," Emerson said to Quinn. "We're going in."

Ava missed everybody living with her. The others - Quinn, Sarah, Julia and Emerson - had recently moved out of Ava's home into their own, newly-renovated Venice Beach home. Since then, Ava had been lonely, even though she entertained superstar actress Fiona Kennedy for awhile while Fiona was hiding out from the paparazzi after a failed marriage. Ava loved having a full and vibrant house, with laughter, music and the occasional meltdown taking place on a daily basis. She was surprised at how much she enjoyed having two 13-year-old girls under her roof. But she did enjoy that, very much. It made her sad to live in her big, empty house all alone.

"Ava, this wine is the bomb," Mia said. It was a bottle of wine created at the Sava Winery, which was Ava and Sarah's winery located in the Santa Monica mountains. It was their Cabernet Sauvignon, a rich red wine that was full-bodied and much milder than many other Cabernet Sauvignons Ava had tried in her life.

"Thanks," Ava said. Then she looked at her glass and towards the now-darkened beach. She took another sip of her wine and closed her eyes.

"Hey," Quinn said. "What's up with you tonight, Ava? I've never seen you so quiet."

Ava shrugged, not quite ready to come clean about her feelings for Elijah. "I don't know. I was just thinking about my trip to the Hamptons with Elijah. I don't really know what to expect."

Sarah and Ava had discussed the prospect that Ava

could leave for a month and they both agreed it was a good time to do so. The grape harvesting was long over, the wines were made and bottled and the crowds the winery experienced during the summer and fall months had slowed considerably. There weren't any events planned at the winery for several more months and, while the winery still did brisk business, it was manageable. So, Sarah was perfectly fine with Ava taking this time off, with the understanding that Sarah would be free to do the same if she ever needed to.

Sarah was looking at Ava with one eyebrow raised. "Uh huh," she said. "I've seen that look in your eyes before. Many times."

"What look?" Ava said in a thin voice. She was transparent. No way could she put one over on one of her closest friends and her sister. Best not to even try.

"You know what look," Sarah said. "And, listen, I've been thinking about it. Yeah, it's kinda weird to be crushing on your stepbrother. But it's not like Greg and Marcia. You were never a part of that family until recently, so you guys were strangers when you met. It's not like you guys grew up together."

Mia just started laughing. "Dude, don't even worry about it," she said. "Seriously. People worry too much about what everybody else thinks. You do you. That's pretty much the advice I've given anybody in my life. You do you."

Quinn looked over at Mia and smiled. Those two were so in sync, Ava thought. They had the kind of easy relationship Ava admired. They laughed at the same things, finished each other's sentences already and just had a comfortable vibe with one another. Ava wondered how they came such a long way in such a short time - they'd only reconnected with one another several months prior- but

Quinn explained they were best friends back in the day and were always like that. They'd always felt a special comfort with each other, like they went way back. Willow, Ava's future daughter-in-law and soon-to-be-mother to her second grandchild, would say Mia and Quinn were old souls linked together in past lives. Willow always said that when two people meet and feel they've known each other for a long time and immediately start talking like friends, it means they were together before.

Not that Ava believed in that sort of thing. Well, maybe she did. After all, she felt that way with Elijah. Right from the start, they conversed like people who went way back. They had a comfort level with each other that was much like with Quinn and Mia. But past lives and reincarnation? Nope, Ava didn't believe in that. She was secretly afraid that this life was all there was. You get one chance to make your mark and then you're gone. You don't come back as somebody else and you don't go to heaven. She wanted to believe there was something beyond this world, but she couldn't make herself believe that.

"Well, sugar, what do you think?" Quinn asked. "You going to be looking at Elijah for the next month with googly eyes?"

Ava smiled as she realized that she didn't have to confess anything to her closest ones. They already knew.

"Am I that obvious?" Ava said.

To that, Quinn and Sarah just rolled her eyes and smiled. "Sis," Sarah said. "You've always been that obvious. I'm your sister, remember? I know all about you. And my memory is longer than an elephant's." She playfully punched Ava in the shoulder. "The question is, what are you going to do about it?"

"Nothing. Listen, I'm going to the Hamptons for a

month and Elijah will be there the whole time. But he's going to be preoccupied with other things, like his sick and possibly dying mother and dealing with two half sisters he doesn't get along with too well. So, I doubt he'll be too focused on me."

Sarah just gave Ava a look. "Better you than me, going back to New York in the wintertime. That's the reason why I think you really have it bad for this guy. You're leaving Southern California in the middle of winter to go to New York. Personally, I think that's crazy, but I wish you the best.'"

Ava laughed. Sarah was right about that. In the middle of January, the weather in Southern California hovered around 65°. She was going to a place where it actually snowed, and snow was one of the things Ava did not miss about the East Coast. Yet she was looking forward to this visit. She had another family. Two half-sisters. Esther was not blood to her, but she'd met the older woman and was completely taken with her. Esther was down-to-earth, funny, lively, and as vital as a 93-year-old woman could be. Now, apparently, she didn't have much time left. While Ava had met her only once, she bonded with her, so she would be very sad once Esther passed away. Not that Ava thought Esther would actually die from her cancer. If there was anybody who could beat cancer at age 93, it was Esther. Besides, it was breast cancer and had not yet spread. It was definitely treatable – just look at Hallie, who beat the very same thing and was in complete remission now.

At the same time, Ava somewhat dreaded the prospect of spending a month with Esther, Deborah, and Rachel. There was a chance that because Elijah didn't get along too well with his half-sisters that there might be some family drama going on. Ava dearly hoped that wouldn't be the case, as there was nothing worse than being in the middle of a family soap opera.

Quinn just smiled and Mia smiled back at Quinn. Ava had a feeling the two of them had discussed her situation with Elijah on more than one occasion. That was the problem with her best friend having a relationship with a woman - two women are going to gossip. When a man and woman are together, the gossiping about one's friends and family usually go nowhere, because the man in a relationship usually couldn't care less.

Ava just took another sip of her wine and turned her attention to the rolling surf. It was now pitch dark outside and the moon was high in the sky. She could hear a distant bark and could smell a bonfire raging just down the beach. She would soon be hearing a different surf on a different ocean as she sat on the deck of a different home altogether. Would she have fun there? Would she be enlightened by her other part of the family? Or would she be caught in some hopeless morass from which she could not get away fast enough?

Ava finally stretched and yawned. It had been a long day at the winery, as most days were anymore. And she was unusually tired. She hadn't been sleeping well at night and often woke up about four in the morning or even earlier, unable to get back to sleep. She didn't know if she just had a lot on her mind or something physical caused her not to sleep well. She would have to figure it out because she was often tired during the day, needing to take a nap while working. That simply wouldn't do – Ava needed her energy.

"I'm heading up," Ava said. "Of course, like usual, you ladies are more than welcome to stay out here as long as you want."

At that, Ava went up to her room and lay on her bed.

But she looked at the other side of the bed longingly. She suddenly realized just how big her bed was. It was a California King and the mattress was a Sleep Number. What was this feeling, that she wanted somebody next to her? It had been so long since she actually had someone next to her in a bed at night. And she really didn't think much about it all these years. Yet, she felt a kind of loneliness that she hadn't felt before. It was as if she was not ready to commit to anybody before and now she was. Something had shifted, and she didn't know exactly why. She only knew it did.

And she knew exactly who she wanted in that bed with her. Elijah.

Oh, she was in trouble.

The Beachfront Crush: Chapter Two

Ava

A week later, Ava found herself on a plane heading east. Elijah was already on Long Island, and it was already decided he would pick up Ava at the Long Island MacArthur Airport. Ava being Ava, she tried to protest and say she could just find an Uber over to Esther's beach house. But, Elijah wouldn't hear of it.

"Are you kidding me?" Elijah said, his voice light. "My mom would kill me if I had you get an Uber here. She'd think she didn't raise me right."

So, Ava was looking forward to the drive over to his mom's beach house from the airport. The airport was about an hour away from Esther's beach house, so Ava and Elijah would have a bit of time before riding into the storm. Elijah told Ava that he would be alone when he picked her up. His two sons, Caleb and Levi, wouldn't be at the house at all. They were in school, so Elijah hired a nanny to watch them for the month.

Ava put some earbuds in and settled in for the long flight. She was in first class, so she had a lot of legroom and a place to sleep. Which was important, as this was a red-eye flight taking off at midnight. She would be arriving before 6 o'clock in the morning in Long Island.

She thought about her friend Hallie. Hallie was having the time of her life working at the retreat. And why wouldn't she be? It was really a dream job, helping people better their lives through healthy living. Hallie seemed interested in her roommate, Conrad, an interesting British man and artist who had his own issues with imposter syndrome and fear of failure. Hallie and Conrad had recently started a romance, and Ava was anxious to see where that went.

It seemed that Hallie was attracted to complicated men. Much like Ava herself.

Not that Elijah was complicated, per se. He wasn't. He was a doctor and an amateur photographer who had won many awards for his photography and had been displayed in different exhibits, including winning first prize for one of his photographs in the San Diego Fair. It didn't seem he had any kind of major issues. He just seemed like a normal man.

No, the complication came from the whole incestuousness of it all. Oh, they didn't have any blood relationship. But would it seem weird if they started dating? Would it be odd considering they both shared the same relationship with Deborah and Rachel? Just like Deborah and Rachel were Ava's half-sisters, they also were Elijah's. Elijah, Deborah, and Rachel had the same mother, but not the same father. Ava, Deborah, and Rachel had the same father, but not the same mother. In the Venn diagram in Ava's head, there was some overlapping in the family tree, and that disturbed Ava.

At some point, Ava just decided to close her eyes and

not worry about it. She was overthinking it. As she usually did.

Around 6 o'clock in the morning, the plane touched down at the Long Island MacArthur airport. Ava got off the plane, got her luggage and saw Elijah standing on the sidewalk, his hands in his pockets. This dark curly hair had grown out a little since the last time Ava saw him, which was several weeks ago. He was wearing a leather coat, jeans, and a pair of Top-Siders that probably cost over a thousand dollars. He was looking for her, and, when he saw her, a large grin spread over his face.

He looked a little bit like a boy to Ava. He had a youthful face, much like Paul Rudd, a Kansas City boy who made really good. Ava's heart quickened. Boy, this would be difficult staying under the same roof as Elijah for an entire month.

She walked over to him and he gave her a big hug. "Good to see you," he said. "How was the flight?"

"Oh, you know, it was a flight. Pretty uneventful. Then again, flights always are uneventful unless they crash."

"True," Elijah said as he took Ava's suitcase she was wheeling behind her. That gesture, just taking her suitcase without her having to ask, impressed Ava. Maybe she wasn't expecting much from a man after having been married to Christopher, the husband who ended up stealing from her, coming back to try to get back with her, then telling her he'd been married to somebody else while married to her. Christopher was never much of a gentleman, on top of everything else. He was too involved with his own self to think about anybody else. But Elijah seemed to be a guy who was raised right. Not that that surprised Ava. Having met Esther, and having known James, the man who raised Elijah, she thought they probably had decent parenting skills.

"You hungry?" Elijah asked Ava. "I'm thinking we should grab some grub before going into the lion's den." Then he smiled. "Just kidding. I just saw the look on your face when I said that."

Ava wondered if he could tell how nervous she was. And she was out of her element. She spent so many years leaning on her best friends and her sister for support, and they were nowhere to be seen right at the moment. As much as she wanted her security blankets, obviously she couldn't have them and didn't know what to expect when she met her half-sisters. She kind of knew what to expect from Esther, having met her once before, but not Deborah and Rachel.

"I'm actually starving," Ava said. "I haven't eaten since yesterday morning."

"Yesterday morning?" Elijah shook his head. "Why yesterday morning?"

"Well, I kinda forgot to eat. It was a busy day at the winery."

It kind of was a busy day, at that. They hosted a family reunion at the winery that was impromptu, because nobody had made a reservation. Basically, 30 people from the same family just appeared, and Sarah and Ava busted their rear, trying to keep everything afloat. After they were slammed like that, Ava rethought the wisdom of just letting Sarah do everything at the winery while she was gone. So, they both decided to hire a temporary wine tender from an agency.

"Well, come on, let's go get some eggs."

Ava and Elijah then headed over to Elijah's Range

Rover, putting Ava's bag in the back. Elijah opened the door for her, another gesture she wasn't used to anymore. Elijah seemed to be a bit of a throwback with his manners, coming from a time when men opened doors, pulled out chairs and took bags without having to be asked.

Elijah looked over at Ava and grinned. "How does it feel, coming from Southern California to a place that's colder than hell's hinges?"

"Yeah, it's kind of weird coming to a place where I can see my breath. But you forget, I was raised in Kansas City, I lived in New York City for many years, and then I lived on Nantucket, so it's not exactly like I'm a Hibiscus flower that will wilt in the snow. But, I have to admit, I've been a bit spoiled by the Southern California weather. But this is home sweet home for me."

"Well, thank you for coming out. I'm really excited you're going to spend some time with the other part of your family."

Ava knew Elijah probably would've liked to have the same opportunity. But his birth father wanted nothing to do with him, so he never got to know one-half of his heritage. Ava realized she was privileged to have this opportunity and would make the most of it.

"Yeah, here I come, the shiksa in the family," Ava said. She wondered how she would feel about that. While she really enjoyed services like Shabbat On The Beach, because it was such a joyful experience, complete with singing, dancing and camaraderie, all on a beach with the sun setting behind the hills, she still wasn't religious. And she didn't plan on becoming religious. She was still her mother's daughter in many ways. Ava's mother, Colleen, who Ava didn't get along with until just recently, was as practical as it comes. And Colleen was not spiritual or religious, to say the least. So, that was another reason for being apprehensive. She didn't think Esther would judge her for her lack of spiritual beliefs, but would Deborah and Rachel?

"Relax, they don't expect you to know Hebrew or even take part in Friday night Shabbat. My sisters know the score and so does my mom. You don't have to go to temple with us, either. All you're expected to do for this month is to relax and do your thing. It'll be great if you really bond with my family, who's part your family too, but if it doesn't happen, it doesn't happen. Not everybody vibes with each other. So just try not to stress."

Oh, if only it was easy as all that. Ava tended to worry a little bit too much about things that she shouldn't be worried about. Of course, one never knows what is worth worrying about until the thing comes to pass. Sometimes her worries came true.

They got to a bustling restaurant. It was a diner, the kind Ava always liked. She really liked the divey places, the kind of place where truck drivers would come in, park their rigs and eat things like biscuits and gravy, corned beef hash and lots of bacon. She loved that Elijah was taking her to a low-key place like this instead of some fancy place on the beach. It somewhat showed they might have the same taste in breakfast outings.

Ava ordered a traditional breakfast of eggs, bacon, hash browns and an English muffin, with a large orange juice. Elijah ordered some pancakes with a side of eggs. Ava looked around and realized how hungry she was when she saw everybody else in the diner digging into their food.

"Okay, tell me what I can expect when I get to your mother's beach house."

"Well, what can I say? My sisters are there. So, there might be fireworks. Just warning you. Rachel is none too pleased that you got the Nantucket house. She always loved that place and couldn't believe James would give it to what she terms a rando. You watch *Downton Abbey*?"

Oh, that was a question for the ages. Did she watch *Downton Abbey*? Yeah, she watched that show. She'd seen every single episode four times now. She still binge-watched it when she was feeling low. "Of course."

"Well, let's just say Rachel is Mary in the situation and you're Matthew. Without the sexual tension, of course. But, yeah, Rachel thinks you took her inheritance. So, she'll be making backhanded comments about that. Strap on a helmet and prepare to take incoming."

In *Downton Abbey*, at the beginning of the show, Lady Mary's possible inheritance of Downton was given to Matthew, who was essentially a rando because he was a distant cousin of the Crawley family. Mary hated Matthew at first for that reason. Of course, they inevitably fell madly in love and got married, but then Matthew died tragically in a car accident. Mary's getting back on her feet after such a tragedy made up much of the storylines over the subsequent seasons.

"Oh, great. Just what I wanted to hear, your sister already has it out for me."

"Just fair warning. Deborah won't hassle you about the house, though. So, who knows, you and Deborah might be allies against Rachel."

Then Ava smiled. "Well, just remember, Matthew and Mary eventually fell in love and got married, even though Matthew took Mary's inheritance, as it were. So, you never know, maybe Rachel and I will become the best of friends. But thanks for the heads up. I'll be prepared to kiss Rachel's rear end."

"Well, it's not as bad as all that. You're not going to

necessarily have to kiss Rachel's butt. In fact, I think you shouldn't. You should probably just ignore her kvetching. And that's all it is – kvetching. That's just how she is. She's a chef, you know. I could just imagine what she's like working. Probably a female Gordon Ramsay without the charm."

Ava laughed. "That's a great picture in my head. Gordon Ramsay in drag and with no sense of humor."

Elijah smiled with a twinkle in his big brown eyes. "Sounds like a pretty accurate portrayal of Rachel."

The food came around and Ava and Elijah dug in. The eggs were amazing - light, fluffy, prepared with butter and seasoned just right. The bacon was crisp and the hash browns were also crisp on the outside, tender on the inside. The orange juice was freshly squeezed. Elijah cut off a part of his pancakes, which were tropical and infused with banana, pineapple and coconut, and put it on Ava's plate.

"Try this," he said. "It tastes like Hawaii."

Ava smiled and took a bite of his pancake and then rolled her eyes with pleasure. "Oh my God. If Hawaii tastes like this, I want to go to Hawaii. That's all I can say."

Elijah smiled. "You've never been to Hawaii?"

"No, can't say I have. But it's on my bucket list, along with going on a European river cruise that stops in Prague."

"Prague? Why Prague, exactly?"

Ava shrugged. "It just looks like a beautiful city." Unlike Ava's sister, Sarah, Ava was not a world traveler. She always wanted to be, but before she landed on Nantucket, she was way too busy raising her triplets and working all the time. So, she'd never been to Europe, even though she always wanted to. And Prague always looked like the most beautiful city in Europe to her.

Elijah winked. "Well, we should go to Prague sometime.

I could show you around. My family originated from Czechoslovakia, so it holds a special place in my heart."

Ava took a deep breath and turned her attention to her food. As much as she wanted to tell Elijah that she would love to go to Europe with him, she couldn't bring herself to say the words. At any rate, Ava was sure Elijah was just making the offer about going to Prague lightly and in jest.

"That would be a lot of fun. And I could probably do it now. The winery I own with Sarah is doing really well and we just found a wind tender who is temporarily working for our winery. I hope she turns out to be somebody we could permanently hire."

"Oh, the flexibility of somebody who owns their own business. I envy you. Me, I have to take a sabbatical whenever I need an extended vacation." Elijah continued to dig into his pancakes, adding extra syrup. "I'm on vacation," he said with a smile. "Time to live a little and add more syrup."

"Oh, it's always time to add more syrup," Ava said, taking a sip of her freshly-squeezed orange juice. "Life's too short not to."

Ava agreed with that sentiment. Life really was too short to not add more syrup. She raised her glass and Elijah clinked his with hers. "To a new family and new beginnings."

Elijah smiled. "I like that. I hope you can get close to this part of your family tree. Everybody deserves to be loved and accepted by their blood. And, by the way, my mother absolutely adores you. She told me the two of you got along famously."

Ava smiled. "We did. I think your mother is an amazing woman."

"Yeah. She's 94 this Saturday and still walks three miles every day. She gets around her brownstone in Brooklyn better than people half her age. She's always told me that age is just a number, and it is. That's no cliché - it's true. Even though my dad is gone, and she mourns him every day, she's in no hurry to join him in the afterlife. She has too much living to do right now." He sighed. "She has breast cancer, but it's Stage 1. She's being dramatic when she says she doesn't have much time left. I think she's just saying that to get her family to spend some time with her. Mission accomplished."

Ava thought about the YouTube video she once saw of a woman who was over 100 years old and dancing a line dance at somebody's wedding. She was the sweetest older lady Ava had ever seen and Ava thought how wonderful it would be if that were her at age 100 plus. Dancing at the wedding of her great granddaughter, whoever that might be. It sounded like Esther, Elijah's mother, might be that 100 plus old woman boogying with 20-somethings on the dance floor.

"Well, it sounds like you have some excellent genes," Ava said.

"Yep. I'm the son of a Holocaust survivor and a 1950s-era socialite. They both have such fascinating stories to tell. And they both were extremely healthy into their 90s. My dad was, you know - healthy. He had no health problems we knew about until he had his fatal stroke. But that's how you should try to live life. Be healthy until your last day and then go quickly. We should all be so lucky."

Grab your copy...
vinci-books.com/beachfront-crush

About the Author

Ainsley Keaton lives with her hubby and two fur-babies in Southern California. When she's not binge-watching *Grace and Frankie*, *Succession* and *Downton Abbey*, she's reading historical and women's fiction and scouring the beach for sea glass and sand dollars.

About the Author